CALLED THIRD STRIKE

LINDA FAUSNET

Published by Wannabe Pride 2022

Editing by Linda Hill

Cover Design by Chuck DeKett

FIRST EDITION.

Library of Congress Control Number: 2022902228

❀ Created with Vellum

1

SARAH

I love this place so much.

Gazing out my office window to the ballpark below, a sense of peace settled over me. To me, Old Bay Stadium was the most beautiful place in the world. The late February sun was just setting over the field. The stands were empty now, but spring training was just a few weeks away. Soon the new season would begin, and the stands would be filled with loyal Baltimore Bay Bird fans. During the off-season, I still had plenty of work to do running fundraising events for the Bay Birds.

Tearing myself away from the window, I focused on the task at hand. I made sure to grab all the paperwork I needed for tonight's event at the Hyatt Hotel, which was located just across the street from the ballpark. Tonight's fundraiser was to support the Baltimore Bay Birds Foundation, our general funds charity account that we used to support a slew of local organizations.

I arrived at the hotel to find everything operating smoothly for the event. My stomach flipped with happy anticipation as I gazed at all the activity going on around me. I adored being so involved with a sports organization, and the charity aspect of my job never failed to warm my heart. I'd left home, clear across the country, in the hopes of making a fresh start. Here in Baltimore I had found a warm and loving community and had made some wonderful new friends. After a year and a half, this place felt more like home than anywhere else I'd lived.

Some of the Baltimore Bay Birds players began to arrive, looking dapper in their tuxes for this black-tie event. I was always so grateful for the athletes who took time out of their busy schedules to support the worthy causes promoted by the Bay Birds organization. Among the first people to arrive were the second baseman, Matt Jovey, and his wife, Julia, who also worked for the ball club. Julia was the head groundskeeper; she did an incredible job caring for the most beautiful ballpark in all of baseball. Matt was a dear friend of mine, and I knew I could always count on him to show up at my events.

"Hey there," I said with a smile as I walked toward the couple. "You guys look great."

"Thanks," Matt said, the hint of a smile at his lips and warmth in his deep blue eyes. He was never one to display a lot of emotion, but he was as kind as he was quiet. The strong, silent type I supposed. Exactly the type of man I was looking for, really. A kindhearted soul who would someday make a terrific father. I dreamed of meeting someone like him who I could settle down with and raise a family.

A *good* family. Not like the horror show I grew up with.

"Look at you, girl," Julia said, her pretty hazel eyes lighting up. "Give us a twirl."

I obliged, spinning to show off my shimmery black dress.

"You are *fine*, Sarah," she said with a laugh.

"You're no slouch yourself," I said. Julia was resplendent in fancy dress slacks and a black and white blouse. She rarely wore dresses. In fact, the only one I'd seen her in was her wedding gown. At the reception, she'd changed into jeans and had worn a cowboy hat while she danced with Matt. That had been, without question, the most fun wedding I'd ever attended.

Several other players arrived, which was wonderful. Gazing across the room, I caught sight of our shortstop, Brady Keaton. I was thrilled to see him as his presence was always a *huge* draw. No doubt we had sold hundreds more tickets the minute he'd announced he would be in attendance. Often, athletes with his level of fame wouldn't bother doing charity events, but he attended as many as his schedule would allow.

It made me so happy to see so many players supporting the Foundation. By now, I knew who I could count on to show up and who I couldn't. I inwardly grimaced as I thought of Trace Ridgerton. The catcher for the Baltimore Bay Birds, Trace was my least favorite type of person. A cocky athlete who thought he was better than everyone else. Too good to attend charity events. He never came to any fundraisers, and I knew better than to ask. He was also quite the womanizer—another reason I despised him. During the off-season, Trace had made headlines for getting into a fist-fight with one of the New York Kings after sleeping with the guy's wife. What a *jerk*.

Love and light, I reminded myself. That was my mantra. I always did my best to wish others love and light, even if they were someone I didn't like. *Especially* when they were someone I didn't like.

Ever since high school, I learned to keep away from the

likes of Trace. I couldn't stand the guy, but that didn't mean I wished him any harm. Fortunately, I rarely had to deal with him since he wouldn't go near an event like this anyway.

Brady smiled when he saw me, and he and his wife, Lyric, headed our way. He was such an oversized presence, that Brady. But in a good way. He was tall and muscular, with dark eyes, dark hair, and light everything else. He had a huge heart and a mischievous personality. He knew how to keep things fun. Lyric was as understated as her husband was outspoken. She had shoulder-length dark hair and pretty blue eyes that were gentle and kind.

"Great job, Sarah," Brady said. "Place looks awesome, and looks like you got a pretty good turnout."

"Oh yah," I said. "We sold a lot of tickets."

"Oh yah, doncha knoooow," he said with a grin. Brady loved teasing me about my Minnesota accent.

"Quit it," I said with a laugh as I gently punched him in the shoulder. Then I turned to Lyric. "Hey, girl."

"Hey," Lyric said with a smile before pulling me in for a hug. "Everything looks beautiful. Do you need any help with anything?"

"No, I think everything's all good. Just relax and have fun. Bars are open on both sides of the room."

"Sweet!" Brady said, making a beeline for the closest one.

As more players began to arrive, Lyric said, "Go. Schmooze. I'll catch you later."

"Thanks," I said with a laugh. My friend knew the drill. As Director of Community Partnerships and Events, I had lots of work to do, but I'd probably be able to have a glass of wine and sit with her later once the party was in full swing.

It turned out to be a wonderful evening, the type of

event where everything happened on schedule and people seemed to be having a great time. The photographer, a recent college graduate named Toby, kept busy taking publicity pictures all night. I smiled as I watched Lyric graciously pose for several pictures with Brady. Unlike her husband, she was uncomfortable with the spotlight. Lyric wasn't crazy about constantly being photographed, and yet she never hesitated to pose with Brady for pictures at these events. She knew it would be terrific publicity for a good cause, and she knew how much it meant to me. Both Lyric and Julia had become treasured friends to me, and I was lucky to have them in my life.

I managed to find a few minutes to sit down and eat at the table with Lyric and Brady. The dinner was delicious, with a choice of steak, chicken, or vegetarian entrées. I indulged in the steak but passed on dessert. It wasn't easy, given how incredible the chocolate cake, cheesecake, and parfait options looked. But I'd struggled with my weight all my life and had to be sure to eat everything in moderation.

After dinner, my turn came to give a brief speech. Public speaking had never bothered me much, and I was grateful for the chance to address my audience.

"Thank you so much to everybody for coming out tonight," I said from the podium at the front of the banquet room. "The caterers, servers, and event staff here at the hotel did a wonderful job, didn't they?"

I paused to allow the crowd to give those hard workers a well-deserved round of applause.

"Every time I work one of these events, I am overwhelmed by the generous spirit of the Baltimore Bay Birds organization. Thanks to all the players who donated signed jerseys, bats, caps, and other memorabilia for the silent auction. We will be able to raise a lot of money for some very important causes tonight. Through our shared love of baseball, we can reach out and share our love with the Baltimore community."

Those weren't just idle words. I often struggled to express my emotions for this ball club and my adopted city of Baltimore without tearing up, but I managed. My prepared speech highlighted some of the terrific causes that the Foundation would continue to support with the money we raised this evening. The funds would help some of the most vulnerable members of the community, like the poor and the homeless. We supported local veterans, as well as those who had been incarcerated and were looking for a fresh start. And then there was the cause closest to my heart: Maryland Kids Kicking Cancer.

I wrapped up by saying, "So thank you once again to everyone who came out tonight to support such a worthy cause. And here's to another year of great Baltimore baseball!"

The audience erupted in applause, and a fresh wave of love and optimism for the future coursed through me. And to think, I almost hadn't taken this job. I had personal reasons for my hesitations, but I was so happy I'd pushed past them and wound up here.

"And how about a round of applause for Sarah Asiago for throwing together this whole shindig!" Brady yelled out, which prompted laughter and loud clapping. That did make me tear up, and I wiped my eyes as I nodded to the crowd before stepping away from the podium.

As happy as I was, when I looked around at the couples in the room, I couldn't help feeling the tiniest twinge of sadness. Still, I enjoyed seeing Brady and Lyric so much in love. And newlyweds Matt and Julia, who couldn't take their eyes off each other. Deep down, I held out hope that I would be in their place one day. Perhaps someday, I would meet the man of my dreams and we could form the kind of loving family I'd been denied while growing up.

As usual, I did my best to remain positive. Yes, I truly believed my Prince Charming was out there somewhere.

2

———

TRACE

"Fuck *me!*" I yelled in fury as my goddamned rental car slid right into the Honda Accord in front of me. I'd only taken my eyes off the road for two damned seconds to change the radio station, and now I'd be tied up for half the night sorting out a fender bender. At least I wasn't in my own car—a Lamborghini. Or worse, my beloved Indian motorcycle. Since I'd been in Florida for spring training for the last few weeks, I'd been stuck with a rental car. Tomorrow I could head back to Maryland for the start of the season.

Riding my motorcycle again was one of the things I was most looking forward to once I got back. Everything made more sense when I could ride free, out on the open road on my bike. Wind therapy, people called it. And it was the truth. Calmed my mind and heart like nothing else.

Groaning in annoyance, I pulled over to the side of the road. Hopefully, the person I'd hit wasn't a total asshole. Paying them off without going through the hassle of insurance would be the easiest thing to do. I could afford to pay to make this go away.

I watched with interest as a pair of long, shapely legs stepped out of the Honda. I slowly slid down my sunglasses to get a better look. This girl was *hot*. It was like watching a sexy woman walk in slow motion in a movie. Maybe this encounter wouldn't be so bad after all.

"Dammit!" Car Crash Lady cried when she surveyed the damage. She had shoulder-length brown hair, light blue eyes, and a killer rack. "Why didn't you watch where you were—"

Then her eyes landed on me. She stared at me for a moment. I knew that look. Seen it all my life. I was what you might call "blessed" in the looks department. Tall and muscular thanks to my day job as an athlete, I had dark brown hair and eyes. Whether or not she recognized me as the catcher for the Baltimore Bay Birds I couldn't say. But I doubted it would matter.

"Ah ... I ... mean ... are you all right?"

Yeah. Didn't matter if she knew who I was or not. I could worm my way out of this one. Easily. My ability to charm women was one of the few things I was confident about in life. Well, that and sports. I wasn't much good for anything else.

"Oh yeah. I'm fine. Are you okay?" I asked, managing to sound sincerely worried about her welfare. Girls loved that.

Nervously smoothing out her deliciously short skirt, she nodded.

"Y—Yes. Yeah. Yes. I'm okay," she said, still staring at me. Her eyes drifted downward to my tight jeans and black button-down shirt. Black was for sure the best color on me. I had to stifle a chuckle as Car Crash Lady took a good look at my package before finally looking back up into my eyes. I didn't understand why women got mad when guys treated them like a piece of meat. I loved it when women did that to me.

"Listen, let me pay for all the damage," I said as if I was doing her a favor rather than doing what I was legally obliged to do. "Just give me your information, and I will get this all taken care of right away."

Please just go with it, lady. Don't mention insurance.

"Um..." She said, gazing nervously at the rear end of her car.

"What's your name?" I asked.

"Nancy Featherstone."

"Nancy." I drew out her name as I said it. She bit her lip and looked me up and down. "I'm Trace. Trace Ridgerton."

I scanned her face for any hint of recognition. Nothing. Clearly not a baseball fan.

"Nice to meet you, Trace."

"Nancy," I said, walking closer to her. "How would you like to go out for a drink?"

And that's how we wound up discussing the details of the car crash, among other things, at a high-class bar in Fort Lauderdale. I'd wanted to take her someplace fancy rather than touristy. Everything was ridiculously expensive in Florida anyway, but this bar was on a whole other level. Women were usually really impressed with places like this. They also seemed to find it alluring that I always ordered a stiff drink like whiskey rather than an ordinary beer.

Car Crash Lady was quite excited, if a bit skeptical, when I told her what I did for a living.

"You're really a pro baseball player?" she asked, her eyes lighting up. I could tell she wanted to believe me.

"Yeah. See?" I said, searching the internet for some photos of me in uniform with the team.

"Oh wow," she said, her face practically glowing. "You're incredible, Trace."

You're worthless. How stupid you are. I took a healthy swig of my whiskey as if that would kill the sound of my mother's voice in my head. Of course it wouldn't. Nothing did. Then there was the all too loud sound of my own voice in my head.

No. I'm not incredible. What happened to Betsy was all my fault.

Another sip of my drink did help shut my mind up for a bit. Sometimes it took a few minutes to get to where I needed to be.

As much as I preferred to sit here talking about how great she thought I was, I knew switching the conversation to her would work to my benefit.

"So, tell me about you," I said, leaning in to pretend to be enchanted by whatever came out of her mouth. Then she proceeded to prattle on, something about being a legal secretary and whatnot.

By the time she was on her second glass of wine and I was on my third whiskey, I figured it was time to make my move. After all, I had to get up somewhat early to head back to Maryland tomorrow.

"I don't know about you, but I feel like we have a real connection here," I said, gazing into her eyes.

"Yeah, me too," she said breathlessly.

"Would you like to come back to my hotel room?" I asked, holding my breath as I waited for an answer.

With hardly any hesitation, Car Crash Lady said, "Yeah. I'd like that."

I paid our tab, and we both drove our cars back to my hotel. Hers was a little banged up but still drivable. My rental car had a few scratches, but I'd paid for the rental insurance so the damage wasn't my problem.

We had an incredible night together, the perfect capper to wrap up spring training. Car Crash Lady had a rocking body, and I loved that she was a screamer in bed. It was always a huge ego boost to think anybody walking by my hotel room would know some lucky woman was getting it good from a guy who knew what he was doing.

Lucky for me, she was a heavy sleeper, so I had no problem sneaking out early in the morning. I left her a note thanking her for a great time along with my agent's contact information. I wrote that she should call him and he would make sure all the car damage was taken care of. She was a great gal and all, but no way was I about to give her my personal phone number.

I headed to the airport to return the car and hop on a plane to Baltimore, ready to start a brand-new baseball season.

JUST A FEW WEEKS into the season, everything was going great. I was settled back into my house, located about twenty minutes from Old Bay Stadium. Opening day had been awesome as always, and it felt great to be back behind the plate in Baltimore. I'd been hitting well, and all was perfect in my world.

Then I got hauled into the owner's office. Gary Devilbuss himself wanted to see me. I told myself he probably wanted to discuss my contract, which was up at the end of this season, but deep down I knew that couldn't be true. My agent would handle that. After the day game ended, I showered quickly and nervously headed over to see the big man.

"Sit down," Devilbuss ordered the second I appeared in his doorway. His gray eyes narrowed as he sneered at me. The fat, graying guy could pass for Santa Claus if he had a beard, except he wasn't exactly jolly right now.

Not good. Not good at all.

I did as directed, taking a seat across from his desk.

"Is everything all right?" I asked.

"No," he said bluntly.

"Oh."

"As you know, you're already on thin ice with your off-season shenanigans," Mr. Devilbuss said.

The word "shenanigans" struck me as hilarious for some reason, and it was a genuine struggle not to laugh. I tried to focus on what he was saying.

"I'm not sure what you—"

"You slept with Kurt McCracken's wife and then got into a physical altercation over it," he said.

Oh. That.

To be fair, I'd had no idea that woman was his wife at the time. Sure, I had my way with lots of women, but even *I* didn't mess around with other guy's wives or girlfriends. The truth was, she came on to *me* in New York. But hell, I didn't blame people for not believing my story. I didn't exactly have the best reputation. No wonder Gary Devilbuss was mad. He took great pride in the Baltimore Bay Birds and wanted us to be squeaky-clean.

"But now you're being sued, and I do not need any more bad headlines about you," Devilbuss said in an angry, clipped tone.

"What are you talking about?" I asked.

"Your agent called and told me a Nancy Featherstone is suing you."

"Who the hell is Nancy Featherstone?" I asked.

"How the hell should I know?" Devilbuss roared, and I realized I better figure this out pretty quick. I wracked my brain, but I simply did not know anybody named Nancy.

The big boss blew air sharply out of his nose, and I nearly expected to see steam come out of his ears.

I was still drawing a blank, leaving me no choice but to wait for the old guy to clarify.

"She claims you hit her car in Fort Lauderdale," he said.

"Ohhh," I said, the light bulb finally coming on in my head. "Car Crash Lady."

"What?" Mr. Devilbuss asked sharply.

"Okay well, yeah. I got into a minor fender bender during spring training. But I gave her my agent's info and told her he would take care of it. That way I wouldn't have to go through insurance. So why the hell is she suing me?"

Even as I asked the question, I knew the answer. Revenge. She was pissed that I walked out the morning after, leaving no return address.

"Ms. Featherstone claims she hurt her back and neck in the accident."

"That is such bullshit," I blurted out without thinking. "I had her in all kinds of positions that night, and believe me, she was *not* injured."

That was the *wrong* thing to say. Gary Devilbuss was notorious for being a family man. Though he knew many of his players weren't exactly choir boys, he didn't want to hear about it. And he certainly didn't want the public to hear about it. That's why he'd gotten so mad about the Kurt McCracken wife incident.

"News has already gotten out about the lawsuit," he huffed. "The woman spoke to local Florida news and now the gossip rags got hold of it. Between this publicity and your other recent indiscretion ..."

Mr. Devilbuss's eyes narrowed into slits as I waited to hear just how much trouble I was in.

"Your contract is up at the end of the season, you know."

Big trouble. That was the answer.

"Yes. I know," I said, sitting up straighter in my chair. This was serious. I loved playing for Baltimore and had no desire to be shipped off somewhere else.

"I'm not happy with the reputation you've managed to get for yourself. That is not the kind of image I want for the Baltimore Bay Birds."

My heart seized in my chest. Playing baseball was all I had. I couldn't let him take this away from me.

"I understand, sir," I said, praying he would let me off with a warning.

"You're going to need to fix this problem and fast. Otherwise, I suggest you tell your agent to start reaching out to other ballclubs for next season."

My mouth went dry.

"I understand," I said quietly. I was willing to do whatever it took to make the Baltimore owner happy, but the problem was I had no idea what to do.

"You can start by doing some charity work for the Baltimore Bay Birds."

"Yes," I said, leaning forward in my seat. "Yes, of course. That sounds like a great idea."

Relief swept over me. He hadn't totally given up on me yet.

"And stay the hell out of the headlines unless it's positive publicity. Do some work for the Baltimore Bay Birds Foundation or something, and make sure it's public so people will see you're not a total jerk."

"You got it. You can count on me, sir."

"We'll see," he said, narrowing his eyes so far they

almost disappeared. Then he stared at me as if to ask *Are you still here?*

I jumped up from my seat, eager to get started on whatever I had to do to fix this mess.

3

SARAH

I smiled to myself as I worked in my office overlooking the ballpark. It was a rare mid-week game day, and I loved when I could open my window and catch the scent of hot dogs in the air and hear the sounds of the ballgame while I worked. Game time was still more than an hour away, but the Bay Birds were at batting practice now and some hardcore fans were already in the stands. In a little while, I would even get to go down to the field for the ceremonial first pitch. Finding Hometown Heroes—people who contributed to the community—to throw out the first pitch was part of my job. Today, I would escort a sweet Black man in his late sixties to the field to toss the first pitch of the game. He had spent his life mentoring Baltimore City youth.

I heard a knock at my door, and I assumed it was my secretary with the information I'd asked her to research about food banks in the area.

"Come on in," I said.

The door swung open, and there stood Trace Ridgerton dressed in his full Baltimore Bay Birds uniform and looking slightly sweaty from batting practice. My stomach dropped.

It was just such a surprise, and not a pleasant one, to see him of all people at my door.

"Hi," I said uncertainly. I knew him of course, but as far as I was aware, he had no idea who I was. He'd seen me around here and there over the last year since I'd started working here, but it wasn't like I ever saw him at any charity events.

"Hi. Ya got a minute?" he asked.

Not really, I wanted to say. I'd been having such a lovely afternoon and Trace was not exactly someone I wanted to be around. But I wouldn't be rude to him, and I was curious about what he could possibly want from me.

"Sure," I said, forcing a smile and trying hard to hide my distaste for him. I did my best to find the good in everyone, but his cocky attitude and the way he treated women really rubbed me the wrong way. That, and I had horrible flash-backs of my teen years every time I laid eyes on him.

It had taken years of therapy, but I had fought to over-come the bullying I endured both at home and at school. Sports had always been a great comfort to me, so it didn't help that my chief tormentor in high school had been the star baseball player. That horrific experience had threat-ened to destroy my love of sports, especially baseball. I was so glad I hadn't let it steal my joy in the end. Not only was I still a huge sports fan, I had landed my dream job and now made my living supporting a wonderful major league team.

"You're in charge of all the Bay Birds charity stuff, right?"

"Yes, that's right."

"I need to do some charity work," he said.

"What do you mean you *need* to?" I asked. "Did you get sentenced to community service by a judge or something?"

Trace laughed. "Well yeah. Kind of. Judge Gary Devilbuss. He's mad because I got in trouble a few times, so he needs me to clean up my reputation."

I sighed heavily. Just when I thought my opinion of this man couldn't sink any lower. Part of my job was to keep up with the comings and goings of the players, and I always read any article about the Baltimore Bay Birds that came up in my online news feed. I knew all about his latest troubles about being sued for some car accident. That, combined with the ugly news about his affair with the wife of a New York Kings player, must have angered Mr. Devilbuss something awful.

"I see," I said wearily.

"What?" Trace said with a smirk. I knew that look. This man knew he was incredibly attractive, and he expected me to fall for his alleged charm like other women did. There was no chance of that.

"So you've never shown any interest whatsoever in any of the community and charity work done by the Bay Birds organization, but now you want to volunteer so it will make you look like a good person?"

I tried to feel bad for being so blunt, but it was hard. I had seen a lot of hardship and poverty in the city of Baltimore, and I'd also seen players like Matt and Brady giving money as well as donating their time to worthy causes. I'd never been a fan of Trace's, and his selfishness seriously annoyed me.

"How do you know I'm not actually a good person?"

I bit my tongue *hard* to keep from answering that question.

"I don't know you, Trace," I said, doing my best to keep my voice even. I generally didn't have much of a temper, but I felt my anger flaring. I had half a mind to turn him down and tell him I didn't want his help.

"Would you like to?" he asked, smirking again.

"No," I said forcefully. "Not especially."

"Damn," Trace responded, holding his hands up in mock defense.

Oh my God, this guy.

My hands clenched, and I fought the urge to toss him out of my office. Not only was he asking me for a favor, but now he was *hitting* on me?

All I knew was I needed to get this guy out of my sight before I killed him.

"Okay, so basically you need the quickest, easiest way to volunteer, to get back in Gary Devilbuss's good graces, correct?"

"Yeah," he said.

Trace was being honest with me. I'd give him that. He could have come in here claiming to be passionate about helping people in the city, which would have been worse.

Sighing again, I pulled up the schedule on my computer.

"We have a food drive coming up. People get a chance to meet some of the players if they bring food for the needy."

"Do you have room for one more on that one?"

"Yah, sure," I said.

He cocked his head curiously. "You from the Midwest?"

I stared at him for a moment before answering.

"Yes," I said. "I'm from Minnesota."

"No kidding!" Trace exclaimed. "So am I."

"I know."

"You do?"

"Yes. I've read your file."

"You did, huh?" he asked, cockiness in his voice.

Don't flatter yourself, I thought. I had to be careful. I'd come darn close to saying that out loud.

"I've read everybody's file. It's part of my job to know

about the players. Their interests, their strengths, and possible areas of interest in charity and community. Things like that."

"What made you come all the way out here from Minnesota?"

I wasn't sure why I did it, but I decided to reply honestly.

"To escape."

"Escape from what?"

"From everything that happened in my life before the age of eighteen," I said sharply.

I supposed I'd told him the truth for shock value. Anything to wipe that stupid smirk off his face.

It worked—he seemed intrigued and leaned forward.

There was a knock on my open door, and both Trace and I turned to see my administrative assistant in the doorway.

"Sorry to interrupt," Brenda said.

"No, it's fine," I said. "Come on in."

Brenda walked over to my desk with some paperwork for me, and Trace wasted no time looking her up and down. She wore a tight skirt, which I was sure he thoroughly enjoyed. She placed the papers on my desk and then looked over at Trace.

"H—hello, Mr. Ridgerton," she said.

"Oh, please," he said, waving his hand in the air and pretending to be modest. "Call me Trace."

"Okay. T—Trace," Brenda said, blushing.

Happy now? Now you have a woman falling all over herself for you. Brenda could do what she wanted, but I sure as heck wasn't about to make a fuss over this guy. Trace was undeniably attractive. Muscular of course, since he was an athlete. With his dark hair and dark brown eyes, he had strong, masculine features and looked great in his baseball uniform. When not dressed for a game, he wore expensive clothes and frequently wore black, which even I had to admit was his color. Still, I didn't find him attractive, because his cocky personality was so unappealing.

"This looks great," I said, looking over the research she had done for the food banks project. Brenda knew I preferred working with actual papers so I could make notes and highlight things, and I appreciated her thorough work.

"Is there anything I can get you?" she asked me while still looking at Trace.

"No, that should do it. Thanks."

"Okay," she said, sounding disappointed. Well too bad. Trace could hit on her during her own time. Right now I just wanted to get rid of him.

Growing more irritated by the minute, I waited while Trace stared at Brenda's backside as she left the room. I did my best to keep my face neutral. The last thing I wanted was for Trace to think for one second that I was jealous of the attention he was showering on Brenda.

"All right," I said once she was gone. "Let's get you scheduled for the food drive. Now, once you commit to this, it is very important that you don't back out. Barring an emergency, of course. Your name will be all over the publicity materials, and your fans will be expecting to get the chance to meet you."

"Got it," he said with a grin.

I hated to admit it, but the truth was Trace did have a very loyal fan base. He was quite popular and, unfortunately, he knew it. We took a few minutes to work out the scheduling logistics and to discuss the procedure for safely meeting with the fans during the event.

"Sounds great," Trace said with the familiar smirk on his face.

I swallowed hard, still struggling to quash my anger. I

couldn't help being upset. There were so many genuinely needy, hungry people in Baltimore, and I felt like Trace was not only using them to get out of trouble, he would get his already massive ego stroked in the process. It simply wasn't fair.

"You can count on me," he said.

"I hope so," I said grimly.

"Catch ya later," Trace said with a wink. Then, at last, he left my office.

Sighing heavily, I got up from my desk and looked down at the field below. I was disappointed in myself. I'd let Trace get to me, and I had failed in my quest to be kind to everyone, even those I disliked.

Closing my eyes, I pictured Trace's face. Just imagining that smirk made my blood pressure rise. Still, I soldiered on.

"Love and light," I whispered. "Trace Ridgerton, I wish you love and light."

I opened my eyes and took several deep, steadying breaths. I reminded myself that I did not know Trace's story. For all I knew, he had reasons for being so insufferable.

Glancing back down at the field, I saw Brady signing autographs. My tension eased as I watched him joke around with his fans.

Most of the Baltimore Bay Birds were a joy to be around. And I was grateful.

4

TRACE

*W**ell that was unpleasant.**

I'd managed to put on a happy face during my meeting with Angry Charity Lady, but it hadn't been easy. You would think someone in that kind of job would enjoy helping others, but not her.

I tossed my regular shoes back in my locker, grabbed my cleats, and then slammed the metal door shut.

"Problem, Mr. Ridgerton?" Brady teased.

"Nothing I can't handle. Just had a run-in with one hell of an ice queen," I muttered.

"Are you saying you found a woman who is actually immune to your charms?" he asked.

Chuckling, I said, "Yeah, I guess you could say that. I had to meet with that head of Bay Birds charity woman. Sharon something-or-other?"

"You mean Sarah?" Brady asked, sounding surprised.

"Yeah, that's the one. What a nightmare she is."

"Wait," Matt said, wandering over to us. "Do you mean Sarah Asiago?"

"Yeah. Her. She's kinda mean," I said, hating how I

sounded like a wounded child. But I couldn't help it. She had been super frosty to me.

"What are you talking about?" Matt asked, his blue eyes wide. "Sarah's one of the nicest people I've ever met."

Brady nodded, as did several other players who were listening.

"Sarah Asiago," I repeated to make sure we were all talking about the same person.

"Yeah. She's a real sweetheart. I helped get her the charity director job," Matt said. "Well, her credentials got her the job. I just told her about the job opening and put in a good word for her."

"She and Lyric get along great," Brady said with a shrug.

"And I consider her to be one of my best friends," Matt said, sounding defensive. He seemed genuinely pissed at me; rare for a chill guy like him. Made me wonder if maybe he had a thing for Sarah, which was kinda messed up considering he'd just gotten married.

Brady slung his arm around my shoulder and said, "Looks like she just can't stand you, champ."

Laughing, he let go of me and headed out to the dugout.

"Son of a bitch," I muttered as I laced up my cleats. I would only have to deal with her for this food drive and then I would be done with her. So I guess it didn't matter what she thought of me.

Well, it shouldn't matter.

Trying to put Sarah out of my mind, I concentrated on the details of the game. It was still early in the season, but the Boston Red Rebels were in our division, so every game we played against them was important. I headed out for the opening ceremonies.

I stood at the railing of the dugout and joked around with Brady and some of the other guys for a few minutes.

Then Sarah of all people came walking out of the clubhouse and onto the warning track. I couldn't help staring at her. She was dressed in a knee-length skirt, which showed off her shapely legs.

"She is attractive, isn't she?" Brady asked, amusement in his voice.

It annoyed me that I'd been caught looking at her.

"Sure, I guess," I grumbled.

Sarah was beautiful. Annoyingly so. There was simply no denying it. She had blondish, slightly brownish shoulder-length hair. Dirty blond, or maybe honey-blond you could call it. Her bright blue-green eyes lit up when she smiled, which she'd been doing since she walked out onto the field. Seriously, she smiled at *everyone,* and she looked like a completely different person than the one I had met in her office a short time ago.

I watched as she joked around with Julia on the sidelines. Julia's pre-game field preparation was done, and now they were just waiting for the usual opening ceremonies. Sarah excused herself from her friend and made her way back over to the tunnel inside the stadium where we had all just come from. An older Black man was being ushered onto the field, and Sarah hurried over to greet him. They stood just a few feet away from the dugout.

"Hello, Mr. Spencer! Are you ready for your big moment?" she asked, still smiling.

"I guess," the man said with a shy smile. "A little scared is all."

"Oh, please don't worry," Sarah said kindly. "You're gonna be just fine. We just want to celebrate you and all the wonderful work you've done for the city. Nobody will be expecting you to pitch an eighty mile-an-hour fastball."

"Lordy, I hope not," the guy said with a grin.

Sarah stood next to him as the announcer introduced him as Mr. Vincent Spencer, pillar of the community. He was selected as one of the Bay Bird's Hometown Heroes. A U.S. veteran, the man was a champion of the homeless in Baltimore City and had done a lot of work in raising funds to educate underprivileged people so they could provide for themselves.

As the announcer wrapped up his glowing words about the man, Sarah coached him on when it was time to head for the mound so he could toss the first pitch. She bit her lip nervously as she watched the man, and I knew she was rooting for him to do well. Funny how we did this Hometown Hero shtick all the time and I never thought much about it, even though I was the guy who tried to catch the ball they pitched. And it was weird that I'd never really paid much attention to Sarah before now. She mostly stood off to the side while talking to the person who would toss the ball to me.

Mr. Spencer pitched the ball. I let out a sigh of relief when the ball actually made it to the plate, and I caught it easily. The crowd went wild, and the man smiled and waved.

"You did great," Sarah said happily as she walked over to us.

"Whew, yeah," Mr. Spencer said. "Yeah, that wasn't so bad."

He turned and gazed out at the crowd. "I do love this city."

His voice wavered a bit, and Sarah smiled.

"Now don't you cry," she said. "You'll make me cry."

Mr. Spencer chuckled softly. "Thanks for all your help. You made an old man pretty happy."

"You deserve it," Sarah told him. Then she turned around and caught a glimpse of me.

A look of utter distaste crossed her face when she saw me. She recovered quickly but not quickly enough. Brady snickered beside me.

Then, to prove a point, he said, "Hey, Sarah. How's it going?"

Sure enough, Sarah smiled at him the way she smiled at everybody but me.

"It's going really well," she said, sweet as honey. "Hope you guys have a great game today. Beat the Rebels!"

"We'll try," Brady said with a friendly wave. He chuckled, and I knew damn well he was laughing at me.

Honestly, I'd have done the same thing if the situation had been reversed. I'd have found it funny as hell if some woman clearly couldn't stand him but was nice to me. But that would never happen. Everybody loved Brady Keaton.

"Dude, what the hell?" I muttered as Sarah walked over and started chatting with our manager, Pete Robards. The old man could be rather gruff and short-tempered, but she spoke to him like they were best friends. Something she said to Robards even got a small smile out of him.

"I don't know man, but she does *not like you*," Brady said. "Hey, good luck at that charity thing, fella."

He cackled and walked away, leaving me to wallow in annoyance.

Sarah stayed through the National Anthem. She walked right by me without saying a word or even turning her head to acknowledge my existence.

"Hey, Clay," I heard her say as she walked into the clubhouse. "Hey, Rusty. Have a good game."

"What the actual fuck," I muttered to myself. I remained in a rather foul mood until it was my turn at bat in the first inning.

As I stepped up to the plate, my signature song, "Back in

Black" by AC/DC blared, and the crowd went wild. Maybe Sarah Asiago hated me, but tens of thousands of fans begged to differ.

Bolstered by the screams of the fans, particularly the high-pitched female ones, I vowed then and there that I would win Sarah Asiago over, no matter what it took.

Sooner or later, she would give in to my charms. They all did.

5

———

SARAH

I arrived early to set up for the food drive, which was located outside, in front of the entrance of a large shopping mall about twenty minutes from Baltimore. Normally, I loved doing events like this, but knowing Trace would be participating today put a damper on it. My usual mental reminders to wish him well weren't working for some reason. I couldn't help it. I just didn't want to see him.

The truth was, he made me nervous.

Every time I saw him, I felt transported back to the most painful time of my life. As much as I tried to put up a brave front, it was a constant struggle to remain upbeat and strong. Being bullied when I was young had left scars that hadn't truly healed, and every time I saw Trace's cocky grin, I felt like the fat, unwanted outcast I was in high school.

Closing my eyes, I drew in a deep breath of the morning air as I leaned against the Bay Birds van in the lot. I needed a moment of reflection.

Being overweight should have nothing to do with how I feel about myself. I need to love myself and my body, whether I'm heavy, trim, or anywhere in between. And as for feeling unwanted, it was not my fault my family was dysfunctional.

I opened my eyes and gazed around the empty parking lot. Trace aside, I was beginning to feel better about today. I loved the Baltimore Bay Birds, and representing them as we helped the community made me feel good all over. Today I would greet excited baseball fans while collecting food for the needy. I was doing important work, and I *was* wanted here. I belonged here.

Trace and people like him can't hurt me anymore. Not if I don't let them.

Fortunately, our first baseman, Rusty Power, would also be here today. He was an enthusiastic rookie on the team, and he seemed grateful to be with the Bay Birds organization. I would be okay if I focused more on him than on Trace.

I smiled when I saw the Baltimore food bank truck roll up right on time. The weather was warm and sunny, which was critical for an outdoor event like this one.

Much to my dismay, Trace arrived while I was still setting up. He came roaring in on a loud motorcycle, no less. Sighing heavily, I watched him glide into a parking spot quite close to where I was standing on the mall sidewalk. I grimaced when he took off his helmet.

He caught me looking and raised a curious eyebrow at me.

I felt terrible. I had a visceral, negative reaction to seeing him, and I knew I had to get a grip. Whatever his personal reasons were for being here, Trace was here to help. The best thing I could do was to treat him like any other volunteer.

"Good morning, Trace," I chirped in my best event-coordinator voice. I nearly added "nice to see you" but I couldn't bring myself to lie. "I'm still setting up."

"Need any help?" he asked with a grin that probably made other women swoon but made my stomach churn with anxiety.

This is not high school.

Mad at myself for feeling so off-balance around Trace, I fought to not only look brave but actually feel it. After all, I'd worked around athletes for most of my life, and Trace Ridgerton was hardly the first cocky jerk I'd dealt with. Back in the old days I'd been powerless, at the mercy of my parents and the cruel kids at school. For what it was worth, I was in charge of the event today. Should Trace step out of line, I could always send him home. Granted, that was a last resort.

"Nope, I'm good," I said, forcing a smile.

I went over to the van and unloaded some folding chairs. Then I started pulling out the table.

Trace sighed audibly.

"What?" I asked.

"Can I please help you with that?" he asked.

I was being ridiculous and we both knew it. The man was a professional athlete, and my insisting on moving the heavy table by myself was silly.

"Sure. Thanks," I said.

The folding table was fairly long, and it really was a two-person job.

"Where to?" Trace asked, hoisting his end like it was light as a feather.

"Follow me," I said, walking backward as I held my end. I stopped at a point near the front entrance of the mall. "Right about here is perfect."

"Let's flip it over so we can extend the legs," he said.

Together, we turned the table over. He went right to work opening up the metal legs. "Okay, flip one more time."

Soon it was upright and ready for action.

"Great, thanks," I said, genuinely grateful for his help. Normally I had some volunteers to help with this kind of thing, but they hadn't arrived yet.

"What's next?" Trace asked, grinning again.

"You can just sit tight. Will be a little while until things get started."

Trace nodded, and I went to work moving empty boxes and bags from inside the van. He sat on one of the metal folding chairs. Crossing his arms, he sighed again. I ignored him.

"I can help with that, you know," he said.

"I'm good," I called out as I leaned inside the van to grab more supplies.

When I emerged with my hands full, he shook his head.

"Why do you hate me?"

There was no way I would answer that honestly.

"I don't hate you," I said. That part was true. I didn't hate anyone. But I did dislike him. Strongly.

"Then why won't you let me help you?"

"There's not that much to do."

Trace's laugh was as snide and cocky as his smile. "Coulda fooled me."

I despised the way this guy tested my patience. Sometimes being positive all the time took more mental energy than I had to spare, and Trace was draining mine pretty quickly.

"I can take care of everything."

"I know you *can*, but why should you have to when I'm here to help?"

Trace's words made logical sense, but they sounded

different coming from his mouth than when other volunteers said them. He sounded more like he was hitting on me than genuinely trying to assist me. And yet, he *was* a volunteer, the only one here so far, and I might as well put him to work. Who knew? Doing some charity work might do him some good.

"Fine," I said, trying not to clench my teeth as I spoke. "Thank you. We need to unload the rest of the cardboard boxes from the van and then assemble them for when we collect donations."

"Cool," Trace said, heading over to the van.

Whatever his reasons for being here, it was unusual for the players to help with the actual grunt work like this. Most of the time, their job was to show their faces and get fans to show up to see them. That, or donate generous amounts of money to the Foundation.

We unloaded the rest of the boxes and sat on the metal folding chairs at the table to assemble them and tape them together.

After several moments of silence, Trace said, "You never answered my question."

"What question?"

"I asked why you hated me."

"I did answer your question. I told you I didn't hate you."

"But you don't like me."

Trace's statement made me sad for some reason. No, I didn't like him. But I felt bad that it was so obvious. I did my best to be kind and like everyone, but I wasn't a saint.

I didn't respond, but my silence said it all.

"Can you at least tell me why? What did I ever do to you?"

All I'd wanted for today was to have a fun event to

benefit the community. The last thing I needed was to dredge up my life story, and Trace was forcing the issue.

"You really want the truth?"

"Yeah," he said. I didn't turn to look at him, because I could tell by the sound of his voice that he was wearing that snarky grin of his.

"You remind me of the kids in high school who were very cruel to me. They bullied me relentlessly, especially the popular athletes. They damn near ruined my love of sports, but I wouldn't let them."

I pulled sharply on the packing tape, angrily ripping off a piece for the box on my lap.

Trace fell silent for a moment, which made me wonder if perhaps he was having a moment of compassion for me.

"Well, that's not really fair to me, is it?"

I laughed bitterly. "No. I guess it isn't."

I didn't know why I had thought for a second that he would understand.

Composing myself somewhat, I set the box down next to me and reached for another one to assemble. I thought back to all my therapy sessions and reminded myself that I could not control the actions of others. But I could control how I chose to respond. Trace could be cocky and obnoxious, and I could choose to be kind. It wouldn't be easy, but it would be making the best of a tough situation. I didn't know how many events Mr. Devilbuss would force Trace to attend, so I'd better get used to his presence.

"Just a few more boxes and we're all done. Thanks for your help," I said sincerely. Funny how I did feel better after I said that. Anger and bitterness could be poisonous to your soul. Choosing kindness brought peace to it.

"You're welcome," Trace said.

I got up and walked over to the food bank truck to talk to

the driver who was sitting in the back of the open truck drinking coffee. We chatted for a few moments, having a pleasant conversation about the plan for the day.

Not long after that, the security guard from the Bay Birds arrived. John Miller was a delightful man in his late 40s whom I'd worked with many times. He would ensure the safety of me and the players, making sure the fans in line didn't get too rowdy.

All the time I was talking to John and the man from the food bank, I could feel Trace watching me. At first, I thought I was being paranoid. But when I glanced his way, sure enough he was staring at me with his arms crossed. He was eying me up the same way he'd been ogling my assistant that day in my office.

What a creep.

No. Not a creep. A man that I barely knew, which meant that I had no idea what was going on in his life. I was constantly battling demons from my past, and for all I knew, he was too. Trace Ridgerton deserved the benefit of the doubt. It had been my experience that people who were cocky on the outside were frequently insecure on the inside.

Sorry for thinking you were a creep, Trace. I wish you love and light.

Once again, my positivity made me feel better. I felt better still when I saw Rusty Power arrive. As I watched him step out of his blue Honda Civic and head over toward us, I noted that even his walk was friendly. He bounded over to us like an excited puppy. Having only recently made it to the majors, Rusty was overjoyed just to be here.

"Good morning," I said as he approached.

"Hey, Sarah." His smile was warm and boyish. He had red hair, which was why people called him Rusty instead of his real name, Russell. His bright blue eyes matched the sky overhead. "Couldn't have asked for a better day, right?"

"Yah," I agreed. "I'm hoping we'll get a big turnout."

I ushered him over to the table where Trace was still sitting, grinning, with his arms crossed.

"Hey, man," Rusty said, and I could see the hero worship in his eyes when he looked at Trace.

I explained to the two of them how the food drive would work. Fans would get in line with their donations, which I would accept from them and put in the boxes and bags for the Baltimore food bank. It was up to the players how much interaction they were willing to permit. In the past, some guys agreed to pose for pictures and sign autographs while others were more standoffish, preferring just a quick hello. On the *very* rare occasions that Brady Keaton participated in a meet and greet, we usually stuck with the quick hello in order to get to as many fans as possible. It wasn't that Brady was unwilling to participate—quite the opposite. He loved the fans and was passionate about helping the Baltimore community. But he was so famous that he required extra security, and any event involving him necessitated careful planning and expense.

Both Rusty and Trace were willing to do pictures and autographs. My stomach quivered with excitement just thinking about all the happy fans that would get to meet the Bay Birds' catcher and first baseman. I advised both players to tailor their fan interaction based on the size of the crowd. If it was a big turnout, we wanted to make each fan feel appreciated while keeping the line moving so as to get as much food for the needy as possible.

"Thanks for doing all this, Sarah," Rusty said with a smile.

"Well, thanks for being here," I said. "You too, Trace."

Trace nodded. And grinned.

That familiar sense of anxiety flowed through me at the sight of Trace's smile. I couldn't help thinking that Rusty was here out of the goodness of his heart and that Trace's presence was practically court-appointed.

Don't dwell on the negative.

While Rusty was still new to the team, Trace was hugely popular with the fans. His presence would be incredibly beneficial to this event. And for that, I was grateful.

"So the Jammerjacks did pretty well this season, huh?" I asked Rusty, knowing he was a big hockey fan like me.

"Oh," he said, moaning and clutching his heart.

"I know, I know," I said with a laugh. The Baltimore Jammerjacks' season had ended in a heartbreaker with the team just barely missing the playoffs.

Rusty and I chatted about the team for a few moments, and I delighted in watching Trace's face as we spoke. At first, he seemed impressed with my thorough knowledge of hockey. Not only did I love the game, my last job had been with the Hershey Growlers minor league team. I knew as much about hockey as I did about baseball, which was a considerable amount. As Rusty and I talked and laughed together, I watched Trace's face go from being impressed to looking grouchy and annoyed. God forbid he wasn't the center of attention all the time. I wasn't intentionally freezing him out or anything. I just enjoyed talking hockey with Rusty.

After a while a few volunteers showed up, and I was glad to see them. Welcoming them and showing them what to do kept me busy and away from Trace for a while. As soon as I was sure they were prepared for the day, I gave them a chance to meet the players before the crowd of people arrived.

Trace leaned back in his chair, grinning and nodding as the two men and one woman approached the table. Rusty, however, jumped out of his seat to shake their hands enthusiastically.

"How you doin' man?" he said with a smile as he shook hands with the first guy. "Thanks for coming out and helping today."

He spent a few minutes chatting with each of them before people started showing up with their donations.

The rest of the morning went pretty much like that. While Trace did pose for pictures and spoke with the fans, he maintained his cool demeanor the whole time. Not cool as in he was frosty with the fans. He was perfectly nice to them. But it was like he was used to being the most admired person in the room wherever he went. He kept his motorcycle jacket on the whole time, even after the weather began to warm up. I guess he thought it made him look tough.

Which it did, I supposed.

Rusty's excitement never wavered during the event. His eyes lit up every time he greeted a new fan, and he was utterly charming and gracious with everyone. What a sweetheart he was. Rusty was passionate about baseball, and I hoped he would have a long and successful professional career. He was the type that wouldn't take a moment for granted.

I couldn't help wishing Trace would get traded to another team. It would be easier to wish him love and light from a distance.

During the event, I stood behind Rusty and talked with him in between fan visits.

Turned out that was the one thing that actually rattled Mr. Cool. He did not like being ignored. The fact that I was happily chatting away with Rusty actually wiped that smirk off his face from time to time throughout the day. He recovered quickly every time I saw him scowling, but he didn't fool me. It was rather satisfying to get a rise out of him. Clearly he was used to women falling at his feet.

Not this woman.

I wasn't interested in him, and he'd best get used to it.

Toby showed up halfway through our food drive to snap some publicity pictures.

"Make sure you get some of me," Trace ordered him without so much as a hello.

Jackass.

Yeah, yeah. Love and light and all that, but his rudeness really got to me. Brady, Matt, and many of the other players knew Toby and the other supporting staff by name. Because they'd bothered to *find out* their names.

My irritation mounted as I watched Trace actually shake a fan's hand for the first time today, just in time for Toby to snap a photograph of the historical event. I knew Trace needed physical evidence that he'd been here to show the press and Mr. Devilbuss, but it still annoyed me.

Rusty greeted Toby with a wave, and then went back to joking around with the fans. No doubt he got some terrific, genuine photos of Rusty's fan interactions.

Fortunately, the crowd began to dwindle by the time the event came to an end. It always broke my heart having to send fans away without getting to meet the players, but I had to draw the line somewhere. This time, we were able to give everybody a chance to say hi to Trace and Rusty, even if the last few dozen people had to be rushed a bit.

"Wow, this is amazing," I said, my heart soaring when I looked into the truck to find it piled high with donations.

Rusty walked over to the truck to peek inside. "Nice. We did have a great turnout."

"Yah. Thanks again for everything."

"Anytime, Sarah. Really. Just give me a holler the next time you've got an event planned. Listen, I hate to rush off, but I've got plans with my niece and nephews."

"Oh, no problem. Go enjoy the rest of your day."

"Thanks. You too," he said and then hurried off toward his car.

I glanced over at Trace, who still sat at the table, hands crossed behind his head, staring at me. Doing my best to ignore him, I focused on helping the volunteers pile a few more boxes of food into the truck. I hoped he would just get up and leave now that his part was over, but no such luck. Trace just sat there with that insufferable grin on his face. He hadn't offered to help us pack up the truck. I figured he didn't want the other volunteers to see him perform menial labor.

My muscles tensed as I had no choice but to send the rest of the volunteers home after we'd packed everything and loaded up the Bay Birds van. We even loaded the table where Trace seemed determined to stay put. The last thing to go was his chair, which he eventually surrendered by standing up.

Now it was down to just him and me. It was unsettling, which was probably what he wanted. Trace seemed to enjoy teasing me, making me feel off-balance. It was the same old thing. The cocky jock teasing the nerdy good girl.

My anger started to rise, and I was tempted to jump into the van without another word to him. Deciding I would not let him get the best of me, I took the high road.

I walked right up to him, trying to exhibit confidence I didn't actually feel, and smiled.

"Thanks again for all your help. Enjoy the rest of your day."

Zipping up his leather jacket, he squinted at me and cocked his head to the side. He reminded me of one of those tough motorcycle guys from a 1950s movie. All he needed was a cigarette dangling from his mouth.

"You still don't like me, do you?" he asked.

I took my time trying to figure out the nicest way to respond to that without lying. He didn't give me a chance to come up with anything.

"Don't worry," he said with a grin. "You will."

He stared at me for moment, and I half-expected him to toss that imaginary cigarette to the ground before walking away. Instead, he shot me a sly look before strutting over to his motorcycle.

I sighed audibly, and I heard him chuckle as he climbed onto his bike.

I was annoyed at myself for letting him get the last word, but at least I was rid of him.

For now.

6

TRACE

A few days after the food drive, I got the chance to see Sarah again. And here I'd thought I would have to wait for the next charity event that I could fit into my hectic baseball schedule. Nope, she came walking out of the clubhouse and onto the warning track shortly before Friday night's game. It was another one of those events where they trot out some kid that beat cancer and let him throw out the first pitch.

Leaning on the metal railing of the dugout, I grinned at her as she walked past.

"Hey, Sarah."

She turned at the sound of her name and then grimaced slightly when she saw me. Her reaction to me hurt more than I'd expected. She adored all the other players on the team. Was I really such a horrible person?

"Hi, Trace," Sarah responded in a clipped tone before hurrying off toward the field.

Brady chuckled from his spot right next to me. "Still hasn't warmed up to you, I see."

"I hear she pretty much ignored you all day at the food drive," Matt teased.

"Who told you that?" I asked.

"Julia. Sarah told her she much preferred talking to Rusty over you," Matt said.

"Damn gossipy woman," I muttered.

Gazing out onto the field with a calm expression, Matt said, "Talk that way about my wife again and I'll break your face."

Matt scanned the ballfield until he found Julia, caught her gaze, and waved. She blew him a kiss in return. Such a simple gesture, but one that seemed unfathomable to me. I couldn't imagine anyone having that kind of affection toward me.

That's because you're a worthless piece of shit.

I swallowed hard, fighting not to let my stepfather's voice drown out my thoughts.

Matt shook his head. He wasn't really mad at me. At least I didn't think so. It was hard to tell with that guy since he was so quiet most of the time.

I watched Sarah speak with Cancer Kid and his family. The boy looked about eight years old, and he smiled excitedly as Sarah motioned toward the mound and explained what to do.

Good thing I liked a challenge, because that was exactly what Sarah Asiago was turning out to be. That woman did not like me.

I tried not to think about her look of disdain. It reminded me of the way my mother used to look at me. Hell, she *still* looked at me like that. I'd never managed to win over Karol Ridgerton. She still despised me.

"What are you up to, asshole?" Brady asked, chewing and popping his bubble gum.

"Figuring out how to bag Sarah," I answered, trying to sound tough. Inside, I felt like that neglected kid I'd been growing up.

Nobody loves you. They never will.

Maybe Karol and Robert Ridgerton had never actually said those words, but they hadn't needed to. It was obvious how they felt about me.

"What?" Matt asked. Now he did sound pissed off, which was rare for him.

"She hates me, so it will be that much sweeter when she finally succumbs to my charms," I said, sounding a lot more confident than I actually felt.

Brady scoffed out loud and popped his gum again.

"She's not going to succumb to your alleged charms, jackass," Matt said, his teeth clenched.

"What's your problem?" I asked. Being annoyed when I talked about his wife was one thing, but he and Sarah were just friends. Or so I thought. What was he hiding?

"I told you before that Sarah is one of my best friends, and I don't want you screwing with her. Physically, mentally, or any other way."

"What is she, your ex-girlfriend or something?" I asked.

"Kinda," Brady said.

Eyes wide, I said, "No shit?"

Matt punched Brady on the shoulder and said, "Sarah is *not* my ex-girlfriend. We went on exactly one date a long time ago. We've never been anything more than friends."

"If you say so," I said. Matt was getting pretty riled up over a woman who was allegedly just a friend. Going on "exactly one date" could still mean they'd slept together. The thought of Matt being able to get her into bed only made me doubly motivated to bag her. It felt like an affront to my manhood that Mr. Shy Nice Guy had had his way with Sarah and I could barely get her to glance my way.

I watched Julia hard at work making sure everything was ready for today's game. She instructed one of her workers to go check on the chalk on the left field line, and then she walked the whole way around the warning track to check it before stopping at the dugout to say hello to Matt.

"Everything looks great, Julia," he said with a smile.

"Thanks," she said, her hazel eyes shining with happiness as she gazed at her new husband.

The twinge of jealousy I felt took me by surprise. I was hardly the type to want to settle down with a wife, but the two of them seemed so happy together.

"So it seems Trace has his eye on Sarah," he said, ratting me out.

Julia's face twisted into a grimace not unlike the way Sarah usually looked at me before catching herself and rearranging her face to pretend to be nice to me.

"Is that right?" Julia said, cocking her head and eying me suspiciously. She seemed as annoyed about the idea as Matt.

"You know Matt dated her, right?" I blurted out.

"Ugh," Julia said, rolling her eyes. She and Matt locked their gaze, and both shook their heads in annoyance. "I am fully aware that my beloved husband went out on one date with Sarah. They were set up by my brother. That's how Matt and I became good friends with her. What's the matter with you, Trace? You deliberately trying to stir up trouble with a newlywed couple just because you're annoyed that Sarah's not into you?"

Julia had a point. I *had* been trying to cause trouble. She and Matt were crazy in love, and it was a shit thing for me to do. Besides, I should have known Matt wouldn't have kept any secrets from her.

I seriously considered apologizing, but just then Sarah waved me over. I grinned. Whether Sarah liked it or not, yours truly got to catch Cancer Kid's pitch. Sometimes it was our other catcher, Tommy Mitchell.

Not today, sweetheart. Today you get me.

"Be nice to her, you prick," Matt warned.

I headed to my place behind the plate, and Sarah stood a few feet off to the side to watch the ceremonial first pitch.

"We meet again," I said cockily.

"Just catch the ball, Trace," Sarah said wearily.

I slid my mask down over my face, crouched down, and prepared to try to catch the ball wherever it landed. I was eager to show Sarah I could catch the baseball no matter how wild the pitch might be. Turned out the kid had a pretty good arm, and I only had to lunge forward a bit to nab the ball. The crowd went wild for Cancer Kid.

I stood up, flipped up my mask, and said, "So Sarah, why don't we—"

Sarah ignored me completely and instead went over to congratulate the boy and his family. She led him to the dugout to greet some of the other players, bypassing me completely. Or trying to, anyway.

"Great job, kid," I said, hurrying over to catch up with him.

"Oh, thanks," the lad said, his eyes lighting up. I held out my hand and he shook it with enthusiasm.

Sarah smiled, never lifting her eyes from the boy. At the dugout, she introduced him to Brady, which nearly made the kid's head explode. I stood off to the side, doing my best not to scowl as Sarah continued to ignore me. Once the boy and his family were finally ushered off the field, I had a quick moment with her before we all had to line up for the National Anthem.

"You're looking lovely today, Sarah," I said, eying her up and down. She had killer legs, and she was quite the knockout in her short black skirt.

"Thanks," she said flatly.

Matt's nostrils flared. I didn't think I'd ever seen that guy look mad before. It was odd and rather entertaining. I always did enjoy getting a rise out of people.

"We should do dinner sometime," I said.

"Why?" she asked bluntly, her blue-green eyes boring holes into my head. Sometimes I got the feeling she was a little afraid of me, but it seemed she'd found her courage today.

"So we can get to know each other."

"That won't be necessary, Trace. I think I already know you well enough."

Brady snickered and Matt glared.

"Sarah, is this guy bothering you?" Matt asked.

"Yes," Sarah said firmly, her eyes still fixed on mine. Then she turned to Matt and said, "But it's nothing I can't handle."

Matt nodded. "I believe it. You just let me know if I need to step in."

"I will," Sarah said with a fond smile at her friend.

"Come on, girl. Let's just grab a quick bite after the game. Or a drink or something."

"I don't think so," she said. Then she laughed. "It's funny. That's not something you do very often."

Grinning, I asked, "Yeah, and what's that?"

"Strike out," Sarah said, before turning on her heel and disappearing into the clubhouse.

Pretty much every player in the starting lineup heard me get shot down, and they weren't shy about letting me know. Loud groans and whistles erupted around me.

"Damn, that was brutal," Brady said.

Matt chuckled but said nothing. He didn't need to.

It was humiliating, but all Sarah's rejection did was redouble my motivation to win her over.

One strikeout didn't mean I'd lost the game.

This was only the beginning.

I WAS all hyped up after the game, especially since I'd successfully managed to pick off the fastest guy on the Chicago team when he tried to steal second. Revving my motorcycle, I roared out of the Old Bay Stadium player's lot and sped off toward my rancher home in Towson. My place was the perfect distance away from the park. The twenty-minute ride was enough to relax me, but not long enough to wear me out having to commute every night.

The early May night was a bit chilly, but my leather jacket kept me warm enough. Breathing in the fresh air as I rocketed down the Baltimore Beltway, I thought about tomorrow's game against the Chicago Eagles. We'd narrowly managed a win tonight, but their lineup was strong. I started running scenarios about what pitches to call for the game, but somehow my thoughts kept returning to Sarah.

She was a tough one, that gal. Still, I would admit that on *rare* occasions I came across a woman who didn't immediately find me attractive and irresistible. Those types needed a little extra effort, but it was nothing I couldn't handle. Sarah was unique in that she actively couldn't stand me. Granted, that happened sometimes *after* I'd slept with a woman and then went on my way. It wasn't like I promised anybody a ring before we went to bed. Not my fault when they sometimes got the wrong idea.

Sarah *hated* me for some reason.

Chuckling to myself, I realized that was a lot more fun than indifference.

Sure, it was flattering when women got all flustered and nervous around me, but there was something undeniably sexy about the way Sarah could meet my eye and glare at me. She was beautiful when she was mad.

She was also beautiful when she wasn't. Her face always lit up when she spoke with one of those Cancer Kids or Community Heroes. She was clearly passionate about her job and was damned good at it. I couldn't help being aroused by her flashing blue-green eyes, not to mention the way her ass and legs looked in that tight skirt. So easy to imagine just taking her right there on her desk, her skirt pushed up to her waist and high heels in the air as I banged that scowl right off her face. After she'd embarrassed me in front of the guys, the sex would be even more satisfying.

Sarah seemed so sure of herself, confident that she could resist me.

In an odd way, I was proud of her for that. She was a lot different than any other woman I'd ever met.

In fact, I was starting to actually like her.

7

SARAH

I was pleased with the way the food drive had turned out. We'd managed to collect a lot of food for the Baltimore food bank while also generating goodwill for the team in the community. I'd asked Toby to please make sure that Trace's face was splashed everywhere for that event, including all our social media accounts, the article for the online newspaper the *Baltimore Bugle*, and for the "Bay Birds in the Community" segment that was featured on the jumbotron during games. Hopefully, Mr. Devilbuss would be happy enough with Trace's good-guy publicity that I wouldn't have to endure any more events with him.

Scrolling through the photos on the Bay Birds' social media accounts, I stopped and stared at Trace's image. Though he still unnerved me sometimes, I found it amusing that he seemed so eager to get my attention. He was such a jerk, so it was funny to watch him try and fail at winning me over. Obviously, it made him crazy that there was one woman on the entire planet he could not have, but too bad. He was wasting his time with me.

I finally clicked away from Trace's picture to check my emails. I was pleased to see I'd received some responses from local military veterans for an upcoming project. I let out a loud groan when I saw I'd gotten an email from Trace Ridgerton. Good thing he didn't have my phone number or personal email.

"Hey, gorgeous. Being around you and your do-gooding has inspired me to do more charity work."

Great.

"I promise, this time I'm not just volunteering to get on Mr. Devilbuss's good side!"

No, you're trying to get on mine. I could practically see that stupid grin of his, even through an email.

Leaning back in my chair, I tried to figure a way out of this mess. As Director of Community Partnerships and Events, I had the right to refuse volunteer service to anyone I deemed unfit. However, my personal dislike of a person wasn't a valid reason. Given all the good work the Bay Birds did, it would be unethical to turn Trace away for no good reason. And yet, that didn't mean I had to subject myself to his harassment just because he was pretending he'd suddenly developed a conscience.

I leaned forward and quickly typed a response.

"Dear Mr. Ridgerton. Thank you so much for your continued interest in volunteering for the Bay Birds organization! You will be happy to know that the Owings Mills, Maryland youth baseball team will be picking up trash on I-795 next Saturday morning. I am pleased to note that, since the Bay Birds have a game start time of 7:05pm, you should be able to attend. Unfortunately, I will not be able to attend because I am otherwise engaged. However, there will be several Bay Bird staff members in attendance to provide guidance at this event. Thank you again for volunteering!"

I hit send with a flourish and a laugh. With any luck, he would get the hint that he would not be working alongside me at any events if I could possibly avoid it.

I finished up with the morning emails, then went to work on my favorite charity, Maryland Kids Kicking Cancer. Opening up the physical files on my desk, I flipped through some of the profiles of the brave kids battling cancer at Johns Hopkins Hospital. Those kids and teenagers had been through so much. I teared up when I saw a photograph of Kristy Anders. Seven years old. I'd met with her a bunch of times over the last year as she fought lymphoma. The sweet girl had lost her battle about two months ago.

My anger flared when I thought of Trace's smarmy face. How dare he try to use charity work as a means of manipulation? He had no clue what it was like to be poor and hungry or terminally ill. As much as I despised him, I hoped he'd never find out firsthand what those things felt like. But I did wish the man would learn some compassion. I felt that way about most people who had wronged me. Not necessarily that karma would catch up with them, though sometimes I wanted that. I was only human, after all. Mostly, I hoped that mean, obnoxious people would stop hurting others after they realized they were doing wrong. I wished all the jerks of the world would get the Ebenezer Scrooge treatment and understand how their actions hurt people. That they'd learn from it and go forward with goodness and kindness in their hearts. Rather than being miserable after a dose of their own medicine, they'd feel peaceful having understood what was really important in life. Love and kindness.

Since it was highly unlikely that Trace would be visited by Yogi Berra, Ty Cobb, or any other Ghosts of Baseball Past, I had to accept that he wasn't going to change his ways. The best thing to do was avoid him as much as possible until he found another female conquest.

So much for avoiding Trace Ridgerton. There I was, having a perfectly lovely time at Brady Keaton's house on a rare night off when I heard the unmistakable sound of a motorcycle come roaring up outside. Though Trace was hardly the only Bay Bird who rode a bike, I just knew it was him. I had that kind of luck. Always.

Brady often entertained players and their families at his house. It was a way to hang out with a bunch of famous people without having to deal with autograph-seeking fans. I'd been sitting at a table with Lyric and Julia in Brady's basement bar having some drinks and some laughs with my good friends when Trace had to show up and ruin it.

No. He wouldn't ruin my good time. I wouldn't let him.

I shot a brief distasteful look his way when he walked in before turning my attention back to my friends. Thankfully, Trace went right up to the bar without noticing me.

I sighed heavily as I picked up my glass of wine and took a sip.

"What's the matter?" Lyric asked.

"I feel like I'm being a total bitch."

"Why?" Julia asked with surprise. "You're one of the nicest people I know."

"I cannot stand Trace Ridgerton, and I feel like I'm being unreasonable about him."

"You're not," Lyric said with an uncharacteristic edge to her voice. Both Julia and I looked at her with surprise. "He's not a bad guy, I guess. Just not exactly my favorite player on the team. Something about him just rubs me the wrong way."

"Exactly," Julia agreed.

Hearing that my friends agreed with me made me feel less like a terrible person. That, and recalling the way he'd treated me, I realized I wasn't being that unreasonable.

"Do you know he keeps volunteering for charity events now just to hit on me?"

"Ugh," Julia said, shaking her head. "That's pretty messed up. I thought he was just volunteering to get out of trouble with the big boss."

"Well, that's how it started. I hoped all the good publicity he got for the food drive would be enough to make Mr. Devilbuss happy. But now Trace keeps asking to do more stuff, and it's clear he doesn't actually care about charity work."

My anger flared when I thought about my precious Maryland Kids Kicking Cancer group. There were plenty of real reasons to get involved in charity work with so much suffering in the world.

I glanced over at the bar to see Trace with a whiskey in his hand, talking with Brady. It was annoying how good-looking Trace was. As usual, he was wearing his leather jacket. He looked sexy and a little dangerous.

Turning back to my friends, I said, "He reminds me of high school, when some of the kids were so cruel to me. This one time ..."

Julia nodded sympathetically as she listened, encouraging me to go on.

"What happened?" Lyric asked gently.

"You guys know I had kind of a messed-up home life. I wanted to get out of the house as much as possible, but it's not like I had a lot of friends. So I found comfort in going to sports games."

"I get that," Julia said kindly. Though I knew she shared my love of sports, Julia was so pretty, warm, and friendly. I got the feeling she was really popular in high school. Not that she would ever point that out to me.

"Once in a while I'd scrape up enough money to go to a Minnesota Wolves game, but most of the time I just attended our high school games. Football, baseball, soccer, whatever they had going on." I smiled at the memories. "There was something magical about having all these people come together rooting for the home team, you know?"

"Brady says that all the time," Lyric said with fondness in her voice. She'd told me that when she first met him, she hadn't known the first thing about baseball. She fell in love with the game due to her husband's passion for it.

"People pretty much ignored me, and I guess I was okay with that. I just sat in the stands day after day rooting for the home team."

My stomach tightened as I went on, wanting to get this burden off my chest and not wanting to talk about it at the same time. I trusted these women with my life, so I knew it was safe to tell them.

"Then one day the first baseman of the team pulled me aside after class. Told me he'd noticed me coming to all the games and said it was cool that I was such a big sports fan. We talked about baseball and stuff for a while, and we really hit it off. We talked every day for two weeks. When I went to see him play, he smiled and waved at me from the field. It was incredible. I couldn't believe a guy like him would notice a girl like me."

Both Lyric and Julia stared at me grimly. Clearly, they'd

caught on to this asshole's game a lot quicker than I had at the time.

"Then one day right after the game ended, he got down on one knee and held up a poster asking me to the prom in front of the whole stadium. For one brief moment I actually thought ..." My throat tightened and tears threatened to spill. Fighting to keep myself steady, I plowed forward, determined to finish my story. "It wasn't until I heard the laughter from the whole team that I realized it had been nothing but an elaborate joke."

Julia gasped in horror and covered her mouth.

Lyric shook her head sadly. "That is one sick joke. Oh, Sarah, I'm so sorry people have to be so cruel."

"It was my own fault. I was so fat and ugly back then. I should have known better than to—"

Drawing in a deep breath, I said sharply, "No." I shut down my negative self-talk right away. "It wasn't my fault. I wasn't fat and ugly. I was a scared, lonely girl who deserved better."

"You're goddamn *right* you did," Julia snapped angrily.

I took another sip of wine and my tense muscles relaxed a little. The next part of my tale would be a lot easier to tell.

"Sports had always been such a respite for me, you know? An escape. And that horrible jerk almost took that away from me. After that traumatic experience in front of half the damn school, I seriously considered dropping out of high school altogether. But you know what I did instead?"

Both Lyric and Julia shook their heads, eying me intensely.

"I went to the very next baseball game like nothing happened. It was the hardest thing I'd ever had to do. I sat in my regular seat and I heard people laughing, talking about me and all that. Sitting there without crying took every ounce of emotional energy, but I didn't shed *a single tear*. I even cheered for the team, just like always."

"You are *badass*, Sarah," Julia said. Then she lifted her beer to toast me, and Lyric did the same.

We clinked our glasses as pride surged through me. I really could be badass sometimes.

"I will say the best memory of my high school experience happened after that," I said. "One of the cheerleaders who had been dating the star pitcher of the team came up to me in the hallway. She told me she dumped her boyfriend after she saw him taking part in that horrible prom stunt. She said what they'd done was, in her own words, 'fucking bullshit' and 'totally messed up.'" My eyes welled up at the memory. "Her simple act of kindness meant more than that girl will ever know. I never forgot it."

"That's lovely," Lyric said.

I glanced over at Trace, who was currently laughing and punching Matt in the shoulder for some reason. "When I see the cocky grin on Trace's face, I see all those obnoxious ballplayers from high school. I can't help it."

"That makes sense," Julia said.

"Naturally, I never did end up going to the prom. Not that it really mattered, I guess. Still, I heard all about the prom the Monday after when it was all anybody could talk about. I couldn't help feeling left out."

"I'm sure you did," Lyric said. "It must have been hard."

"Yah," I said. "The big story was apparently one of the jocks got down on one knee during one of the songs and serenaded his girlfriend. It wasn't my tormentor. One of the guys on the team. I just ... I can't imagine what it would feel like to be that kind of girl. Just *once*, you know? Instead of being the girl who gets mocked and made fun of, I'd love to be the one who has a guy sing to her." Laughing bitterly, I said, "I know it sounds stupid."

I was embarrassed at having said that last part out loud in front of two of the strongest, most independent women I knew. They were both killing it in male-dominated fields, with Lyric studying to be a doctor and Julia being only the second female head groundskeeper in all of Major League Baseball. And here I was talking like a wannabe Disney princess.

"Not at all," Julia said firmly. "I think what you're describing sounds incredibly romantic. Just because women like you and Lyric and me are strong and independent doesn't mean we don't want to be romanced once in a while."

Julia's words made me smile. She couldn't know how much having her include me in her group of strong women meant to me.

"You know what I hate?" Julia asked angrily.

"Uh-oh," Lyric said with a laugh. "You got her going now …"

Julia giggled. "I know, I know. But hear me out. I hate that anything girly like proms and romance and stuff is considered weak just because women tend to like that sort of thing. Like anything feminine is bad. You should never feel bad about the stuff you like, Sarah. You do you!"

Laughing, I said, "Okay, I will. I promise."

It occurred to me that Julia did know what it was like to be the kind of girl who was serenaded in public. After all, Matt had gotten down on one knee and proposed during a game at Old Bay Stadium. It was beautiful.

"Oh God," Julia groaned.

Following her gaze, I turned to see Trace heading toward us. He was grinning, because of course he was. When he got to our table, he grabbed an empty chair, spun it around, and sat down on it backward. I stifled a sigh. Sitting like that was such a bro move.

"How's it going, ladies?"

"Very well, thank you," I said brightly, determined not to show my anxiety or dislike of him.

"When are you gonna let me volunteer again?" Trace asked, leaning forward on the back of his chair.

"I already said you could pick up trash on the highway next week."

Julia laughed and I had to bite my cheek to keep from smiling. It was fun to tease him.

Trace grimaced, and I rolled my eyes.

"So much for the joy of giving," I said dryly. "I've done trash duty before and it's kind of fun. Hanging out with the youth baseball players can be very rewarding."

"Oh, I'm sure it is," he said. "But it's not exactly what I had in mind."

"I know what you had in mind. You like the events where fans come up and fawn all over you and stroke your big fat ego while you get your picture taken for publicity. And if you happen to collect some food for people along the way, so be it."

So much for me hiding my dislike of him. I'd lasted ten seconds with my resolve.

Trace shrugged. Sometimes his face was *so* punchable.

"Sarah, when are you gonna give me a chance and go out with me?"

"When you become as charming as you think you are."

Julia chuckled and sipped her beer. Lyric simply smiled.

Trace grabbed his heart dramatically. "You wound me, girl. Truly."

My stomach quivered with a sudden, annoying spark of

attraction. Trace was undeniably gorgeous and cool, looking tough wearing all black per his usual. I'd never been attracted to his type before, and I rather hated it.

Suddenly all my old memories and insecurities came flooding back. My muscles tightened, and I was afraid that maybe Trace was simply making fun of me when he was flirting.

Trace's expression softened for a brief second as he looked at me, and I realized I must have looked as afraid as I felt. Quickly recovering, at least on the outside, I stared into his eyes.

"You know, it's not easy, but I'm doing my best to feel sorry for you," I said in the most confident voice I could muster.

"What do you mean you feel sorry for me?" Trace asked, sounding genuinely offended. Good. I hoped he felt as knocked off-guard as I did. This was not a man who wanted to be pitied.

"I like to believe there's a reason you're such a jerk all the time. I've found that most people are obnoxious for a reason. I don't know what your problem is, but I wonder if you had a rough home life. Maybe something terrible happened to you." I quickly added, "I sincerely hope that isn't the case. I hope you're all right. But I wonder ..."

For once, Trace didn't have a snappy answer to that. And honestly, that made me a little sad. Because it meant I was probably right about his past.

Then he grinned again.

Oh, here we go.

"I know you don't believe it, Sarah Asiago," Trace said with tremendous confidence. "But one day you're gonna give in. One of these days you're gonna wind up in my bed."

Julia slammed her beer down, clearly ready to tell him off.

"Don't worry," I told her. "I got this."

Seconds earlier, I'd genuinely felt sorry for him. Now I'd had enough. Tired of this back-and-forth crap with him, my emotions were raw from this stupid game. It didn't matter if he was just screwing with me or if he genuinely found me desirable, because it was never going to happen between him and me.

"Look," I said, speaking louder than I'd intended but too mad to care. "I know you think you're every girl's dream, but you're not mine. You think so damn highly of yourself that you can have any woman in the world in your bed. Well you *can't have me!*"

The entire bar had gone silent. My adrenaline pumped throughout my body as I fixed my angry gaze on Trace Ridgerton.

Slowly, he got up from his chair. He grinned and spoke two words: "Challenge accepted."

Shaky but determined, I got to my feet. I looked up at him, fixing a steely glare on him. As much as I fought it, I couldn't keep my voice from shaking and my eyes from watering.

"You have absolutely no right to speak to me like that."

His eyes grew wide, and he looked taken aback. He seemed surprised at how upset I was.

"I am not a conquest, and this is not a game. All I want is to do my job in peace and be here with my friends without being harassed. Now *leave me alone.*"

Trace stared at me for a moment and then, at last, he turned to leave.

8

TRACE

On the plane to California with the team, I didn't flirt with the flight attendant because all I could think about was Sarah. I stared out the tiny window, picturing her face the last time I saw her.

She'd had tears in her eyes.

My God, I'd made her cry.

I hadn't meant to upset her. Most women loved it when I paid attention to them. And yet, Sarah had made it clear she didn't want my attention, and I'd refused to respect her wishes.

I felt horrible. That wasn't unusual, since I frequently thought I was a terrible person. But this time it wasn't my mother or my stepfather's voices in my head. Now it was my own thoughts.

Sarah was such a sweetheart the way she always looked out for other people. And not just because of her job. She did it because that was her nature. And here I was, giving her a hard time for no reason. Well, for no *good* reason. I could always count on women being attracted to me, and Sarah's rejection hurt. Besides baseball, attracting female attention was my only skill. Sarah made me wonder if I was losing my touch.

For some reason, I simply could not stop thinking about her. I wanted her attention so bad, more than any other woman I had ever met. That was why I'd behaved so terribly at Brady's bar when she'd turned me down yet again. I couldn't help being taken with her. She was so unlike any woman I'd ever known. She seemed scared of me sometimes, and yet she never backed down. As much fun as giggling and blushing women could be, there was something infinitely more exciting about a lady who could stare me right in the eye without backing down.

Sarah was strong; she'd obviously been through some shit in her life. She'd been roughed up in high school, by guys like me, no less, and I remembered her telling me she'd moved to Baltimore to escape everything that had happened to her before the age of eighteen.

Maybe she endured what my sister Betsy went through.

I shuddered just thinking about it. Nobody deserved that kind of hell. My chest ached when I thought about my baby sister. It hurt too much to think about her, so I did what I always did. Tried to forget.

Though I thoroughly enjoyed having Sarah spar with me, I didn't want her to fear me. Gazing out at the clouds, I thought about that look on her face when I'd teased her at Brady's bar. For a brief instant, her expression had gone dark. Like she was remembering something terrible. The look disappeared as quickly as it came, but I knew I hadn't imagined it.

Yes. Sarah had been through some shit. No doubt about it.

And she sure had my number. She'd zeroed right in on my hellish home life growing up. Nobody else had ever questioned why I walked around with such bravado all the time. Women seemed to love my cocky, tough-guy demeanor. None of them seemed to realize I didn't always feel as confident as I acted.

Until now.

You're such a fucking pussy.

As usual, it felt like a contest in my head to see whose voice was the loudest. My mother's, my stepfather's, or mine. Right now my punkass stepdad seemed to be the frontrunner. Funny how even though I was a pro baseball player, had bagged tons of women, and I owned a motorcycle old Robert would have killed for, sometimes I still felt like that scrawny-ass kid he used to beat up.

The way Sarah seemed to see right through me sometimes was unsettling, but it was also oddly comforting. Like maybe she would understand since she'd made it clear her early life hadn't been ideal.

I had to figure out a way to see Sarah again, and not just in Brady's basement bar when she was with her friends. As smitten as I was with her, I wasn't eager to be humiliated in front of the whole team yet again when she inevitably shot me down. She didn't understand that I was legitimately into her and she wasn't just a conquest to me.

I needed a chance to spend some real time with her so I could show her I was capable of being more than just a cocky prick in a leather jacket. But the baseball schedule was jam-packed, leaving little time to do any volunteer work. And even if I could find the time, Sarah kept shutting me out. There were no sports banquets going on where she couldn't stop me from buying a ticket to attend. Those happened primarily in the off-season.

There had to be some way I could connect with Sarah.

I pulled out my phone and found the link to turn on the

airline's Wi-Fi. I searched up Sarah's social media accounts. No use sending her a friend request on any of the networks that required the person's approval, because I knew that wasn't going to happen. I followed her on Instagram and started scrolling through her pictures.

"Stalker much?" Rusty said from the seat next to me. He *would* pick now to wake up from his nap.

"I like looking at pretty girls, that's all," I said.

"Don't we all? But you can't have *that* pretty girl, and you know it," he teased as he gestured at my phone. "And you know why?"

"Because she hates me?"

"Correct," Rusty responded gleefully.

"Yeah, right now she does. But she'll change her mind. They all do."

I felt a twinge of guilt when I said that. It was shitty of me to talk about Sarah like she was just another potential notch in my belt.

He snorted. "Whatever. Good luck, pal."

"Thank you," I said as if his well-wishes had been sincere. "Go back to sleep."

Rusty didn't go back to sleep, but at least he flipped open his laptop to play some computer game.

Scrolling through Sarah's Instagram feed made me smile. Most of the things she posted were pretty images of nature and positive-thinking memes. I should have known her posts would be all touchy-feely stuff. As bitter as I could be sometimes, I had to admit it was a welcome change from all the political nastiness people posted these days. My body relaxed as I flipped through her Instagram. Positivity could be contagious, I supposed.

She also posted photos of other people—some Baltimore Bay Bird players and her friends, including Lyric and Julia. At last, I came across a selfie.

Sarah Asiago was a beautiful woman, and it was deeper than just her pretty blondish hair and nice body. Her blue-green eyes somehow radiated ... *love.*

I was embarrassed to have such a cornball thought, even silently, but it was true. She had something purely *good* about her. Like she was an angel.

An angel who wasn't afraid to sass me back right to my face.

God, I was crazy about this woman. Too bad she hated me.

Sighing heavily, I clicked on the Instagram direct message button, despite the fact that I had no clue what to say.

"Sarah, I swear I'm not a complete and total asshole once you get to know me"?

It would be hard for me to type that when I didn't really believe it myself.

"Sorry I kept telling the whole world that you were my sexual conquest"?

My finger hovered over my phone keyboard for a ridiculously long time before I finally typed *"Hey."*

Brilliant.

"I really do want to help you with more volunteer work. Let me know what I can do."

I hit send, hoping she wouldn't block me from her Instagram. She didn't block me, but I did get a response just a few minutes after I sent the message.

"NOT GONNA HAPPEN."

Rusty cackled.

"Shot dowwwwn!" he said in a too-loud-for-an-airplane voice.

"Will you mind your damn business?" I said, smacking him on the back of his stupid ginger head.

"Boy, does *she hate you*," Rusty said with another laugh.

Yeah. She sure did.

Fuck.

9

SARAH

My morning at Johns Hopkins Hospital visiting the pediatric cancer patients was both inspirational and emotionally exhausting. I couldn't imagine how tough childhood cancer must be on the parents of these brave kids. I'd met some of the most courageous people I'd ever known in these halls.

Saving my favorite patient for last, I knocked gently on the hospital room door. A weak voice said, "Come in."

My throat tightened when I saw fifteen-year-old Flynn Bishop lying in his bed looking frail and tired. He must have recently gotten through a tough round of treatment for his leukemia. Flynn was a tall, skinny kid with brown hair and sweet, inquisitive gray eyes. At fifteen years old, he was a sophomore in high school.

Poor sweet soul.

I adored him and his doting parents, and it hurt like hell to see him in this condition. The last time I'd visited, he'd been a bundle of energy. Flynn was a huge baseball fan, and he loved it when I told him all about the team. His dream was to someday throw out the first pitch at a Bay Birds game. I would make sure that happened the moment he was well enough.

Fighting hard not to look as horrified as I felt, I walked over to his bedside. His nurses had assured me that Flynn was up to seeing visitors, but it didn't look that way to me.

"How are you feeling?" I asked.

Flynn let out a groan, but then laughed weakly. "About as good as I look."

I wasn't sure how to answer that. Flynn smiled. "I'm doin' okay I guess."

"I won't stay long," I told him.

"No, it's cool. Really. I feel like crap, but I'm sooo bored."

"I'm sure you are."

I had an important decision to make today, but as soon as I locked eyes with Flynn, I knew I'd already made my choice. This sweet boy had me wrapped around his little finger. Such a dear, funny kid who didn't deserve to have his body ravaged by such a horrible illness. Of course, nobody deserved to have cancer. There was just something about Flynn that made me want to protect him.

"You know," I said with a smile, "I can arrange to have one of the Baltimore Bay Birds come visit you in the hospital."

"Really?" he asked, his eyes wide. Flynn's voice sounded stronger now, and it filled me with hope for his future.

"Yah," I said. "You betcha I can. We can only do it once in a while because the guys have such a tight schedule, but the organization will let me arrange a visit now and then. And I get to pick the patient they visit."

"And you picked me? Oh God, I must be dying," he said with a wink.

"Of course not," I said quickly, just in case he was actually worried that might be the reason. "I just know how much you love baseball, and I knew you would really appreciate a visit from one of the Bay Birds."

"Who's gonna come see me?" Flynn asked, sitting up in his bed. He let out a sigh, looking utterly exhausted. Then he pressed the button to tilt the head of the bed up to support his back.

"Anyone you want, as long as their schedule allows," I told him.

I knew who Flynn was going to pick. Brady Keaton. He asked about him all the time, and he was quite impressed that I was good friends with his wife. Brady was quite the character, so I usually had good stories to entertain Flynn with. My mind was already whirring, trying to figure out how to swing a visit from the most famous player in all of Major League Baseball. Brady would be more than willing to do it. I had no doubt about that. He would need extra security and all that, and we had to make sure the medical staff was prepared for everything. We certainly didn't want to interfere with their important work.

"Really? Anybody I want?" Flynn asked, his gray eyes lighting up with excitement.

That look right there was the number one reason I adored this job.

"Yes," I said, knowing I would move heaven and earth to make this kid happy.

"Oh man, I would love to meet Trace Ridgerton!"

Staring at him, I took a few long seconds to respond.

"You want to meet Trace Ridgerton?" I asked, hoping I'd heard him wrong.

"Yeah, that guy is so *cool*," Flynn said. His exhaustion seemed to fade a bit.

Cool.

I pictured Trace looking tough in his leather jacket and riding around on his sleek motorcycle and understood why Flynn would see him that way. Trace was a lot of things, but even I had to admit to his "coolness" factor.

Clinging to hope that Flynn might change his mind, I said, "I had no idea you liked Trace. You've never mentioned him. I really thought you'd choose Brady Keaton."

I watched Flynn's face carefully, hoping he would get excited at the mention of our star shortstop.

"Brady is cool too. He's great and all, but Trace Ridgerton is my favorite. No doubt about it."

"Wow," I said, trying to keep my voice even. "I had no idea."

Those darling gray eyes filled with hope, Flynn asked, "Do you really think you could get him to come see me?"

"Oh, I'm sure I can," I told him. "In fact, he recently contacted me asking if there were any volunteer opportunities he could help with."

"Yeah?" Flynn asked, sounding positively giddy. "That's awesome. I had a feeling he was a good guy."

Trace is not a good guy. He's a pompous, selfish prick who only wants to do charity work so he can get into my pants.

I had absolutely no choice but to grant Flynn's wish and bring Trace to the hospital to see him. And I would do everything in my power to protect Flynn's fantasy of Trace Ridgerton as a great guy. No matter what it took, I would make it my mission that he never found out what kind of man his hero really was.

"You get some rest, okay?" I said, my stomach filling with dread at the idea of having to involve Trace in my most beloved charity.

"Thanks, Ms. Asiago. I can't believe it! I'm gonna meet

Trace Ridgerton!" Flynn somehow found the energy to pump his fist triumphantly in the air.

That's when I knew whatever torture I would have to endure with the most obnoxious player on the team would be worth it. I would do just about anything to make my sweet Flynn Bishop smile.

10

TRACE

I woke up groggy and disoriented, not even sure where I was. Were we still in California? No. We flew back to Baltimore late last night. It was all coming back to me, including the generous amount of whiskey I'd indulged in when I got home after midnight. My body clock was still messed up after being on the West Coast for a week.

I sat up in bed and checked my phone for the time. It was just before noon, so I had some time to chill before tonight's home game. My notifications showed a missed call and a voice mail from an unfamiliar number. Weird. I punched in my pass code to unlock the phone so I could listen to the message.

"Hi Trace," the weary voice said. "It's Sarah Asiago."

"Holy shit." I sat up straighter, as if that would help me hear this important call better.

"Look, I need your help with something. Can you come to my office sometime soon? Thanks. I appreciate it. Talk to you later."

Wow. The last thing I'd expected was a phone call from Sarah after she'd brushed off every attempt I'd made at helping with her charity work. And from her personal phone number, no less. At least I thought it was. I knew her office phone number by heart. My mind whirred with the possibilities.

It seemed unlikely that she actually needed my help with anything. Not after all the times she'd basically told me to take a hike. Was this an excuse to get me to come see her? Did she actually want me to have her personal number? Her tone of voice in the message hadn't made her seem excited to see me, but maybe she was just too proud to admit she was into me.

Grinning, I realized there was only one way to find out. As soon as I'd showered and grabbed a bite to eat, I'd just have to hop on my bike and head on over to see her.

GUNNING MY MOTORCYCLE ENGINE, I zoomed down the beltway toward Old Bay Stadium. I couldn't wait to see Sarah again and see what this was all about. She'd been maddeningly immune to my charisma so far, but I knew I could wear her down if I just had enough time.

As much as I felt like sprinting down the hall toward her office when I got there, I made sure to slow my roll. Sarah didn't need to know I was as giddy as a schoolboy with a crush. I had a reputation for being tough and cool, and it was vital that I maintained my composure around her.

Sarah's administrative assistant—Barbara, or whatever her name was—looked up from her desk in the lobby.

"Oh, hello, Mr. Ridge— I mean, Trace," she said, blushing and smiling nervously.

Now why couldn't I have that effect on Sarah? As soon as that thought crossed my mind, I realized that wasn't what I wanted at all. The real turn-on was the way Sarah challenged me at every turn. Making her blush would be a huge accomplishment. That would actually mean something.

Glancing at her nameplate, I saw her name was Brenda, not Barbara. Whatever.

Brenda typed in something on her computer. "I just messaged Sarah that you're here. You can go knock on her door. She should be available right now."

"Thanks," I said, winking at her, making her giggle again. Sometimes it was too easy to get a rise out of women. I turned eagerly on my heel and walked as smoothly as I could toward Sarah's office. My heartbeat sped up, which was a strange feeling. With Sarah, *I* was the one getting nervous.

I knocked on the door, rapping harder than was probably necessary.

"Come in," Sarah said, sounding as weary as she had on the phone message. Either she was a good actress, or she really wasn't thrilled to see me again.

I strolled into her office and plopped down in the seat across from her. Grinning, I said, "You wanted to see me?"

"Yes, I needed to see you."

She made it sound like she needed to see me like somebody needed to see a dentist.

"What can I help you with?"

"As you know, one of the Bay Birds Foundation's partnerships is with Maryland Kids Kicking Cancer."

"Yeah. Like those kids you drag out onto the mound to toss out the first pitch."

"We do not *drag* them out there, Trace," Sarah said. She was clearly annoyed, and it was exciting to see her getting riled up already. No stammering and blushing from this chick. "They are invited to throw out the ceremonial first pitch in celebration of their triumph over childhood cancer."

"Okay, cool. Good for them," I said with a nod. It was tempting to say something more just to watch her get madder, but I didn't want to be a complete and total jerk. And yet, my mind drifted to thoughts of how exhilarating having angry sex with her would be.

"When possible, we like to arrange to have one of the players come visit the kids in the hospital. It means a lot to them to get to meet one of the Bay Birds."

"I see."

"There's a very sweet boy at Johns Hopkins right now battling leukemia," Sarah said, her expression softening as she spoke of the kid. "He's a huge baseball fan, and I knew he would love to meet one of the guys from the team."

"Uh-huh."

"And for some inexplicable reason, he's chosen you."

A slow grin spread across my face. Was this a lucky break or what? The bad news was that Sarah obviously had not changed her opinion of me and hadn't called me because she'd wanted to see me. The good news was that she could not possibly say no to some sad sack cancer patient. This was my chance.

Thank you, Leukemia Kid!

"So you want me to go to the hospital to see this boy."

"Flynn would very much like to meet you, yes," Sarah said, choosing her words in such a way to avoid admitting she wanted me there.

"Anything you want, baby."

Sarah's eyes flashed and my cock stiffened instantly.

"Do. Not. Call. Me. Baby," she said, making my insides go all mushy. "It's sexist and degrading."

She was right, of course. But she was the only one to ever call me out on it.

"Okay. Sorry, Ms. Asiago."

She huffed irritably through her nose.

"Sarah," I said, holding up my hand in mock defense. "Sorry, *Sarah.*"

"So you'll do it?" Sarah asked.

"Of course I will. You tell me when and where, and I'll meet with the kid."

Nodding, she said, "I'll check your baseball schedule and coordinate with his medical team."

"Sounds good," I said, not wanting this meeting to wrap up. I tried to think of something to prolong it but came up empty.

Sarah stood up, which was my cue to leave. Damn. I got to my feet too.

"Don't you worry," I said in a teasing tone. "I'll take good care of this kid."

Sarah's eyes flashed again. She took two steps forward and stood directly in front of me. Even in her high heels, she had to look up to meet my gaze.

"You better take care of him," she commanded. Her steely-eyed stare turned my insides to jelly all over again. "He is a wonderful child who's been through hell and back again."

I gazed down at her and practically got lost in those passionate blue-green eyes of hers.

"If you're gonna do this, Trace, you need to do it *right*. Be good to him."

"Sarah, I'm not a monster. I'm not gonna be mean to some kid with cancer, for God's sake."

Sarah nodded, still looking worried. She obviously cared deeply for this boy.

"I hope not. If you do anything to hurt Flynn, I will make sure you suffer."

Once again, I was tempted to say something to tease her further, but I held back. I saw the fear in her eyes, and it finally dawned on me how hard this must be for her. Here she was doing her best to help this Flynn boy and everybody else in the city, and she was forced to reach out to the one guy who did nothing but torment her.

"I'm not gonna hurt him, Sarah," I said gently. The anxiety in her eyes eased a bit. "You set everything up, and I'll make sure he has a good visit, okay?"

"Thank you," she said, relief shining in her eyes.

"Anything for you, Sarah," I said with a smile.

She huffed through her nose again.

I walked out of her office, feeling her eyes on me as I left.

11

SARAH

I was a nervous wreck as I drove to Johns Hopkins Hospital on the day of Trace's meet and greet with my favorite patient. Why did Flynn have to pick him of all the players on the team? I envisioned Rusty having a joyous, upbeat visit, sharing his passion and excitement for baseball with everyone around him. Matt would have had a pleasant, low-key chat with my kid. Brady would have blown in like a tornado, but Flynn and the medical staff would have had so much fun with him.

Drumming my fingers on the steering wheel as I waited for the red light to change, I worried about Trace's behavior today. No doubt he would flirt with every female doctor, nurse, and staff member in the place. It was aggravating how much that bothered me.

I felt the tiniest bit sad thinking about the day that would eventually come when he quit asking me out. That annoyed me all over again. I had to stop letting this guy get under my skin. He had a way of being completely and utterly obnoxious and then pulling back at the last minute.

Like his insistence on helping me with the heavy stuff at the food drive. And especially his backing down when he saw how upset I was about him having to meet with Flynn.

I parked my car in the visitor lot of the hospital and walked toward the entrance. Just as I reached the door, I heard the unmistakable roar of Trace's motorcycle. Sighing, I turned around to watch his approach.

My nerves tingled at the sight of him, clad in his black leather jacket, gliding into the lot. The man oozed sex appeal from every pore. No use denying it. Unfortunately, Trace was fully aware of how gorgeous he was.

And his motorcycle made him look sexier than ever.

I had to be careful with those thoughts. Not that I would ever give into temptation with him, but I found it alarming to be even slightly tempted. After all, I couldn't stand the guy. He was a total jerk.

Well, maybe not a total *jerk,* I thought as I watched him dismount and take his helmet off.

I remembered the look in his eyes when he said quietly, *"I'm not gonna hurt him, Sarah."*

For a brief second, he'd been thinking of someone other than himself. He'd clearly been thinking about Flynn. And maybe even about me.

Ugh. *Why did I care?*

Crossing my arms, I hoped I was giving off a halfway believable indifferent vibe. Thanks to my mirrored sunglasses, I was free to eye him up and down as he approached.

"Have you been waiting for me long?" Trace asked with a snarky smile. He made it sound like today's visit was all about me wanting to see him.

"Nope. Just got here when I heard your bike."

"Cool," he said.

"Let's go." My stomach quivered with nervousness as I led him inside. Only part of my anxiety was due to my growing yet undeniable attraction to Trace, which felt like coming down with some infectious disease. Honestly, I preferred the flu over admitting this man turned me on.

Most of my nerves were due to his meeting Flynn. Trace could torment me all he wanted, but if he dared do anything to upset that sweet boy, I would destroy him.

"Okay," I said wearily once we reached the outside of Flynn's hospital room.

I was acutely aware that an unusually large number of people were gathered at the nurse's station, and they were all staring at us. Not that I could blame them. It was exciting to have a celebrity here, and it was a welcome respite from the daily emotional and physical drain of dealing with critically ill children. Now a small part of me hoped Trace *would* flirt with some of the staff. It would be worth it just to see them smile. God knew they deserved something to brighten their days.

"Flynn's expecting you, of course," I said, my anxiety going into overdrive at the idea that I had to turn Trace loose on my precious kid. "He's been looking a bit stronger since he got through his last round of treatment."

I was near tears just thinking about how weak he had looked. Hopefully, he was strong enough to enjoy this visit that he'd been so excited about.

"Sarah," Trace said gently, looking alarmed at my expression. "I know I give you a hard time, but I'm not gonna hurt this little boy, okay? Seriously, what kind of man do you think I am?"

I nodded. Maybe I was being unfair, but I was scared to death. Trace was so abrasive sometimes. I couldn't bear the thought of Flynn being disappointed after meeting his hero.

"I'm sorry, Trace. I just ... could you not ..." I tried to figure out a nice way to say *Could you just not be yourself when you're with Flynn?*

"I'll be good to him, Sarah. I swear. You think this is the first time I've met with a fan?"

"I know. It's just that Flynn is very special to me," I said, still struggling not to tear up. "I mean, they all are of course. But—"

"He's in good hands," Trace assured me with a smile. And it wasn't his usual jerky grin for once. This time, he seemed sincere. "Now, will you just let me go do my thing?"

"Yes. Of course," I said, tugging my canvas bag onto my shoulder. "I brought my laptop, and I'll be just down the hall in the waiting room. Take your time with him and come get me when you're finished. Okay?"

"Will do," Trace said with a cocky grin and a salute. Then he knocked on the hospital room door.

"Come in!" came Flynn's enthusiastic reply. He sounded strong and happy. If I found him to be anything less than that after Trace's visit, there would be hell to play.

"Hey there," I said, forcing a grin, hoping I could hide the fact that I was worried sick about him.

"Hey," he said without looking at me. His eyes were wide and fixed on Trace.

"I don't need to introduce this guy because you know who he is," I said.

Flynn nodded excitedly, still transfixed by his hero.

"I'll be just down the hall if you guys need anything."

"Uh-huh," my boy said.

As much as I hated leaving the two of them alone, I realized the more I stood here the more I was torturing the kid.

He could see me anytime, but his time with Trace was limited.

"Okay then. See you guys in a little bit!"

I drew in a shaky breath as I walked out, shutting the door behind me.

Please don't hurt him, Trace.

Please.

12

———

TRACE

As Sarah shut the door, I heard her sigh deeply. Poor girl was totally freaked out about my meeting with Flynn, and I felt bad about that. It would have been a lot easier on her nerves if the kid had chosen Brady instead of me. Brady put everybody at ease. I made Sarah nuts, and not in a good way.

Now that I was here, I realized I had absolutely no idea what to say to the kid. I'd been so focused on seeing Sarah again that I hadn't thought much about the sick kid part. Time to turn on the charm.

"So you're the Flynn guy I've been hearing so much about," I said to the gangly teen in the bed.

"Yeah," he said, his gray eyes lighting up. Flynn stared at me like he couldn't believe he was actually seeing me in person. I got that a lot. It can be surreal for people to see a celebrity in real life after seeing them on TV for so long.

Flynn sat up in bed and straightened out his hair.

Neither of us said anything for a few seconds, and I realized I should probably get the ball rolling. When it came to flirting with women, I never had trouble coming up with stuff to say. When I met kids at a baseball event, I gave them a quick smile, a hello, and an autograph before sending them on their way. I hadn't sat down and had an actual conversation with a teenager in quite some time.

"So, how are you feeling?" I asked.

"I'm doin' okay," Flynn said. I'd hoped for a longer response, like maybe he would tell me all about his treatments and that would eat up some time. No such luck.

"That's good, that's good. Sooo, tell me a little about yourself. What kind of things are you into? Besides baseball, of course."

Flynn's eyes flashed with excitement again, and I was relieved to have stumbled on the right thing to say.

"I like theater and stuff. Like I've been in a bunch of shows in grade school and high school and stuff. And me and my friends like Dungeons and Dragons."

"Oh. Wow."

So the kid's a major geek. Reminds me of the kids I used to beat up in high school.

Flynn's face darkened a bit. "Not that any of that stuff matters anymore."

"What do you mean?"

"Hobbies don't really mean much when you'll be dead in a few months."

Holy hell.

I'd had no idea Flynn's prognosis was so bad. I knew the kid had leukemia, but it hadn't dawned on me that the kid could actually *die.*

"I'll be lucky if I see another Christmas," Flynn said, sounding understandably bitter. In that moment he appeared much older, probably having suffered through more shit than many people see in a lifetime.

Then he laughed heartily.

"Dude. I'm fucking with you," he said, shaking his head and grinning wickedly.

I blinked.

"You are? Why?"

"I dunno. Maybe 'cuz of that look on your face when I said the words Dungeons and Dragons. I'm not stupid. I see that look on people's faces at school all the time. Usually before they start beating me up."

Shit. This kid was perceptive.

"Oh. Sorry," I mumbled.

Flynn shook his head wearily. And just like that, his hero worship of me had vanished. I was afraid he just might kick me out of his room. Sarah would never speak to me again if that happened.

"Look, I didn't mean to be insulting. I guess I just never knew a theater gee— I mean *fan* could be into D & D and also like sports."

"Surprise," Flynn said, still sounding annoyed.

"Can we just kind of start over here?" I ask, trying to figure out how the hell to salvage this situation.

"Sure," he said flatly.

"Do-over!" I yelled so loud the kid jumped. I got up and walked over to the door. Then I turned back around and walked back to his bed. "Hi, I'm Trace Ridgerton. I'm really glad to meet you, Flynn. Sarah told me all about you and, though I know she's not supposed to play favorites, I'm pretty sure you're her favorite sicko up in this bitch."

Flynn laughed and shook my hand. "Good to meet you, man."

That glimmer of excitement was back in his eye. Not only did I not want to anger Sarah, I found I really did want to make the kid happy.

"So how *are* you doing. Healthwise," I asked, sincerely wanting to know. "Are you gonna be okay?"

"Yeah, I think so. I got acute lymphocytic leukemia, or what they call ALL. I have good days and bad days, and I am so damned sick of being in the hospital."

"Gonna level with you. I don't technically know what leukemia is."

Flynn smiled. I think he liked when I was straight with him.

"The short answer is that it's blood cancer."

"Shit," I said, making him laugh.

"Exactly," Flynn said.

"Are you in pain?"

"Yeah. My bones literally hurt right now."

Flynn's expression darkened, and I got the message right away. This kid did not want my pity. From what Sarah had told me, Flynn had wonderful parents who took good care of him. And I knew Sarah fussed over him as well. I got the feeling that what Flynn wanted most was to be treated like a normal person.

Yeah. I could do that.

"I gotta ask," I said. "What made you choose me out of all the players on the team? You know, you coulda had Brady Keaton."

"Not gonna lie, dude. I seriously considered Brady. It was a toss-up."

I frowned as if I was hurt by his confession. Flynn chuckled.

"In the end I chose you."

"But why?"

"Cuz I think you're badass."

"Good answer!" I was genuinely flattered. When a

fifteen-year-old boy calls you a badass, that really means something.

"I love watchin' you behind the plate, man. Nothin' like watchin' you pick off runners," he said, miming the way I threw the ball toward first base to pick off wannabe base stealers. "And I love your motorcycle, man."

"Yeah?" I enjoyed talking about my bike more than anything. "You ever been on a motorcycle before?"

"No, but I'm dying to," he said. "I want to get my motorcycle license as soon as I'm old enough. Like, I could care less about driving a regular car."

"Well, you're probably gonna have to drive a regular car first. It's not like you can ride a motorcycle year round, ya know. I mean, I don't care about the cold or anything," I added quickly, lest Flynn think I was a pussy who wouldn't ride in the winter. "But ya can't exactly ride in the snow."

"Yeah. And it's not like my parents are gonna let me get a motorcycle license any time soon," he grumbled.

"Give them a break. I'm sure they worry enough about you as it is."

"They do," he said, suddenly getting quiet. "This whole thing is really hard on my mom."

"The last thing she needs is you riding a bike and crashing and turning yourself into street pizza."

Flynn burst out laughing at that, and it made me feel like a million bucks. I liked this kid.

He gazed at me with admiration, like he had when I'd first walked in the door. I was so glad hadn't completely blown this visit for him. My do-over seemed to have done the trick.

"It's funny how I always wanted a Harley until I saw your bike."

"Nah, man. Indian's the way to go," I said, pulling out my phone to show him some of the pictures I'd taken of my bike. I had more photos of my motorcycle than some people did of their children.

Unlike most people, Flynn didn't get bored, even after seeing dozens of pictures. We spoke at length about motorcycles, and I was truly impressed by his bike knowledge.

This kid was into sports, theater, Dungeons and Dragons, *and* motorcycles. Flynn was far more interesting than I had expected.

I would never have known he was in pain if he hadn't told me. Flynn was the badass here, as far as I was concerned.

After a while, Flynn started to look a bit fatigued. He probably didn't want to admit to being tired, and I knew better than to bring it up, lest he mistake my concern for pity.

"Man, this was fun," I said with a grin. "I better be heading out soon, though. Got some stuff to do before the game tonight."

"Okay. Cool," Flynn said, and the disappointment on his face nearly broke me. I didn't know a thing about cancer treatment, but I was pretty sure it was time for him to rest for now.

"I had a blast talking with you, Flynn."

"Me too, man. This was so great. Thanks for coming to see me. I really appreciate it."

"Maybe I'll come back and see you again sometime."

"Yeah, that would be great," Flynn said, but he didn't believe I'd be back. I could tell by the look on his face.

"You take it easy now. Maybe next time you can tell me all about Dungeons and Dragons."

Flynn laughed, looking weaker by the moment. Yeah. It was definitely time to go.

"Sure thing."

"Later, dude," I said, waving at him on my way out.

13

SARAH

I tried to concentrate on my work, but it was tough. Trace had been in there with Flynn for a really long time, which I hoped was a good thing. Maybe I should have stayed with them longer, just to make sure everything went smoothly. I'd arranged these player visits before, and I usually just stayed out of the way. The Bay Birds were professionals, and I'd never worried about how any of the guys would treat a cancer patient.

But I'd never had to deal with a visit from Trace Ridgerton before.

My head whipped around when I heard footsteps in the hallway. I'd know those biker boots anywhere.

Trace marched into the room and stood towering over me at the table with my laptop and work spread everywhere.

"You don't have to look so panicked, Sarah. The kid's fine."

"That was a pretty long visit. How did it go? What did you talk about?"

Trace's lips curved into a sly smile. "Why don't we discuss this over coffee or something?"

"Would you stop hitting on me for five minutes?" I snapped angrily as I jumped to my feet. I couldn't help it. My protective instincts kicked into overdrive, and I felt like running down the hall to check on Flynn. He wasn't a baby, and he was capable of handling himself. I knew that. But I still felt the need to take care of him when his parents weren't around. They doted on Flynn, but both his mother and father had to work all the time to pay his medical bills. I knew for a fact that it had broken his mother's heart that she couldn't be here today for this visit that meant so much to her son.

But I was here. And it was my duty to make sure everything was okay.

Trace chuckled at my outburst, but I could see the hint of compassion in his eyes no matter how hard he tried to suppress it. He looked down at me. It was so annoying that he was so much taller than me.

"Flynn's a helluva kid. We had a great time. I took good care of him, just like I promised you I would. We talked about all kinds of things. He's really into motorcycles."

I watched Trace's face carefully, and he seemed to be telling the truth as far as I could tell.

"That boy's a fighter. He's in pain, but he tries not to show it. Doesn't want any pity. Just wants to be a normal kid. I hope I made him feel that way, even for just a short time."

I sighed with relief, and the tension in my shoulders eased.

"I like the kid," Trace added. "I really do."

I stared into his deep brown eyes for several seconds too long. It was hard to tear my gaze away for some reason.

"Thank you for doing this for him," I said softly.

He smiled, and I could tell he was truly fond of my sweet boy. For a brief instant, I saw the real Trace Ridgerton under all that macho bluster. Like maybe deep down he wasn't such a bad guy.

"Sure thing. See ya around, baby." With a wink and then a quick glance up and down my body, he turned and walked away.

Then again, maybe not.

With a weary sigh, I packed up my belongings and headed down the hallway to see Flynn. I'd gotten Trace's side of the story, and now I needed to see what my patient had to say.

I knocked on his door. There was no response. After a few seconds, I knocked again.

"Come in," came a weak voice. I winced, realizing I'd probably woken him up. Flynn often put on a brave face, but he tired easily. No doubt he was wiped out after his long talk with Trace.

Flynn smiled when he saw me, warming my heart. He looked tired but happy.

"I'm so sorry to wake you," I said.

"No, no. It's okay. Come in."

He sat up in bed and looked at me with bright, excited eyes. He was wide awake now.

"I'm glad you came in. I really wanted to thank you for bringing Trace to see me. That was awesome!"

"Really? You had a good time?"

"Hell yeah. It was amazing. I still can't believe I got to meet him. We talked about all kinds of things, and he showed me tons of pictures of his badass motorcycle."

"That's nice."

"I'm so pissed that I didn't think to take a selfie with him," Flynn said. "But other than that, it was incredible. It was cool of him to stay with me so long. I kinda lost track of time, and I hope he didn't get too bored with me."

"I'm sure he didn't. Trace said you were a helluva kid and that he really liked you."

"Yeah? He really said that?" Flynn's face lit up like a kid at Christmas.

Oh thank you, thank you, thank you Trace for doing this for him.

I'd never seen Flynn so excited and happy. His mother was going to be so thrilled when she visited him after work and heard all about it. This was the beautiful ripple effect of kindness. Trace's simple good deed had brightened my day, Flynn's day, and would later delight Flynn's parents.

"Yes, he certainly did," I said. "Trace seemed quite taken with you."

"Wow. Cool."

"I'm so glad you had such a wonderful visit. Now you get some rest and then later you can tell your mom all about it."

"Yeah," Flynn said with a nod. He was fighting it, but I could see his exhaustion had returned.

I squeezed his hand and smiled at him before turning to go. When I looked back, his eyes were closed.

But he was still smiling.

I GOT BACK to my apartment in Owings Mills, exhausted but happy. After a quick dinner and some television, I was still tired. Washing my face to get ready for bed, I thought over today's events.

Overall, it had been a wonderful day. It was a huge relief to have Trace's visit over with after worrying about it for so long, and seeing Flynn's reaction had made all that stress more than worthwhile. Yet another reason to love my job. Some days I could hardly believe I got to work with a professional baseball team and make a difference in the world at the same time. No doubt Flynn would remember today for the rest of his life, and it was an honor to have played a small part in that.

As I plugged in my phone to charge overnight, I saw a text from Trace. I'd been dumb enough to call him from my cell phone, and now he had my number. For once, I didn't mind terribly that I'd gotten a message from him. He'd redeemed himself a bit in my eyes today with how well he had taken care of Flynn.

It was great meeting with Flynn today. He's a good kid, and I'd like to go see him again.

My mind raced. Why would Trace want to see my kid again? It could simply be a ploy to force me to see him. Part of me hoped it was, and then I felt like an idiot for feeling that way. Had I learned nothing from my traumatic high school experience? Guys like Trace did not go for women like me. He'd made it clear from the beginning that I was a conquest to him. A game. He only wanted me because he couldn't have me. If I gave in to him and agreed to go on a date, no doubt he'd brag to the whole team that he'd won. For all I knew, he would tell everyone we'd slept together.

Even the smallest bit of attraction for Trace was not only stupid, it was dangerous. I'd spent half my life learning to distance myself from toxic people, and I could not afford to forget everything I'd learned. Maryland was my home now, far enough away from my biological family that they could no longer hurt me. I had friends here that were closer to me than my real family had ever been. No way in hell would I let an arrogant jock try to poison my love of sports or otherwise ruin the good thing I had going in Baltimore.

And yet, remembering Flynn's darling smile as he drifted off to sleep after meeting his hero, I knew I could not possibly stand in the way of him seeing Trace again. For all I knew, *I* was the one being an egomaniac and Trace's request had nothing to do with me.

I groaned, that familiar tension returning to my body. I knew I had to endure another hospital visit from Trace. At least this time I wasn't too worried about how he would treat Flynn. They'd obviously gotten along really well today, and Flynn would be thrilled at the prospect of another visit. It would give him something to look forward to between his awful chemo treatments, and any amount of stress I would have to endure would be more than worth it. I just had to be very careful not to fall under Trace's charismatic spell. Sure, I was more resistant than most women, but I wasn't made of stone. I'd felt invisible at best and unwanted at worst for most of my life, and the way Trace constantly flirted with me could be addictive. But this was nothing more than a game to him, and I would do well to remember that.

Staring at the text, I decided to wait until tomorrow to answer him so as not to appear too eager. I turned out the bedroom light and lay back on my pillow. I drew in several deep, cleansing breaths to steady my nerves. It would be a privilege to walk into Flynn's hospital room and tell him that Trace wanted to see him again. Just thinking about the look on my kid's face was enough to help me feel at peace, and soon I drifted off to sleep.

14

TRACE

Sarah's car was in the parking lot of Johns Hopkins, but she wasn't out front this time. I parked my bike and hurried inside. Seeing Flynn was the only way I could get anywhere near Sarah these days since she wouldn't let me do any of the other charity jobs she was directly involved in anymore. Good thing I actually liked this kid, because it would really suck having to pretend to be interested in talking with him for another lengthy visit. I'd actually had so much fun with Flynn that I really had lost track of time the first time I came to see him. After a rocky start, we'd really hit it off. He'd treated me like his cool uncle, and we had more in common than I'd originally thought.

When I got to the Cancer Kid floor of the hospital, I was hoping to see Sarah out in the hallway so I could flirt with the nurses and maybe make her jealous. No such luck. I figured she was either in the waiting room with her laptop or she was in Flynn's room.

"Excuse me," I said to one of the nurses at the station at

the end of the hallway. "Do you know where Sarah Asiago is?"

I wasn't even remotely tempted to flirt with the attractive, dark-haired nurse. I just wanted to see Sarah.

"She's in Flynn's room. You can go on in. They're expecting you," Dark-haired Nurse said with a smile. She gazed at me fondly, and I realized visiting sick kids in the hospital really was a terrific way to impress women. They loved that touchy-feely stuff. I hoped Sarah felt the same way despite her whole hating me otherwise thing.

Sarah came out of the boy's room as I walked down the hall. My heart lurched in my chest when I saw her. I'd been attracted to her since the moment we first met, but this gut reaction went further than simple desire. The more I got to know her, the more I liked and admired her. It was such a foreign feeling. All the women I'd slept with over the years had been nothing more than a wild night or two.

I was falling for Sarah, and it was like a shock to my system. Unlike with other women, I wasn't quite sure how to handle her.

She walked up to me, a mixture of worry and relief on her face. Had she really thought I might flake out on Cancer Kid? Just thinking about the look on Flynn's face if I'd bailed on this visit made my stomach hurt. I would never do a thing like that. Especially not to him. Did Sarah think so little of me that she'd actually been worried I wouldn't show up?

"Hey," she said softly. "I'm glad you're here."

"Are you now?" I said with a grin.

She grimaced. "I really hope you're not just using him to see me, Trace."

I leaned against the wall and cocked my head at her. "You think highly of yourself, don't you? You would be pretty sad if I was only here to see the boy, wouldn't you Sarah? You're attracted to me, baby, whether you're willing to admit it or not."

Yes! At *last* I'd gotten the reaction I'd been dying for.

"Finally, I get to see you *blush*, Sarah Asiago," I said in triumph.

She averted her gaze, her face growing redder. Sarah could say whatever she wanted, but her body had betrayed her and she knew it. I resisted the urge to pump my fist in the air. I talked a good game, but I really hadn't been totally sure she found me attractive. Until now.

"Flynn is very excited to see you," she said sharply. "Don't blow it."

My mind buzzed with all kinds of sexual innuendo over her last statement, but she stalked off before I could say anything more.

Oh well. It didn't matter. The important thing was that I'd gotten under her skin, and she clearly felt as off-balance as I did. I figured we could do this dance of sexual tension only so long before she eventually gave in.

Chuckling, I rapped on Flynn's door.

"Come in!" he said excitedly, which helped me remember the other reason I was here. To see my Cancer Kid.

Flynn and I had another fun visit. He really was a joy to be around, and I could only hope my coming to see him helped take his mind off his treatments for a while.

I CAME BACK to visit him several more times over the next few weeks. I even got to meet his mom once, which was cool. I did flirt with her, but it was all in fun. Not only was she Flynn's mother, but she was happily married to his father. I simply couldn't resist, because she was visibly affected by my good looks. I told her she looked way too young and sexy to have a teenaged son, which made her blush and Flynn laugh. The woman loved Flynn with all her heart and was worried sick about him, and I felt good all over to see her so happy when I joked around with him.

Sarah was always there, at least for the beginning of my visits with Flynn. She was a busy woman, so she often wouldn't stick around the whole time, but she always made an appearance to make sure I showed up.

"You know, you don't have to chaperone my visits with Flynn," I told her one day. "It's not like we have shared custody of him. But then again, I do like seeing you as often as possible. And maybe you like seeing me too."

I'd hoped to make her blush again, but so far it had only been that one time.

"I'm here to see Flynn and all my other kids," Sarah huffed. "Way to make childhood cancer all about you, Trace. Just take good care of him, okay?"

"I always do," I said with a wink. "And I'd take good care of you, too, if you'd only let me."

A rosy hue bloomed on her face, but she turned on her heel to walk away before I could be sure. Still, that little sign filled me with hope that maybe she had sexual fantasies about me. I often had them about her.

I knocked on the door and Flynn invited me in.

I sat down in the chair next to him, noticing right away he looked tired. I was about to ask how he was feeling, but he spoke first.

"I get it now," Flynn said.

"Get what?"

"Why you keep coming back to see me. You're tryin' to get into Asiago's pants."

I felt like shit. Flynn was a perceptive kid, and I should have known he would figure it out. I genuinely did enjoy coming to see him, but he'd never believe me if I said that now. I tried to figure out how to explain the truth—that I visited so often both to see him and Sarah. I didn't come up with a response fast enough, though, because the boy plowed ahead.

"Okay, so let's figure out how you can get her." Flynn said. Then he laughed and shook his head. "She doesn't seem to like you very much. And she doesn't really trust you with me yet."

I heard the unmistakable sadness in his voice, and I knew he no longer trusted me so much either.

"You're right. On all counts."

"She's a hottie. Can't say I blame you for goin' after her."

I stared at Flynn in surprise. I'd always thought of Sarah as kind of a mother figure to him. That was definitely how she thought of him.

"I didn't think you'd noticed."

"I'm sick, dude. I'm not blind," Flynn deadpanned, making me laugh. "You want my advice?"

"You want to give *me* advice?"

"What, you think just because I'm a fifteen-year-old virgin who's never had a girlfriend that I have nothing to contribute?"

I laughed. "Well, kinda."

Flynn studied me for a moment. Then he said, "She's not impressed with your fame. She works around professional athletes all the time, and she's used to them. And she's not the type to care about money. She cares about people."

"I know," I said quietly, remembering how Sarah's face had flushed with excitement when she surveyed all the food we'd gathered for the hungry. And the way her expression softened when she looked at Flynn or talked about her other little patients.

"If you want her to give you a chance, then you have to be real with her."

"What do you mean 'be real with her'?"

"I mean you need to drop the cocky, macho bullshit," Flynn said firmly. "I hear the way you talk to her. It's the same way you talk to the other women here when you're flirtin' with them. You act like all you want to do is fuck her."

I was slightly taken aback by Flynn's blunt language, though I probably shouldn't have been. I'd heard kids his age say much worse.

Flynn paused for moment and eyed me suspiciously. "I mean, that's not all you want from Ms. Asiago, is it?"

"No."

"I hope not," he said, his voice taking on a hard edge. "She deserves better than that. She's really sweet and she takes good care of us at the hospital. You can tell she's not just doing it because it's part of her job. She's the type of person who feels stuff deeply, and you can hurt her real bad if you use her."

As usual, Flynn sounded wise beyond his years. Staring death in the face will do that to a person.

"Seriously, if she's just another girl to you, I hope you'll just leave her alone," he said, his expressive gray eyes filled with concern and a spark of anger. I had no doubt this kid would jump out of bed and physically fight me if I ever did anything to hurt Sarah.

Though there was nothing I hated more than talking

about my feelings, I knew I needed to tell Flynn the truth to put his mind at ease.

"Sarah's not just another conquest to me. I promise. I don't know what it is, but it's just ... different with her." Averting my gaze, I forced myself to continue. "I don't think I've ever felt this way about a woman before."

I sounded like such a sap, and I couldn't bear the idea of Flynn thinking I was a pussy. I was supposed to be his badass hero.

"Don't get me wrong," I said, meeting his gaze. "I've been with tons of women."

Flynn nodded, looking suitably impressed.

"But normally I don't feel much of anything for them. But with Sarah ..."

"You like her because she doesn't take any of your shit."

I chuckled, marveling once again at Flynn's insight. "Yeah, pretty much."

"You swear that you're actually into her and not just tryin' to get her to sleep with you?" Flynn asked.

"I swear. I think Sarah's amazing and no matter what I do, I can't stop thinking about her."

Flynn smiled at me. "That's cool."

It was weird how talking to Flynn about Sarah made me feel better. I did think about her all the time these days, and it was driving me crazy. I always felt the need to act tough around the guys on the team, and it wasn't like I was gonna talk about my feelings with any of them. Somehow, talking to Flynn felt safe. Like he would still think I was cool even if I went all gooey over a pretty girl.

"I'm tellin' you, man, the way to win her over is be real with her. If you keep teasing her and acting tough, she's never gonna go for you. *Be real.*"

"How do I do that?" I tried not to think about the fact

that I was actually asking for advice on women from a fifteen-year-old virgin.

He shook his head. "Damn, Trace."

I believed it was the first time he'd ever called me by my name. Usually it was "man" or "dude."

"You been acting so tough for so long it's like you don't know who you are anymore."

"What are you, my therapist?" I asked with a grin.

"Sure seems like it," he said with a laugh.

The idea of being the real me around Sarah was terrifying. Hell yeah, I'd been acting tough for a long time. My whole life I'd been told by my mom and stepdad that I was a stupid, worthless loser. All the money and athletic success never seemed to drown out those painful words and feelings of the past. And I was supposed to be *real* with Sarah? I couldn't be honest with her about who I really was, because beneath my cocky exterior, I knew I had nothing to offer her.

"It's gonna be okay," Flynn said, his eyes filled with compassion. I must have looked as discouraged as I felt. "You're a good guy. I've gotten to know you pretty well now and you're different than you were at first. Takes a while, but once you let your guard down, you're actually a cool guy with a good heart. She'll see that if you just give her a chance."

"I guess," I said glumly.

Flynn winced slightly and his eyes drooped a bit. He was a stubborn kid, but by now I'd learned to pick up on his subtle signals. He was tired. And he was hurting.

"I've taken up enough of your time today, boy-o," I said, standing up to leave. I headed toward the door and then turned around. "Sarah's not the only reason I still come to see you. I hope you know that."

Flynn locked eyes with me for a moment, as if scanning my face to see if I was telling the truth. Then he smiled.

"Cool," he said.

Relief swept through me. Perceptive as always, my kid knew I was telling the truth.

"You know," Flynn said with a sly grin. "I can always help grease the wheels with Ms. Asiago. She'll probably listen to me, especially if I whip out the old cancer card." He coughed dramatically into his fist, then said in a weak voice, "You know, Trace really is a good guy. He cheers me up when I'm not feeling well."

I laughed out loud as I opened his hospital door. To my surprise, Sarah was standing there at the nurse's station.

"I love that kid," I said, still laughing.

Sarah's beautiful face lit up with the loveliest smile I'd seen from her yet. She'd heard me laughing with Flynn on my way out, so she must have known I wasn't putting on an act for her. Most of the time, she had left the hospital by the time my visit with the boy was over. I'd had no way of knowing she was still here.

"Ms. Asiago?" Flynn called from his room. "Can I talk to you for minute?"

"That's my boy," I muttered as Sarah rushed past me to see Flynn.

I felt touched to my very core that Flynn was going to bat for me, so to speak. He was tired and in pain, and I knew he wouldn't bother to hide it from Sarah. He would use it to weaken her resolve when it came to me.

Chuckling to myself, I headed down the stairs.

The kid was smooth. We had a lot in common that way.

15

SARAH

I rushed into Flynn's hospital room and shut the door behind me. I was so glad I'd stuck around long enough to be here when he needed me. It was unusual for him to specifically ask me to come see him, and I hoped he was all right.

I could tell immediately that he was overtired and in pain.

My poor sweet angel.

Trace had been laughing on the way out, and Flynn's eyes shone with happiness. It was clear they'd had a good time, thank goodness. I had to admit that Trace was right about not needing me to chaperone him. He always showed up when he promised to come, and Flynn assured me they had a great time together. I was still afraid that Trace was using my poor, sick patient to try to get to me, but as long as Flynn wasn't aware of it, it was safe to continue on with the visits.

"How are you feeling?" I asked.

"I'm okay," he said. "Just one of those days when everything hurts, ya know?"

"I'm sorry, sweetie," I said, wishing so much that there was something I could do to ease his suffering.

"Helps when Trace comes to see me," Flynn said.

"Oh, I'm so glad. He's definitely taken a shine to you. I arrange these player visits all the time, and you are the only one who's had a player keep coming back."

"That's cool," he said, a hint of pride in his eyes. Trace made him feel better, and that was all that mattered to me. "He's a great guy."

"Oh yah," I said. "A great guy."

"You don't really mean that, do you?"

"What are you talking about?" I asked. I didn't know why I was surprised that Flynn had picked up on my distaste for Trace. He was a smart kid who didn't miss much.

"You don't like Trace very much," he said with a weak laugh. "He really is a good guy. You should give him a chance. He's really into you."

Anger surged through my body. Fists clenched, I fought the urge to go storming down the hall after that bastard.

How dare he use Flynn to get to me?

"Hey, hey. Chill out. Don't go off and murder him or anything," Flynn said, looking alarmed at my expression. "Look, I'm not stupid. At least part of the reason Trace keeps coming to see me is that he wants to get to you. It's cool, Ms. Asiago. It's not the only reason he stops by, and I'm cool with it anyway. Just be sure and invite me to the wedding, okay?"

"Ugh," I said, unable to even attempt to hide my disgust at the idea.

Flynn laughed. "He's not that bad, I promise. You just have to get to know him."

"I've known him for quite a while, Flynn. And I've seen more than enough."

"Tell me why you don't like him," he said with amusement in his eyes. "Don't lie or sugarcoat it. What is the number one thing you don't like about Trace?"

Looking into my kid's eyes was like being injected with truth serum. Flynn was impossible to resist.

"He reminds me of the bullies who used to torture me in high school."

Flynn's expression softened, filled with empathy for me. Dear God, how I adored this wonderful boy. Talking with him felt like therapy sometimes.

"Believe me, I get that. You know what? I felt exactly the same way when I first met Trace."

"You did?"

"Hell yeah, I did. I mean, he's really cool and smooth and all that. But he's got that way of grinning at you like he's mocking you."

"Yes! Exactly," I said, relieved to find someone else who found that as maddening as I did.

"At first, I felt like he was judging me for being a theater and Dungeons and Dragons geek."

"I was afraid of that," I said, my stomach knotting with worry. It had felt like I was sending the captain of the high school football team in to meet with a chess nerd. A sick chess nerd at that. One who might be too weak to defend himself.

"Trace looked at me like I was some pathetic nerd. And I called him out on it," Flynn said with pride.

I smiled at him, feeling proud of him too. As usual, I had underestimated him.

"And after that, everything was great. He's cool, Ms. Asiago. Once you get him to drop all his bullshit, he's pretty awesome."

"I see."

"And he really likes you," Flynn said, sitting up

straighter in bed. He winced in pain, and my throat tightened. I hated seeing him like this.

"Sure he does," I said, rolling my eyes.

"Look, I know he hits on everybody, but it's different with you. It really is. I can tell."

I eyed him curiously. Had anyone else told me that, I would have brushed it off. But between Flynn being naturally perceptive and the fact that he'd gotten to know Trace fairly well over the last few weeks, it was possible he knew what he was talking about.

"Trace only wants me because I keep turning him down. It's like a game to him. He wants what he can't have."

"I get why you think that," Flynn said with a nod. "I'm pretty sure that's how it started out with him. But he feels differently about you now."

My heart surged with hope, and it scared me. Why did I care how Trace felt about me?

"What makes you think he feels differently about me than every other woman on the planet that he flirts with?"

"The way he looks at you, for one. And the fact that he actually talked to me about what to do and how to get you to give him a chance."

I thought about that for a moment. On the one hand, I was furious that he was using Flynn as an excuse to see me. On the other hand, it was endearing that he'd asked Flynn for help.

"One quick date with him. Would that be so bad?" Flynn asked with a sly smile that looked a little too familiar.

"You're quite the smooth talker, kid. I think you're picking up some bad habits from Trace."

"Is it bad that I take that as a compliment?"

I laughed, and he did, too.

"What have you got to lose?" Flynn said with a shrug.

"More than you think," I said quietly.

Flynn eyed me curiously, waiting for me to elaborate.

I sighed, not wanting to get into too much detail. "I've worked hard to keep toxic people out of my life. I've even had to cut some family members loose. I can't afford to let somebody into my life who might do me harm."

"Oh," Flynn said thoughtfully. Then he looked me directly in the eye and said, "I wouldn't tell you to go out with him if I thought he might hurt you."

Something in Flynn's gaze told me that maybe it was okay to trust Trace. Like he knew something I didn't.

"Just promise me you'll think about it, okay?"

"Fine. I promise. Now you have got to get some rest."

"Okay," he said weakly. He was such a fighter, but even he had his limits.

I squeezed his hand gently before leaving. My chest tightened with stress as I quietly shut the door behind me.

I had just promised a kid with cancer that I would give Trace Ridgerton a chance.

16

TRACE

I grabbed a paper cup and filled it with water from the cooler in the dugout. The July sun had been beating down on me for the last three hours, and today's game had ended in a tough loss to San Diego. It was the first game of a back-to-back doubleheader, so it would be a long night for both teams. After tossing back several cups of water, I headed into the clubhouse.

Relief swept over me as I walked into the much cooler air. I couldn't wait to hit the showers and rinse off the dirt and grime from the game. I couldn't find my duffel bag in my locker. I'd left it in the weight room.

The moment I stepped out into the hallway, I almost ran right into Sarah. I hadn't expected to see her today—maybe she was overseeing a ceremonial pitch for the second game.

Clad in a lovely green dress that brought out the color of her blue-green eyes, Sarah looked heart-stoppingly gorgeous. I was caught off-guard, and it took a moment to catch my breath.

"Hey," I said, feeling underdressed in my filthy, dirt-stained Bay Birds uniform. I hoped like hell I didn't smell too terrible. After my last talk with Flynn, I'd resolved to formally ask Sarah out again. I planned to be more sincere this time. Of course, I'd also planned to wear my usual black clothes with a splash of cologne, as opposed to being sweaty and gross.

"Hey," she said as she eyed me up and down. I waited for that typical look of disgust to cross her face, but instead I got quite a different response.

Sarah drew in a sharp breath and her eyes flashed with interest.

No. Not interest.

Attraction.

Sometimes I forgot how much she loved sports, and it hadn't occurred to me that she might find a sweaty athlete in a baseball uniform sexy. Now was my chance.

"So, Sarah ..." I began.

She drew in another quick breath, and I got the feeling she liked when I said her name.

Awesome.

She could fight it all she wanted, but she was hot for me and she knew it. And yet, I had to reign in my cockiness, or she would never give in to me, out of sheer pride.

"What's it gonna take for you to go out with me?"

"Flynn told me I should give you a chance," she said, sounding annoyed. "I can't believe you would use him like that."

"I'm not using him, Sarah," I said, determined to say her name as much as possible. "He told me I should ask you out because he could tell I liked you. He said he knew I was genuinely into you. You know how sharp that kid is. Not much gets by him."

"That's true," Sarah said, her expression softening at the mention of her favorite boy.

"Flynn's a terrific kid, and he volunteered to be my wing man. It wasn't my idea, I swear."

Sarah laughed, and I knew the fondness in her eyes wasn't for me. Still, it was an excellent start.

"Answer my question, Sarah. What is it gonna take for you to agree to go out with me?"

Sarah's eyes bored into me, and I nearly took a step backward. That woman could be intense when she wanted to be.

"I'll go out with you if you agree to tell me the truth," she said firmly, her gaze never wavering from mine.

"The truth about what?"

"Why do you walk around with a swagger in your step, acting like you think you're better than everyone else?"

I had absolutely no idea how to answer that question. Standing there, frozen in her steely gaze, I tried to figure out what it was she wanted to hear.

"I figure it's one of two reasons. You act that way because you actually believe that you're better than everybody else just because you happened to be born with good looks and athletic ability, *or* you do it because you're compensating for the fact that you had a messed-up home life. Now, which is it?" Sarah asked, her gaze still locked on mine.

My breath caught in my throat as I fought the urge to fall back on my usual cocky mannerisms. It would be so easy to tease her about saying I had good looks and athletic ability even as I could hear the cruel voices of my mother and step-father ringing in my ear.

And yet, the loudest voice in my head was Flynn's.

Be real with her.

"The home life thing," I forced myself to say. "My family was shit."

"I'm sorry to hear that, Trace," Sarah said gently. "But

like I told you at Brady's house, that's kind of what I suspected."

I laughed and shook my head. "Dammit. I shoulda thought of that a long time ago. That's what I've been missing. The *sympathy* angle. Have I learned nothing from Flynn?"

Sarah laughed. "The boy's a charmer, no doubt about it. He laid it on pretty thick when it came to you."

Leaning in close to her, I said, "I had a really rough home life. My mom and stepdad were horrible to me. And that is why I cannot love!" I tossed my head dramatically, making her laugh again.

"Is that right?" she responded, with both amusement and sympathy in her eyes.

"Maybe you can teach me how to love, Sarah."

Her breath hitched again when I said her name.

"I don't think so."

She hesitated for a moment, and I could see she was on the fence about giving into me. Then she started to walk past me into the clubhouse.

"See ya 'round, Trace."

"Sarah," I said firmly, making her stop in her tracks.

She turned around to face me.

"Just give me one chance. Please."

That was the most vulnerable I'd felt in a long time. At last, I was being real with her. And it wasn't easy.

Sarah gazed at me. That look of fear was back in her eyes. God, I hated when she was afraid of me.

"One quick drink after the game tonight," I offered.

She paused, and I steeled myself for rejection.

"It's a doubleheader. You'll be exhausted."

That was *not* a "no."

"No, I won't," I said, fighting to keep my voice even. "I'm

not even catching the second game. All I have to do is hang around in case I'm needed."

"Still, it'll be a long night." I was about to argue, but she held up her hand. "Not tonight, Trace."

I nodded, knowing I had her on the hook now, and I had to carefully reel her in.

"How about tomorrow night? We can grab a drink after the game," I suggested, watching her closely as she considered it. "It'll make Flynn happy."

That made her smile.

"You don't play fair," she said.

"Nope."

Sarah drew in a shuddery breath. She was still afraid, and it made me want to pull her into my arms and hold her. Which would have probably terrified her further, so I kept still.

"Okay," she said at last. Then she added, "Flynn promised you wouldn't hurt me. I just hope he's right about you."

Then she walked away without looking back.

17

SARAH

Trace offered to drive his car to tonight's game instead of taking his motorcycle in case I wasn't comfortable riding on the back of the bike. I was *not* comfortable with the idea of straddling Trace with my arms wrapped around his waist, but that was neither here nor there. I made it clear I would take my own car and meet him at the bar after the game. Carpooling with him would leave me effectively at his mercy. If I drove myself, I'd be free to leave if I felt the need.

We agreed on a place about fifteen minutes away from Old Bay Stadium since it was a Friday night and the bars near the stadium would no doubt be packed with Bay Birds fans. The bar was in Towson. Trace said it wasn't too far away from where he lived. I hoped he hadn't told me that because he expected me to wind up at his place. No way in hell was that going to happen.

I parked my silver Toyota in the parking lot and walked on shaky legs toward the entrance. Trace's Indian was in a biker parking spot toward the front, so I knew he was already inside. He really did have Flynn to thank for this date; I never would have agreed to it otherwise. I'd been a nervous wreck ever since I'd decided to have a drink with him, and I was still second-guessing my decision right up to the last minute.

My whole life I'd trusted the wrong people, and I was terrified of doing it again. For all I knew, Trace's allegedly bad home life was a lie to garner sympathy. Lying would be a rotten thing to do. I really did have a terrible upbringing, and I did not appreciate the thought of him making up stories about his own family to get to me. Trace struck me as the type of man who would stop at nothing to get what he wanted, and I was worried that he was still just trying to get me into bed.

But Flynn genuinely believed this time was different.

Sighing heavily, I opened the glass door to the bar and looked around the place. I immediately spotted Trace at the bar, clad all in black, and I hated the way my knees went weak. Why did he have to be so devastatingly handsome? I watched him toss back the rest of his whiskey as he joked around with the bartender. Even his drink was sexy. Most of the men I knew drank beer.

I suddenly felt completely out of place. I was dressed appropriately and all, wearing jeans and a simple blouse. But something about Trace's cool manner and sleek look made me feel like I wasn't good enough. As always, my mind whirred back to high school and my deep-seated fears that this was all a joke. The hotshot baseball catcher had asked the goody-goody charity lady from work out on a date just for a laugh.

I decided since I had come this far, I might as well see it through. I drew in a deep breath.

"Hey," I said uncertainly when I reached the bar.

Trace spun around. His eyes lit up, and his reaction seemed real. Like he was genuinely happy to see me.

"Wow, Sarah. You look gorgeous." He eyed me up and down appreciatively. For once, it didn't feel creepy. I felt flattered. "I was hoping to get us a table so we could talk, but the joint is slammed tonight."

"Yes, I see," I said, scanning the crowded room.

"I did manage to nab you a seat here, though," Trace said, patting the stool next to him. "What's your pleasure?"

"Uh, white wine I guess," I said.

Trace nodded and signaled the bartender, who rushed over like his life depended on it. I hoped that didn't mean Trace was one of those obnoxious customers that demanded to be catered to. I watched his interaction with the bartender carefully. I had no interest in men who treated me like a queen but the waitstaff like garbage.

"A white wine for the lady," Trace said with a smile. "And I'll have another."

"You got it," the man said, looking excited.

I relaxed a little, pleased with what I'd seen so far. The bartender probably knew who Trace Ridgerton was and got a kick out of serving him. Trace didn't seem to be abusing his celebrity privilege.

"Glad you made it," he said with a smile. "I was a little afraid you might bail on me."

"I wouldn't do that. Flynn would be so disappointed in me."

"Ah, I see," he said. Now Trace was the one who looked disappointed by my words. I felt bad about that. I'd agreed to give him a chance, and not insulting him was the least I could do.

My glass of wine arrived quickly, giving me something to do while I tried to think of something to say.

"So," Trace began, but he never got a chance to finish his thought.

"Excuse me," an attractive blond woman said to him. Her sudden appearance startled me.

Trace turned and graced her with a smile. My insides tightened. This was not helping with my feelings of inadequacy.

"Hi," Trace said flirtatiously, embarrassing me. It was disrespectful.

"Could I have your autograph?" she asked, thrusting a paper napkin toward him.

"Sure." Trace glanced up at the bartender, who came rushing over with a pen. I got the feeling Trace came here often and that this happened a lot. Great.

I turned back to my wine, not wishing to see the rest of this little interaction.

"Sorry about that," Trace said, not sounding the least bit sorry. He loved the attention. "Happens all the time. At least that girl brought me a napkin to sign. You wouldn't believe some of the requests I get ... and the body parts women ask me to sign."

"That's interesting," I said.

Trace laughed heartily. "I'm from Minnesota too, remember? I know 'that's interesting' is code for 'that sucks.'"

I chuckled. He wasn't wrong. In the Midwest, we used "that's interesting" the way southerners used "bless your heart." It wasn't a compliment.

"How's work going?" Trace asked.

"It's going okay," I said, not bothering to elaborate because I figured he didn't actually care and was just making conversation.

"I guess Maryland Kids Kicking Cancer is your favorite

charity, but are there other ones you really like working with?"

My eyes widened with surprise. I hadn't thought he knew the name of the project that connected my patients to the Baltimore Bay Birds. Trace usually just referred to "those Cancer Kids." And the way he'd asked the question made it sound like he honestly wanted to know.

"I love helping Andre Jones with all the great work he does," I responded, and Trace nodded.

Andre was an outfielder for the Bay Birds and was passionate about Baltimore. Though he hadn't grown up here, his childhood home in the inner city of Philadelphia had shown him what it was like to live in poverty. The man had a special place in his heart for inner-city kids, and he frequently paid for them to attend games. As a Black man, he also understood how it felt to deal with racism in sports, and he was passionate about equality. The guy was a born leader, and I was honored to help plan projects for him in conjunction with the Bay Birds Foundation.

"That guy's a rockstar, for sure." Trace sipped his whiskey. "Those kids adore him."

I opened my mouth to tell Trace about an upcoming event for Andre's Kids to sing the National Anthem at a game later in the season, but we were interrupted again. This time, I heard the clack of the woman's high heels. She had tight jeans, a tight shirt, and a tight body.

Ignoring me completely, the lady gushed over my date. "Ooooh, you're Trace Ridgerton, right?"

Trace nodded and grinned.

The woman blathered on about having seen him play in a game recently and how she'd thought he was cute. I studied my wineglass and tried to block out the noise. I could not imagine walking up to a man who was clearly on a date and starting to talk to him. How incredibly rude. Of course, Trace did nothing to discourage her, so there was blame to share here.

It was a shame, because for a few seconds, Trace had seemed like a halfway decent person. Now, he was back to hotshot baseball catcher, and I was about done with him. I didn't have the mental or emotional energy to deal with any of this, and I wished I'd just stayed at home. I'd been single for a long time, and I was totally fine with it. Though I'd eventually love to find a great guy to settle down with, I was rarely lonely. My work and friends kept me busy and happy, so I never minded having time by myself at home to unwind.

Since Trace was clearly not going to suddenly turn into Mr. Right, this whole exercise was pointless. Thank goodness I'd brought my own car.

I downed the rest of my wine, and turned to tell Trace I was leaving only to find him staring at me. His adoring fan had left while I'd been lost in thought.

"I'm so sorry, Sarah." The sorrow in his voice took me by surprise. I'd never seen him look so serious. "Bringing you here was a mistake."

Finally, something we could agree on.

"You seem to like when I'm honest, so ..." He raked his hand through his hair. It was a maddeningly sexy gesture. "I come here a lot, and this happens all the time. Fans approaching me. People know I hang out here, so they come and bring their friends to ask for my autograph and ..." Trace paused to smile at me. And it wasn't his usual smirk, either. I saw a fondness in it that I hadn't seen from him before.

"Sometimes I forget you're not like other women. My fame doesn't impress you." He swallowed hard, and I got the feeling it was tough for him to speak freely to me. Then he spoke so quietly that I could barely hear him. "You were right about my family. The whole time growing up I was told I was stupid and worthless, and that it would be better if I'd never been born."

I drew in a sharp breath. Trace's words were powerfully sad, and the darkness in his eyes told me this was not a ploy for sympathy. This was a deep pain, and it was one I understood completely.

"When I go to places like this and fans fawn all over me, it makes me feel like maybe I'm not totally worthless after all."

I nodded slowly, my mouth suddenly dry.

Trace winced, and a few seconds later I understood why. This time, three people had walked over to talk to him.

"Hold on a sec," he said to the fans with a wink and a smile. Then he leaned over and whispered in my ear. "I'm gonna deal with these people real quick and then pay the tab. Meet me in the parking lot. Please, don't leave. *Please.*"

"Okay," I said, my voice barely a whisper. The intensity in his voice made me feel weak all over.

I slid off my barstool and headed out to the parking lot.

Once outside, I walked over to my car and leaned against the driver's door. I still had no idea what to make of Trace Ridgerton. He'd seemed honest and sincere, but it was hard to be sure exactly what his game was. If I'd learned one thing the hard way in life, it was that people were not always what they seemed. Trusting the wrong person could lead to disaster.

I considered a quick getaway. But something made me stay. It was the look in Trace's eyes when he'd said, *"Please don't leave."*

I looked up when I heard someone approach. It was Trace, but not with his usual casual stroll. I'd never seen him move so fast when he wasn't on the baseball diamond.

"You're still here," Trace said, relief in his eyes.

"For now," I said cautiously.

"I'm sorry about all that. I don't always get recognized when I'm out. Kinda depends on where I go."

I nodded. A part of me did understand why Trace felt the need to bring me to this particular bar where he knew people would make a fuss over him. Deep down he was insecure, just as I'd suspected.

"This is gonna sound like such a line, but really, Sarah. The best place for us to go is back to my house where we can talk in private."

My body tensed at the mere thought of being totally alone with Trace. The thought was both exciting and terrifying. I was frozen with indecision.

"Look, I've done my best to be honest with you. And believe me, it's not easy. Will you return the favor and be honest with me?"

"Honest about what?"

His deep brown eyes stared into mine as if searching for answers. Then, very slowly, he lifted his hand to my face and gently caressed my cheek. "Why are you afraid of me?"

His tone held no arrogance. It was a legitimate question.

"I told you why. You're exactly like the kids who were so mean to me in high school."

"That was a long time ago." He lowered his hand from my face but his eyes stayed locked with mine.

"So I should just get over it? Is that what you're saying?" I snapped, my fear and indecisiveness quickly turning to anger.

"No, I just mean—"

"You don't know what happened, so you have no right to judge me."

"Sarah, what *did* happen?"

"I'm not talking about that with you. *Ever.*"

My hands shook with all the adrenaline pulsing through my veins. Why did Trace insist on asking me personal questions and getting me all worked up?

My shoulders shuddered as I sighed. I knew Trace had a right to at least some honesty from me. I wouldn't tell him everything, but I would clue him in a little about my background.

"I used to be a lot heavier than I am now, and I'm not used to men like you giving me the time of day. For most of my life, if a good-looking man—or even a woman for that matter—gave me any attention at all, it was usually to make fun of me. I'm scared your pursuit of me is some colossal joke to you."

My throat got tight, and I fought the urge to break down in tears. Somehow, I held it together.

"That's not what this is, Sarah. Not at all." Trace said it so gently, it was hard not to believe him. Still, I had to keep my guard up.

"Trace," I said, my voice sounding stronger than I felt. "You vowed in front of half the Bay Birds team that you were gonna get me into bed. I mean, what am I supposed to think when you say things like that?"

He nodded, and a look of understanding crossed his face.

"That makes a lot of sense. Thanks for explaining it," he said. "I acted like such an idiot. I'm not gonna lie to you. At the time, I meant every word. I was really embarrassed when you shot me down in front of the guys, and I made it my mission to get you to sleep with me just so I could say I told you so. And so I could brag about it to every man on the team."

Trace shook his head, looking disgusted with himself.

"It was a shit thing for me to say. And now, knowing what you've been through in your life, I feel especially awful about it. All I'm asking now is for you to give me one more shot. A chance to show you who I really am."

"I don't know," I said.

"I'm trying so hard not to play the Flynn card."

I groaned. "That really would be unfair."

Trace eyed me thoughtfully for a few seconds. "Okay. I'm gonna try a do-over."

He pulled his hand down over his face dramatically and closed his eyes as if he were an actor trying to get into character. I struggled not to laugh, the way you do with a person you want to stay mad at.

He opened his eyes and said, "Sarah, I think you are such an amazing person. The first time I saw you, I was struck by how beautiful you were with your pretty blue-green eyes and soft, shiny hair. I see lots of pretty girls, so that didn't mean much. But when I got to see you in action at your job, I was totally blown away. I've never seen somebody so passionate about their work, and I loved watching your eyes light up when you saw how much food we collected for the food drive. And I especially admired when you looked like you would claw my eyes out if I dared do anything to hurt Flynn. I can't stop thinking about you, and all I want is a chance to get to know you even better. And to let you get to know me."

I stared at Trace, hardly believing the words that had just come out of his mouth. Either he was an incredible actor who was highly skilled at improv, or he had really meant the things he said to me.

"I know you're scared. All I'm asking is to spend a little time with you. Maybe just one more drink at my place, just because it might be the only place nearby where we can have some privacy."

Everything he'd said made so much sense that it was hard to find a reason to turn him down. Still, I couldn't quite bring myself to say yes.

"Come on, Sarah," he said with a wink. "Do it for Flynn."

"Dammit," I muttered, and he laughed. "Fine. One drink."

18

SARAH

I followed Trace to his place, hoping like hell I hadn't made a mistake and yet feeling much calmer than I'd expected. Though I'd never been the greatest judge of character, something told me that he was being sincere. I still felt nervous about trusting him, but I also worried about potentially missing out on a great guy just because I was afraid. I'd spent so long protecting myself that I was starting to wonder if I was losing out on opportunities by playing it safe. I would approach this situation with caution while still keeping an open mind.

Trace rode his bike more slowly than normal to make sure he didn't lose me on the way. I was grateful for the security of driving my own car, and yet I wondered what it might feel like to ride on the back of his motorcycle. His impressive arm muscles bulged in his black T-shirt as he gripped the bike's handlebars. The heat of the July night made his trademark leather jacket unnecessary, and I was grateful for the unfettered view of his body. I'd never ridden on a motorcycle before, and I wondered what it would feel like. I quickly warmed to the idea of holding Trace tight as we tore down the road together.

My anxiety ramped up a bit when we got to Trace's house, but I knew there was no turning back now. I had agreed to come here partially because of Flynn. Not only would it make him happy that the two of us had gone on a date, but my kid trusted Trace. Flynn didn't think Trace would hurt me, and I trusted his gut instinct more than my own.

Trace opened his garage door remotely and rode his bike inside. I parked my car just behind him in the driveway. My heart skipped a beat when he took off his bike helmet and shook his hair. He looked like something out of a shampoo ad. I wondered if he'd gotten any commercial endorsement deals like Brady. Trace had the looks, not to mention the body, to model men's underwear and things like that.

"Maybe sometime you can ride with me on the bike," Trace said as if he'd read my mind. I felt myself blush.

"Maybe," I said.

Trace led me inside his home. His rancher house was lovely, and the living room smelled faintly of his cologne. He had a black leather couch and matching chair, which certainly suited him. There were framed photographs of him with various sports players as well as some other minor celebrities. No pictures of family members; that saddened me but it didn't surprise me. I didn't have any of those at my apartment either.

"Oh, I love this," I said, walking over to a large framed black and white photograph of a sleek motorcycle traveling down a winding road.

"Thanks," Trace said. He joined me and we gazed at the picture. "I love this one too."

"I've never been on a motorcycle," I said.

"Aw, you gotta try it," he said, his eyes flashing with excitement. "There's a reason they call it wind therapy. Really makes you feel better. Calms your nerves. That's why I love riding to Old Bay Stadium for the games. It's a great way to unwind on the way back."

"Nice," I said, enjoying his enthusiasm. He seemed so different from the cool, composed Trace I usually saw at work. I loved to hear him talk about his motorcycle like this, when his focus was less about being a badass biker and more his passion for riding.

"You want a drink? Sorry, I don't have any wine. Just beer and whiskey."

"No, I better not. I've already had wine on an empty stomach."

"Oh man, are you hungry? We should order some food. I ate a little at the ballpark after the game, but I definitely could eat again."

"Who delivers around here?"

"You like Thai food?"

I nodded.

"Great. There's a local place I order from all the time." He pulled out his cell phone to find the menu, and we ordered online.

"You sure you don't want a drink while we wait? I'm gonna grab a whiskey."

"Sure, I guess a drink would be okay. Since we're eating soon, and I won't be driving for a while."

Trace got himself a glass of whiskey and me a beer, and we settled in on the leather couch. Close, but not too close for comfort. I could tell he was being cautious with me, and I appreciated that.

"Your house is beautiful." I took a sip of beer, and it was quite good. I rarely drank beer, and when I did, it was usually the cheap stuff. This microbrew was higher quality than I was used to.

"Thanks," he said. "It is nice, and I love that it's close to the park. I have a bigger house in Minnesota, though. That's where I live in the off-season."

"Wow," I said. Sometimes I forgot just how rich Trace must be. The salaries of baseball players were unreal.

Trace shrugged modestly.

"Have you always wanted to play baseball?"

He considered the question.

"I can't say I always wanted to play. It wasn't my lifelong dream or anything. I saw other kids playing soccer and their parents were all into it. You know how it is. You see these parents taking their kids to practice all the time and then cheering them on at games. People love to make fun of soccer moms and all that, but I would have loved to have had one of those kinds of mothers. Those kids are really lucky."

"I know exactly what you mean," I said, remembering the tug of longing I had as a kid when I saw parents like that.

Trace took another healthy sip of whiskey, like he was gathering his courage to go on.

"Then in high school, I tried a few sports and it turned out I was good at baseball. I mean, really good. And I'm not saying that to sound arrogant. You were right that day when you said I was born with good looks and athletic ability, and I know it seems like I take those things for granted. But I really don't. Being good-looking opens a lot of doors for me and being naturally good at sports has paid off in ways I never could have imagined when I was growing up. I'm very lucky, and I try never to forget that."

He paused again. I could see he was gearing up to tell me something difficult.

"My mother, Karol," he said, shaking his head. "She was really abusive to me. She never actually said so, but I'm pretty sure I was an accident." Trace avoided my gaze, and it broke my heart to see him struggle to talk about his past.

"My mom had no trouble telling me that," I said.

"Really?" Trace looked up at me somberly.

"Oh yah. It was casual dinner conversation to her. She'd say stuff like 'You're lucky you were even born,' and 'I never planned on having you, you know.' Or my personal favorite she'd save for when she was really mad: 'I should have gotten rid of you when I still had the chance.'"

"Jesus," Trace said, letting out a long breath. I hoped he didn't think I was trying to one-up him with my sob story. All I wanted was for him to know he wasn't alone. I kept quiet for a moment, hoping he would feel safe enough to continue telling me about his life.

"Baseball was an escape for me in school. It gave me something to concentrate on that had nothing to do with my home life."

"I understand. Though I never played any sports myself, I definitely loved to escape into the games as a spectator. Still do."

"That's cool," Trace said with a smile. "Playing baseball made me feel that maybe I wasn't completely worthless like my mom and stepdad always said I was. I was *somebody* when I was on the team and helping us win. If the guys on the team ever noticed that I never had family show up to any of my games, they were too nice to say anything. It was so bizarre how I was this hotshot at school and a total loser at home."

Once again, Trace lowered his gaze, looking uncomfortable.

"If it makes you feel any better, I was a loser at school *and* at home."

Trace laughed softly, but not in a mean way.

"That sucks."

"Yeah," I said. "That's why I moved so far away from home, and it's worked out incredibly well. I love my job, and I have wonderful friends here."

"That's good," he said, gazing into my eyes. Sitting here with him one-on-one, it felt as if Trace was a completely different person. Well, not completely *different*, just a better version of the Trace I knew. He was still smooth, sexy, and incredibly handsome, but he was more real than I'd ever seen him.

"Did you come here from Minnesota for the same reason?"

"Not intentionally," he said. "But it's worked out well for me the same way it has for you. You know how it is for sports players. We go wherever we're drafted. I've made lots of friends too, and my family members are thousands of miles away."

Trace lifted his whiskey glass to toast my beer.

I laughed. "Cheers to family being far away."

We both drank to that.

"So what's the deal with your family?" he asked. "You don't have to tell me if you don't want to, though."

"No, it's okay," I said. "Like I told you earlier, I used to be really fat— I mean, I weighed a lot more when I was a teenager." I laughed nervously. "I know it sounds stupid, but I've spent a lot of time in therapy learning to stop all the negative self-talk. Like I'm not supposed to disparage myself by calling myself fat. I'm supposed to try to love my body no matter what and all that."

"I don't think that sounds stupid at all," Trace said kindly.

I was overwhelmed with the feeling—the knowledge, even—that I could trust him. It was strange and sudden. I'd been so terrified of this guy for so long, and now something deep inside told me that he was a good man underneath all that swagger. That Flynn's intuition was right. Trace wasn't going to hurt me.

"Thanks," I said, feeling relaxed by the alcohol and the company. "My mother's dream was to be a fashion model. She's pretty and all that. At least she was quite pretty when she was younger, but I'm not sure she actually had the ambition to become a model. To hear her tell it, she could have been a famous supermodel if she hadn't gotten knocked up with me."

"Convenient for her to be able to blame you for her failures," Trace said, tipping his glass at me.

"Exactly. But you know how it is when you're a kid. For a long time, you believe everything your parents tell you. And it can take a long time to get past that. If you ever do."

Trace nodded.

"So you can imagine how Heather Robertson reacted to having a fat daughter," I said, my anger rising just thinking about it. "Like I told you, I try not to use the word fat in a derogatory way about myself, but that's the way she saw me."

"Something tells me your mom had no problem calling you that to your face," Trace said, sounding angry on my behalf.

"No, she sure didn't." Tears filled my eyes. "She was so

ashamed of me. You wouldn't believe how many of her friends didn't even know she had a daughter."

"Wow," Trace said softly.

"She thought it was hilarious that I loved sports so much. Loved the irony that I liked to watch other people exercise while I was so fat and hideous. Again, her words, not mine. Like I said, I was a loser at home and at school. My mother would bully me at home and then I would go get tortured at school by the other kids. When the popular athletes did it … Well, that hurt the most."

Trace nodded slowly, pain etched deeply into his face. He understood what I was saying, and yet I still needed to say the words out loud.

"Th—that's why I've been afraid of you, Trace," I said, breath hitching and tears falling.

He put down his whiskey glass and pulled me into his arms and let me cry.

"I'm sorry, Sarah. I'm so sorry. No wonder you've been so upset that I kept pursuing you."

Trace rubbed my back for a while until I calmed down. Eventually, I started to pull away and he released me.

I wiped my eyes with a tissue from my purse and then checked my face with my compact mirror. My eyes were red, but at least my makeup had held up pretty well.

"I didn't mean to upset you," he said. "But I hope it made you feel a little better to talk about it."

"It did, Trace. It actually did."

"I know how bad it messes you up when your parents are so awful. Makes you scared to trust anybody," he said bitterly. "I got sick with strep throat once, and my mom said I wasn't worth the cost of the medicine."

"When I broke my leg and wound up in the hospital for

a few days, my mother stole most of my hospital food so I could lose some weight."

Trace winced and shook his head.

"My mom and stepdad used to leave me and my sister alone at home when they went out on dates when I was four years old and my sister was two."

"My mom used to disappear for days at a time," I said. Then I burst out laughing at the absurdity of this entire conversation. "This is like the worst contest *ever*."

Trace threw his head back and laughed. "You're right. Scary how we could probably swap horror stories all night."

"No doubt."

He fell silent for a moment. "I might have the winning story, but I'm not sure I'm ready to talk about it yet."

"I understand," I said.

We gazed at each other for a moment, but the silence was anything but uncomfortable. It was lovely, in fact. We'd bared our souls to one another, and it was cathartic. I felt relieved, cleansed. And I was pretty sure he felt the same way.

The doorbell rang.

"Thank God," I said. "My head is spinning from all the beer and wine I've had. I need food."

"Coming right up." Trace went to answer the door.

I lay back on the couch for a moment, feeling emotionally spent. I marveled that most of the fear I'd had about Trace had disappeared after talking openly with him.

Gazing around at his living room, I was amazed at how comfortable I felt already. I had never set foot in here before tonight, and yet I loved his place.

Somehow, coming here felt like coming home.

19

———

TRACE

I brought the food back to the couch and we dug in. I hadn't realized how hungry I was until I smelled the delicious Thai food. Sarah giggled as she watched me practically inhale my food.

"Sometimes I forget what huge appetites you athletes have," she said, sounding impressed.

"Yah," I managed to say between bites. I was usually pretty good at hiding my midwestern accent, but it came out when I was around people who made me feel comfortable.

Though Sarah had said she was hungry—and that was over an hour ago—she still took her time eating. She even put her fork down between bites. I'd heard that was a weight loss tip to help you slow down and eat less, and it made me sad to watch. No doubt she'd battled her feelings about her weight her whole life thanks to her bitchass mother.

I wiped my mouth after I'd devoured my meal. "I don't know about you, but this first date has been *way* more intense than any first date I've ever been on."

Sarah laughed. "Oh, fer sure. I dated a guy for eight

months, and I didn't tell him a lot of the stuff I told you tonight."

I was incredibly honored by that. As much as I loved that she knew she could confide in me, the last thing I wanted was to see her cry again.

"Okay, so let me pretend I'm a halfway normal date," I said. "What kind of music do you like?"

"I know this will make me seem like an old biddy, but I like oldies. My favorite era of music is actually the '50s, '60s, and some '70s. This will sound so pretentious, but I cannot stand modern pop music. I try to listen sometimes, but I swear it feels like work and I have to change the station. I like songs that sound like actual music, if that makes sense."

"Are you kidding? That makes perfect sense. It's so funny. I love '80s music because I don't like the modern stuff either."

"We're a couple of old souls, I guess," Sarah said.

"I love Metallica, Pantera, and Anthrax. I even love Journey, but if you tell anyone that, I will deny it to my dying day."

Sarah laughed.

"But my favorite '80s band is—"

"AC/DC," Sarah finished for me.

Eyes wide, I said, "Yeah."

"'Back in Black' is your signature song," she said, taking another tiny bite of her food.

"Right," I said with a grin. All the guys had a song that played when they stepped up to the plate at home games. I was thrilled that Sarah had remembered mine.

"The song definitely suits you," she said, eying my black clothes. "You always look very sexy in the batter's box, Trace. I'm not sure what looks better on you—your Bay Birds uniform, or your leather jacket and black clothes. But you always look good."

Sarah blushed slightly as she spoke, and I was tempted to tease her about it. But I was so damned flattered by her words that I held my tongue.

"So what's your favorite musical group?"

"I would have to say The Platters."

"And I would have to say I have absolutely no idea who they are," I said.

Sarah laughed. "It's okay. I can't imagine there are many people our age who are familiar with them. They were a group from the 1950s, and they had such beautiful vocal harmonies. The group is still around today, believe it or not. With all new members of course. But I really adore their older stuff."

She spoke fondly of the music she loved, and as always, I admired her passion.

"I think one of the reasons I like the older music is that it has no connection to my past, you know what I mean?" Sarah said. My mother listened to all the current stuff. I don't know. Maybe that's part of the reason I never liked it. And of course, the kids at school made fun of me for having no idea about popular music."

I nodded sympathetically as I listened to her.

"The '50s and '60s music is from a bygone era that had nothing to do with my parents or the kids at school. It felt like it was just ... mine."

"Hmm."

"What?"

"I never thought about it that way, but maybe that's why I like '80s music. Or at least that could be part of the reason. All that stuff is from before my time too."

"Could be," Sarah said with a warm smile.

In fact, everything about this woman was warm. Sitting here and talking with Sarah, I felt more connected to her than I had with anyone in my entire life. The guys on the team were cool, but I wasn't close with any of them. I felt jealous sometimes of how close Matt and Brady were, as well as the tight friendship Brady had with Angel Jimenez, one of our pitchers. I'd always had plenty of women to sleep with, but sex only eased my loneliness for a short time. For the first time in my life, I felt like I had a real friend. I was so incredibly grateful that Sarah had agreed to give me a chance.

Thank you, Flynn.

Of course, I had a lot more on my mind with Sarah than simply friendship. I ached to make love to her, but I knew I had to tread carefully. She'd been through so much in her life, and it was clearly hard for her to trust anyone. The last thing in the world I wanted was to hurt her, and I had no intention of pressuring her into anything physical.

Well, I *did* plan to kiss her goodnight if she let me. I suppressed a smile at the thought. I almost always scored with a woman within hours of meeting her, and now I felt like a schoolboy with a crush, hoping for a simple kiss. I was crazy about Sarah, and I would take whatever she was willing to give me.

Sarah stared at her half-finished takeout containers. After a moment of contemplation, she put them on the coffee table.

"You're still hungry, aren't you?"

"What?" she asked, looking confused.

"You're still hungry, but you're trying not to eat any more."

Sarah nodded sadly, and I wanted to track down her

stupid mother and give her hell for what she'd done to her precious daughter.

"Is every meal a struggle like this?"

"Not always. Some meals are harder than others. Sitting here with a man with movie-star good looks makes me self-conscious about my weight."

"Oh man," I groaned. "I hate that you feel that way. I want you to eat as much as you want."

"I appreciate that," she said. "But it's not that easy."

I nodded, knowing I could not possibly understand how she felt.

"Our parents really did a number on us, didn't they?" I asked bitterly.

"Yah."

All this talk about our dark pasts had been cathartic, but it also dredged up a lot of painful memories. Dizzy and over-whelmed, I leaned forward and put my head in my hands.

"Trace?" Sarah said, sounding concerned. "Are you all right?"

"Yeah, I'm all right," I said wearily. I lifted my head and let out a deep breath.

"What is it?"

"It's just ... It's hard to talk about, you know?"

"Yes," Sarah said softly. "I understand."

She gently rubbed my back. I knew I was safe with her.

"There's something else," I began shakily. "Something else that happened that ... Well, I feel like if I don't talk about it now I never will."

Sarah nodded and kept rubbing my back.

"I never knew my real dad because he bailed before I was born. So I guess I should feel at least a little sorry for my mom for being saddled with me."

Sarah groaned softly. "Oh, Trace. It's not your fault your mother treated you like you were a burden. You deserved so much better."

I shrugged. Intellectually, I knew a baby was innocent and shouldn't be blamed for being born, but that didn't erase the feeling that my entire existence was a mistake.

"Then she married my stepdad and they had another baby. I was never sure if my little sister was planned or not, but they treated her like she was nothing more than an inconvenience to them."

I got up from the couch and began pacing, knowing I could never get through the rest of this story if I was looking at Sarah. A quick glance her way confirmed that she was listening with pure compassion in her eyes.

She cares about people.

Flynn's sage words rang in my ears. Yes, she sure did care about people and not money or fame. Sarah was the first woman I'd dated who'd been perfectly happy with takeout food instead of being paraded around on my arm in public and spending my money. And she was certainly the only woman who actually cared one whit about my personal life.

"My mom and Robert, my stepdad, they loved to drink and party all the time. Acted like they had no kids and no responsibilities. I bet they had friends who never knew they even had kids, just like you said about your mom. I had to take care of my little sister, Betsy, but I wasn't very good at it."

"Because you were a child, Trace," Sarah said softly. "You shouldn't have had to be the parent. It wasn't your job."

"But it *was* my job. It was my job to protect her," I said, my voice taking on a hard edge.

Sarah drew in a shuddery breath.

"Karol and Robert were barely ever home, and when

they were home, all they did was call me worthless and a waste of space. That, and my stepdad would often just beat me up for no damn reason. That was another reason I turned to athletics. Worked out so I could get big enough to kick *his* ass. Anyway," I said, swallowing hard and gearing up for the worst part of the story. "I was so busy trying to stay out of his way that I never realized ... I didn't know he was ... *touching* my little sister."

"Oh, Trace, I'm so sorry," Sarah said quietly.

"I should be sorry. It's my goddamn fault!"

"The hell it was!" Sarah shouted, jumping up from the couch. I'd never heard her yell before.

She grabbed my shoulders and forced me to look at her. "You were an abused little boy who was constantly in survival mode. What happened to your sister was in no way your fault." Her voice softened. "You feel responsible because you're a good man, and you are nothing like your parents."

I hadn't known how much I needed to hear that until Sarah said the words out loud. She pulled me into her arms and held me for a moment.

When I let go of her, she led me back to the couch and we sat close together.

Sarah tenderly brushed the hair from my face and asked, "Where is your sister now?"

"Betsy's in rehab. Her way of coping with it all was drugs and alcohol. We're not really close. I pay for all her rehab stints, making sure she gets the best care and all that. I'm lucky she's still alive."

"Drug addiction is tough to beat, but there's hope if she's in rehab."

"She blames me for what happened. Told me I should have stopped my stepdad from hurting us."

"It's sad that Betsy blames you. But that still doesn't make it your fault. She's hurting. Her words are just her pain talking."

"Yeah. I guess so."

"I always had a feeling that maybe something terrible had happened to you," Sarah said. "Like the saying goes, you should be kind to people because everybody is fighting a battle you know nothing about. I do my best to give everybody the benefit of the doubt when they're being mean, because you never know what demons they're battling."

"That's pretty cool, Sarah."

"Thank you for telling me all this. I know it wasn't easy."

"So ... do I win?"

"What?"

"Earlier when we were trading horror stories, you said this was like the worst contest ever. So did I win?"

Sarah laughed, and my heart swelled with joy. I loved that she understood how dark humor could be healing, and that she didn't think I was crazy.

"Yah, Trace. Fer sure. You win."

I was utterly, emotionally spent, and I was sure she probably felt the same way.

Sure enough, she said, "I guess I better get going. It's late."

I stood and offered her my hands so I could pull her up.

"I'm sorry tonight was so intense. Believe me, it's not what I intended when I asked you back to my place."

"I know," she said, gazing into my eyes.

"I promise our next date will be a lot less depressing. I mean ... if there is a second date?" I asked hopefully.

Sarah smiled. "I think Flynn would like that."

I laughed. "Only Flynn?"

"I would like it too, Trace. Very much."

"Would you also like it if I kissed you right now?" I asked, gently tracing her lips. Her body shivered at my touch.

"Yes," she whispered.

I dipped my head down and pressed my lips to hers. Wrapping my arms around her, I felt her body relax and melt into mine. Her kiss was so warm and inviting that somehow it felt like I was home. Like I'd found a real home, and not the dark and frightening place I'd grown up in.

Our kiss progressed from warm and sweet to hot as hell. My mouth devoured hers and my cock stiffened. My exhaustion vanished, replaced with white hot desire. A soft moan escaped Sarah's delicious lips, thrilling me. She sounded as desperate as I felt.

She broke off the kiss, looking flushed. Had she been any other woman, I would have carried her into the bedroom, and she'd be on her back in a matter of seconds.

But this wasn't any other woman. This was Sarah Asiago, an incredibly passionate, sexy woman who had been badly wounded in the past.

"I'd better go," she said breathlessly. I got the feeling she was fighting to keep control, and I loved it.

I understood that Sarah needed more time. She was worth waiting for.

"So are you gonna go to the ballpark tomorrow and tell everybody about this?" she asked, her forehead creased with worry.

"Tell them what? I didn't get anything."

Her face fell. "Trace ..."

"I'm only joking, Sarah. And no, I won't tell anyone if you don't want me to."

"I don't," she said. "This is just ... too new. And I don't want to deal with—"

"Sarah, it's fine. I understand. I won't breathe a word to anyone. Well, except Flynn. You gotta let me tell him I kissed you."

Her face relaxed and her lips blossomed into a beautiful smile.

"Yah. That's okay."

Sarah touched my face affectionately and then walked out the door.

"Good night, Sarah," I said softly, even though she couldn't hear me.

20

TRACE

I woke up the next morning with the memory of Sarah's sweet kiss fresh in my mind. Last night had turned out to be wildly different from anything I had expected, and that was putting it mildly. I could hardly believe I'd told her everything about my past. I rather expected to regret that in the morning, but I didn't. Had it been anybody else, I would have felt vulnerable and exposed. But not with Sarah. She had not only listened to my tale of woe with compassion, she understood my pain on a deeper level because she'd been through a similar experience with her own dysfunctional family.

Though I wanted to tell everyone on the team that I'd made out with Sarah Asiago last night, I would keep my promise to her and not breathe a word. I understood that she needed more time to really trust me. That, and after I made that stupid vow to get her into my bed, telling the guys I'd kissed her would only embarrass her. Like I'd scored a win in the battle to get her to have sex with me. Not that the players on the team would be mean to her. They were good guys, and everybody liked Sarah. Still, knowing what the athletes in her high school had done to her, the last thing she needed was to feel like she was being mocked by professional ballplayers.

I took a shower, indulging in a healthy jerk-off session while I fantasized about sex with Sarah. I had a feeling I'd be doing this a lot, since it was unlikely Sarah would be ready to go to bed with me any time soon. Frustrating, but understandable. She had a lot of issues to work through first.

After I got dressed, I made some breakfast and ate while I watched the TV that was mounted on my kitchen wall. Everything was going great until I got around to checking my phone messages. My good mood evaporated as soon as I saw the missed call.

"Shit."

Gary Devilbuss had left me a voice mail. Having the big boss call was never a good sign.

"Come to my office today before the game," was all he'd said.

Sighing heavily, I hung my head.

I SAT down in front of Mr. Devilbuss, and he cut right to the chase.

"She's suing for more damages, mental anguish, and lost wages."

Car Crash Lady had resurfaced again, adding more charges to her lawsuit. I had nearly forgotten about her, figuring no news was good news and that my agent was handling things.

"That is so unfair," I grumbled.

"How is it unfair?" the big boss asked angrily. "You did smack her rear end, did you not?"

I bit the inside of my cheek, knowing this guy would blow his stack completely if I so much as smirked.

"I did, sir. You're right. I did cause an accident, and for that I'm truly sorry."

I didn't much care that I'd tapped the lady's bumper, but I did care that my career here with the Bay Birds could be in jeopardy because of it.

"I just meant it's unfair because, I'm *telling* you sir, that woman was not injured." We'd had sex for hours after the accident that had allegedly caused her so much injury and mental anguish. I hadn't heard any complaints when she was having her third orgasm of the night.

"Well, I suppose the courts will determine that."

"Yes, I suppose so."

So what do you want me to do about it?

"You need to do *something* to distract from this nonsense. This Featherstone lady is making the media rounds, saying you were drinking and driving recklessly."

"I was not drunk when I hit her!"

"Does it matter?" Mr. Devilbuss yelled. "This is the court of public opinion here."

"Yeah. I know what you mean."

"You've done what, *one* charity job with the Bay Birds Foundation? You gotta do more. Something to show you're not a complete jerk."

I thought about what Brady Keaton had done when he'd been in almost exactly the same situation. Back when he was still playing for the Richmond Dominos, he *had* been a drunken partier who'd gotten into all kinds of trouble. His boyhood dream was to play for the Bay Birds in his home-town of Baltimore. At first, Mr. Devilbuss wouldn't even consider him for the team. Then Brady got the idea to pretend he'd settled down and fallen in love with a nice, stable girl. Enter Lyric Rivers, a squeaky-clean medical student who fit the bill. The scheme had worked better than he could have imagined. He got a Bay Birds contract and a wife out of the deal when the two had fallen in love for real.

Sarah was a goody-two-shoes charity lady. I would certainly look like a changed man if everybody thought the two of us were in love.

I dismissed that idea in about two seconds. No way in hell would I use Sarah like that. I harbored no judgment about what Brady had done with Lyric. That had started out like a business deal, where she would play the doting girl-friend and he would pay for all her schooling. It wasn't like he'd tricked her into anything. He'd made the offer and Lyric had accepted.

Though Sarah might be willing to help me out in a similar manner, it was still a terrible idea. We'd taken the first shaky steps last night toward a relationship, and I couldn't bear the idea of her thinking for one second that I was just using her to fix my own mess. Sarah had been used and abused by so many people in her life, and I was not about to become one more person to betray her.

"Hello?" Mr. Devilbuss said, waving his hand in front of my face. I'd gotten lost in thought there for a moment and missed whatever he'd just said.

"Do more charity work or something. I know you're busy during the season, but you gotta do something. I don't know ... visit those sick kids in the hospital or something. We still do that stuff, right?"

Funny that he had no idea I was already doing that on a regular basis.

It would sure look good for me if word got out that I'd developed a special relationship with one of the sweet Cancer Kids and visited him all the time.

Using Flynn for my own purposes would be even worse than using Sarah. Even I wouldn't stoop to using a kid with a life-threatening illness to fix my life.

"I'll see what I can do about getting involved in more charity work," I said without offering any specifics.

"See that you do, Trace. You know what's at stake here."

"I do, sir," I said, standing up. "And I hope you know how much I want to stay here and play for the Baltimore Bay Birds. Please don't give up on me."

The boss eyed me curiously. Like everybody else, he was used to me sounding arrogant and cocky. I rarely spoke from the heart, but I'd meant what I said. The idea of leaving Sarah behind was unbearable, and I loved being on this team.

"We'll see what happens, I guess," the old man said. "You're dismissed."

I left his office and headed straight for Sarah's office, which was downstairs in the same building. I told her assistant—Bridget?—that I was here to see Sarah, and she let her know I was on my way.

I knocked on Sarah's door and walked in when I heard her cheerful voice say, "Come in."

"What are you doing here?" Sarah asked with a smile, a far cry from the way she used to look at me. In the past, I'd been greeted with annoyance at best, disgust at worst.

"Just wanted to see you," I said as I closed the door behind me. If she knew I'd been here to see Mr. Devilbuss, she would figure out I was in trouble.

"That's really nice." She got up from her desk and walked over to me.

I pulled her into my arms and kissed her. Sarah's body melted into mine, just as it had last night. I loved how easy it was to get right back to where we'd left off. Kissing her was far more exciting than any other woman, and I'd kissed one hell of a lot of women. Sarah was beautiful, but it was so much more than that. For the first time in my life, I was attracted to the person, not just to the body that came with it. It was desire on a whole other level, and I found it a struggle not to sweep all the stuff off her desk and take her right then and there.

"You're such a good kisser, Trace," she murmured in my ear.

"So are you, baby." I chuckled softly. "Is it okay if I call you baby now?"

"I guess so," she said, smiling and tracing my lips with her finger. "But only in private."

"It's a deal. Can I tell you something else if you promise not to get mad?"

"I can't promise if I don't know what it is. But I will promise to keep an open mind and try not to get mad."

"I'll take it." Running my fingers through her pretty honey-blond hair, I said, "I just wanted you to know I have this fantasy about having sex with you in your office."

Sarah's eyes widened as she listened to my words.

"I love to think about just taking you on your desk. Pounding into you while you try not to scream and let everyone in the building know you're in here having wild sex with the catcher of the baseball team who cannot get enough of you."

She stared at me, a reddish hue blooming on her face.

"You're so beautiful when you blush, Sarah."

She lowered her eyes, and her body stiffened a bit.

"I'm sorry. I didn't mean to upset you."

"It's okay ... It's just ... that sounds a bit forceful, especially from the guy who bragged in front of the whole team that he would get me into bed."

"I really am sorry about that. It was a stupid thing to say, and honestly, I've regretted it ever since."

"Really?"

"Yeah. Was just me and my dumb ego getting in the way as usual. I'm sorry, Sarah."

"Thanks," she said. "That does make me feel better. And really, the idea of sex in my office sounds kind of exciting. Just a bit scary, too, I guess."

"I get that. You're not mad?"

"No, I'm not mad," she said, meeting my gaze again. "Maybe I should be, but ... I'm not used to having men think of me that way. It's kind of flattering."

I leaned in and kissed her neck, eliciting a sensual moan from her. "I have those kinds of thoughts about you all the time," I murmured in her ear. "Especially when I'm in the shower, touching myself and imagining I'm inside you."

A small gasp escaped her throat. Since I was still feeling out her comfort zone, I lifted my head to check on her reaction.

"Trace," she said looking away. Her blush had deepened, but she was smiling.

"I can't help it, baby. You are one damned sexy woman."

"Thank you." She stood on her tiptoes to kiss me again.

"I better let you get back to work," I said, liking the idea of leaving her a bit flustered and wanting more of me.

"Good idea," she said breathlessly. "Talk to you later."

I nodded and slipped out the door.

Yeah. No way was I going to tell her about my troubles with Devilbuss. I couldn't have her thinking I was only using her for her charity connections.

I adored Sarah Asiago, and I wouldn't do anything to mess that up.

21

SARAH

I leaned, breathless, against the back of the door after Trace left. Crazy how he could get my heart pounding, not to mention my panties wet, with just his words. Well, his words and a powerful kiss that would bring any woman to her knees. Glancing over at my desk, I wondered how I was supposed to get any work done with fantasies running through my head of having desperate, animal sex with Trace on top of it.

What had gotten into me? I was literally panting with desire.

I sat down at my desk and grabbed my water bottle. I laughed as I pictured spraying water all over my face to cool down like the players did.

Kissing Trace would have been unthinkable just a short time ago, but it seemed like my whole world had changed last night. He'd been brave to tell me all those things about his past, and I knew now why he was so over-the-top with machismo all the time. Trying to compensate for all the damage caused by a toxic family was hard work, and I understood completely. My heart broke for him, but I was honored that he'd opened up to me.

I leaned back in my chair, reliving the sensuality of Trace's incredible kiss. I'd never been kissed like that before, with such a sense of urgency. The way he'd pressed his lips to mine and held me tight made me feel like he didn't just want me. He *needed* me. A girl could get used to that feeling.

Shaking my head to erase naughty thoughts of Trace, at least for now, I got back to work. It wasn't easy. My cheeks grew hot every time I recalled his admission that he thought of me while he showered. Biting my lip, I thought of my shower massager at home. That thing did wonders for gratifying my needs when I didn't have a man in my life, which was most of the time. I promised myself a nice long shower when I got home.

I'd put that massager to good use so I wouldn't find myself giving into temptation with Trace. It was something I was simply not ready to do.

Yet.

Sunday's baseball game was rained out, and Julia texted me to ask if I was up for a girl's day with her and Lyric. During the season, it was tough for Julia to find time to hang out— she worked more hours at Old Bay Stadium than the players did. When there was a rainout, there was nothing to do on the field until the weather cleared up.

A day with my girlfriends sounded wonderful. Trace's earlier text had warmed my heart; he was going to use the surprise day off to go visit Flynn. Who knew that Trace Ridgerton, of all people, would turn out to be a wonderful guy?

Of course, I was still proceeding with great caution. I wanted to trust him, but I'd been through way too much to get attached too quickly. I still didn't know Trace all that well, and I needed to be careful.

Julia, Lyric, and I had a lovely shopping spree, then Lyric told us she'd like to take us to a fancy Italian restaurant that she and Brady had discovered in Gaithersburg. She insisted it was her treat, which was incredibly sweet. Since the place was about an hour away from Baltimore, we all rode together in Brady's Maserati.

Sometimes my life was positively *surreal*. Days like this felt like I was a million miles away from my life in Minnesota.

Good.

Even the ride to the restaurant was a blast with the three of us singing along to the radio and giggling like schoolgirls. When we got to Carmelo's Restaurant, Julia and I marveled at how beautiful—and expensive—the place looked.

"I know," Lyric said with wide eyes. "Isn't this place wild?"

Lyric had also come from humble beginnings. Though she and Julia were both married to multi-millionaire athletes, neither seemed jaded by their wealth. All three of us were equally impressed with the high ceiling, chandeliers, and exquisite Italian decor. I'd never even seen a place like this, let alone dined in one. It was easy to picture Trace here, though. Sitting at the bar, sipping his whiskey. The thought made me smile.

We were seated at a table with a fancy tablecloth and more utensils than most families might use at Thanksgiving dinner. For a second, I was afraid I might use the wrong fork or something and embarrass myself. Then I remembered who I was with and realized I had nothing to fear. My girls would never laugh at me. They would only laugh *with* me, which was why I adored them.

Lyric and I ordered wine, and Julia asked for a beer. After a few sips, I felt more relaxed and happy than I had in a long time.

"Here's to the rain," I said, lifting my glass to toast my friends. We clinked joyfully to that.

"Whew, it is nice to have a day off," Julia said. "I love my job, but I am really looking forward to the All-Star break. Three whole days off in the middle of the summer will be so nice."

"It's nice in theory," Lyric said with a weary smile. "Not as much of a break for me."

Julia and I nodded sympathetically. Brady had made the All-Star team *again,* which was impressive and wonderful. It also meant Lyric would have to fly to California. San Diego was hosting this year's game.

"Not that I'm complaining," Lyric said. She worked at a hospital during the summer, but at least she was on break from medical school. "I'm so proud of him, and I love how excited he gets about this honor, no matter how many times he's voted to the All-Star team. He's like a kid at Christmas."

"Matt's an amazing ballplayer, too," I said. "Does it bother him that he's never been nominated?"

"Not really," Julia said. "Well, maybe a little. You know how he is. He's not big on attention, but I know it would mean a lot to him to be nominated for the team someday."

"I have to admit, it is partly a popularity contest," Lyric said. "Not that Brady isn't a terrific shortstop. He's incredible. But you know how outgoing he is, and because of all the celebrity endorsements he gets, everybody knows him. Matt is every bit as good an athlete, he's just not a show-off."

Lyric laughed and shook her head. I could see how much she loved her husband when she spoke about him.

"That's true," Julia said with a smile. "Matt's a lot quieter, so he can get overlooked sometimes."

"Exactly," Lyric said.

"Matt and Brady are both great guys," I said, trying to make a smooth segue into what I'd been dying to talk about all day. "So, I actually met someone recently."

"You did?" Lyric asked, looking excited.

"That's great," Julia said, eyes shining. "Tell us all about him."

I'd already decided I wasn't going to tell my friends *all* about him. This thing between Trace and I, whatever it might be, was hardly official. And I wasn't sure I trusted him yet. Still, I had the feeling it could turn into something amazing, and I desperately wanted to talk about it.

"Where did you meet him?" Lyric asked.

"At one of my charity events," I said, which was mostly true. Though I'd known who Trace was before, it was in planning and executing the food drive that I'd gotten to know him better. "And he's done more charity things since then. Like he visits the pediatric cancer ward at the hospital."

Lyric sighed dreamily. "Oh, he sounds wonderful."

"Yeah, he does," Julia said.

I felt slightly guilty about the picture I was painting for them of Trace. He wasn't exactly the do-gooder I was making him out to be. Yes, he'd done both those charity projects, but he'd attended the first one only to get out of trouble with Mr. Devilbuss. The hospital project he'd done at least partly to try to get to me. Neither Lyric nor Julia would guess in a million years that the man I'd described was Trace Ridgerton, the arrogant catcher who hit on anything in a skirt. But there was so much more to the man than most people realized, and I really wanted my friends to know that.

"We went out to a bar for our first date, but it was too … crowded, so we went back to his place."

"Really? On the first date?" Julia asked, eyes wide.

"I didn't sleep with him or anything," I explained quickly.

"Hey, I'm not judging you. Nothing wrong if you did have sex on the first date," she said with a warm smile. "I just know you tend to take things slowly, that's all."

"You're absolutely right. I do prefer to take things slow, and I was pretty nervous about going back to his house. It wasn't like I knew him all that well yet."

I almost mentioned that I'd followed his motorcycle to his house, but I worried that might be too much of a clue. I was being paranoid, though. Lots of people rode motorcycles. If I'd specified that it was an Indian, that could have given him away.

"We just went back to his place, had a few drinks, and ordered some food," I said. "Sounds so basic, but it turned out to be an incredible night. I went there not knowing all that much about him, and then we got to talking."

"You really hit it off, huh?" Lyric said, her eyes bright with happiness for me.

"More than I could have possibly imagined," I said dreamily, recalling how Trace and I had bared our souls to one another.

"Wow," Julia said thoughtfully, sipping her beer.

Lowering my voice, I said, "You guys know what kind of upbringing I had."

Both women nodded somberly.

"Even with you two, it took a while for me to get the

courage to talk about it. But I ended up telling him pretty much everything on that first date."

"No kidding?" Julia asked.

"That's no small thing," Lyric said with interest.

How wonderful it was to have friends who understood me so well.

"Sadly, he's been through the same kind of thing."

"So he really understood how you felt and what you've endured," Lyric said.

"Exactly. It's easier to talk about traumatic stuff with someone who knows what it feels like," I said. "It's funny. He ended up being an entirely different person than I expected. I almost didn't go out with him because I thought he was a jerk."

Lyric laughed. "It is funny how that goes sometimes. So do you think this could turn into something serious?"

"I do," I said, surprising myself at how quickly I'd answered that question. "But I'm still taking things slow. It's hard for me to trust anybody."

"I know it is," Julia said, her voice filled with sympathy. "And I think it's great that you're giving this a shot anyway. That's the definition of being brave. Being scared and going for it anyway."

"Thanks," I said.

Our food arrived, and it smelled *divine*. I'd ordered the penne pasta with vodka sauce, and it looked spectacular. I didn't often indulge in such rich food, but this was a special occasion.

I tried to put my fork down between bites to slow myself down, but the trick didn't work and I soon gave up. I rationalized that Lyric was spending a lot of money on this meal, and I should get her money's worth. Truthfully, it was hard to care about my weight when I was in the company of friends who would love me no matter how big I got.

But would Trace still find me attractive if I got fat again?

I knew the answer: who cares?

I'd never changed my appearance for a man, and I wasn't about to start now.

It hurt my heart to think Trace might lose interest in me if I gained a few pounds. But I knew if he did, then he wasn't right for me after all. It had taken years of therapy to learn to love myself and to undo some of the damage my parents had done to me.

And no man would ever take that progress away from me.

As I gazed at my dear friends, I took a moment to revel in this beautiful moment, when both my heart and my belly were full.

22

TRACE

I drove my car to the hospital to visit my favorite guy. I couldn't wait to tell him about my date with Sarah, both because I knew he would be pleased and because I was dying to talk to somebody about it.

I'd managed to make things so complicated by bragging to the guys about bagging Sarah. It had never occurred to me that I might actually fall for her.

Nice trap you set for yourself, you idiot.

Shaking my head as I entered the hospital through the glass doors, I figured I'd work it out somehow. No sense telling anyone in the Bay Birds organization anything about the two of us until we saw where the relationship was going. In the meantime, at least I had Flynn to talk to about it.

The minute I entered his room I could see something was terribly wrong. His agonized expression made my gut clench.

Oh God. The cancer is spreading. His treatment isn't working.

The whole drive over here I'd been thinking about myself, and I'd forgotten the most important part about visiting a sick kid in the hospital. I was supposed to be making *him* feel better.

Dear God, he could be dying.

"Hey, kiddo," I said as I pulled up the visitor's chair to be closer to him. I tried not to look or sound as panicked as I felt. "Tell me what's going on. You don't look so hot."

"I knew it was gonna happen, but ..." Flynn began. He was fighting tears, and it damn near broke me. I could tell he was trying to be tough in front of me. I wanted to tell him he could cry all he wanted to, but I didn't want to embarrass him.

"But what?" I said, steeling myself for the worst.

"It's not that big of a deal," Flynn said bitterly. I started to hope maybe he was screwing with me like he had on the day we met. But something in his eyes told me this was no act. "It's just ... my hair's starting to fall out."

"Oh," I said. My entire system flooded with relief. I wanted to yell *Thank God that's all it is*, but at the same time, I didn't want to minimize his pain. Looks were important to a teenaged boy.

Who am I kidding? Hell, even I might cry if my hair started falling out.

"That sucks, man," I said with genuine anger and sorrow on his behalf. "It really does."

"Yeah," he said. His sad gray eyes met mine, and I saw gratitude in them. I was glad I hadn't said anything stupid like it could be worse. Flynn needed to mourn this latest cancer loss, and I needed to let him. "It doesn't happen to everybody on chemo. I guess I thought maybe ..."

"That maybe you'd be one of the lucky ones."

Flynn nodded.

"You deserve better, man. I'm really sorry."

He winced, and I remembered how much this kid hated

pity. There was a fine line between commiserating with him and feeling sorry for him. I wasn't sure what to say to make him feel any better. So I figured the best thing to do was treat him like a normal person and not a poor, sick kid. I plowed forward like this was any other visit.

"So I went out on a date with Sarah."

Flynn's eyes went wide. "Shut the fuck up!"

I chuckled. There was the Flynn I knew.

"Yeah, and I'm pretty sure you greased the wheels there for me. I don't think she ever would have given me a chance if it hadn't been for you. Sarah really trusts your judgment."

"Wow. Cool."

Two simple words, but I could tell by the look on his face that he felt a little better already. Everybody wants to feel valued, like their opinion matters. Especially a kid in the hospital who doesn't have a whole lot of control over his life.

"She said you didn't think I would hurt her, and that if you felt I was okay, then she would give me a shot."

Flynn smiled, and a fresh wave of relief swept over me. I never wanted to see that awful, depressed look on his face ever again. It thrilled me to be able to help my guy in any way I could.

"Where did you go? What did you do? More importantly, did you do *it*?"

Cackling, I said, "Do you really think I would tell you about that?"

"Yes," he said bluntly. "I don't think you'd have the restraint not to."

"That is a fair point. No. We did not do *it*," I said with a smile. "But we had a wonderful time. I took her to a bar where I knew I would get recognized by lots of fans, especially women."

Flynn made a face. "Why the hell would you do that?"

"Because I'm an idiot."

"That's what I was thinking."

I laughed. I liked that Flynn didn't kiss up to me like most other people. He had no problem calling me out when I was being stupid.

"Yeah. I figured it would make me look like a big shot, but it ended up making her feel terrible when all these women kept coming up and asking me for my autograph."

"Aww," Flynn said with a pained expression. He really did care about Sarah.

"It was a shit thing for me to do. I would have been upset if she was the famous one and had lots of guys coming up and hitting on her when we were out on a date." I paused for a moment. "Some of those women were really disrespectful. I never really thought about it, but they come up and start talking to me and ignore the woman I'm with."

"And you let them," Flynn said.

"Yeah, kinda."

He shook his head.

"Okay, Dad. I get it."

Flynn laughed and so did I.

"As soon as I realized Sarah was not impressed, I suggested we leave."

"I told you she wasn't impressed by your money or fame."

I shot him a look.

Flynn held his hands up. "Sorry, sorry. Continue."

"Thank you, Mr. Bishop."

He laughed, and I was thrilled that his eyes were a lot brighter than when I'd first entered his room.

"We ended up going back to my place."

Flynn sat up straighter and leaned forward.

"I told you we didn't have sex. Get your mind out of the gutter."

He grinned.

"I figured it was safest to go back to my house because we could have some privacy. To *talk*, Flynn. Believe me, it wasn't easy convincing her to go home with me. But I did, and it was really nice. We had a few drinks, ordered some food, and talked for a while."

"That's it?" Flynn asked, sounding disappointed.

"I know it doesn't sound like much, but it was a pretty awesome date. Talking with her was amazing. I had a pretty messed-up childhood, and it turns out so did she. I'm not gonna get into any details about her personal life or anything, but she opened up a lot. And so did I. I told her a lot of stuff I never really told anybody before."

Flynn smiled. "You were real with her."

"Yes, dear boy. I took your advice. You happy now?"

"Very much so," he said smugly.

"Sarah wouldn't let me pick her up for that first date. I guess she wanted to be able to escape if she needed to," I said with a laugh. "But she didn't. Stayed at my place for a long time, which was cool. She told me she's never been on a motorcycle before. Man, I would love it if she let me pick her up on the bike sometime."

"Oh I bet you would. That way she could wrap her legs around you," Flynn said with a wicked grin.

I chuckled. I was still getting used to hearing Flynn talk about Sarah that way. He was a teenaged boy, after all.

"That bike is sweet," he said with admiration in his voice.

"You never been on a motorcycle, right?"

Flynn shook his head.

"Aw, man. I wonder if your doctors would let me take you for a spin sometime?"

"It's not my doctors you have to worry about. It's my mother."

"You could convince her." Putting on my best London orphan accent, I said, "Oh please, mothah. I have canceh. Cahn't I go on one quick motorbike ride before mah next chemo treatment?"

Flynn cracked up laughing at that.

"You're a theater geek, boy. You could pull it off."

For a second, I worried he might be offended that I'd called him a geek. But he was still smiling.

"You're right. I could talk her into it."

"Too bad it's raining today. Had to drive my car here. Then again, if it hadn't rained, I'd be at the ballpark right now instead of here with you."

"True. Thanks for hanging out with me when you coulda just had the day off."

"It's not like talking to you is work, Flynn."

"I'm just happy you scored a date with Sarah, and you still came back to see me anyway."

"Did you really think that was the only reason I kept coming to see you?"

"I wasn't sure."

My chest ached with sorrow when he said that. Especially because there was some truth to it. But it was also true that I enjoyed visiting with Flynn and had no intention of stopping, no matter what happened with Sarah.

"Please tell me you at least kissed her goodnight," he said.

"Yes, I did."

"Good."

Now I had two reasons to be happy I'd kissed Sarah. Not

only did I ache for any physical contact I could get from that beautiful woman, but Flynn would have been sorely disappointed in me if I hadn't.

"Sarah's been through a lot in her life. I gotta take things slow with her, you know?"

"Yeah," Flynn said with a sad smile. "That's cool. She's lucky to have you."

"I guess," I said with a shrug. "Pretty sure I'm the lucky one."

23

SARAH

The All-Star break occurred not long after my first date with Trace, so we had three whole days to spend together. It was the longest break in the entire six-month baseball season, with only the occasional day off every few weeks otherwise. Last night, we'd shared a cozy evening at his place again. Now, I lay on the couch watching TV, waiting to hear his motorcycle arrive at my apartment. We were still keeping everything on the down low. Trace had kept his word; as far as I could tell, nobody on the Bay Birds knew we were dating.

We'd been hanging out at his house, both to avoid his fans and to keep the secret that we were together. And we *were* together, officially, even though we hadn't been intimate yet. During one of our late-night talks at his place after a game, he'd told me he wanted to be exclusive. I wanted that too, but deep down I feared he wouldn't be faithful. I berated myself for not trusting him, but it was still so hard for me. I'd always been aware of his reputation as a womanizer, and I found it nearly impossible to believe he would change his ways just for me. Did I honestly expect him to give up wild sex with who knows how many other beautiful women just to hang out with his frigid girlfriend who wouldn't go any further than a good night kiss?

I drew in a deep breath and let it out. Once again, I tried not to be so hard on myself. I wasn't frigid. I was scared. It was okay for me to take my time in this new relationship, and it was fine that I wasn't ready for sex yet. Trace had been incredibly patient with me. If he was upset about not having sex after numerous dates, he didn't show it.

My eyes opened wide when I heard the roar of Trace's motorcycle. I sat up and fluffed up my hair, hoping I looked all right. My heart pounded at the thought of seeing him, and the noise of his bike was such a turn-on. It took effort not to run to the door when he knocked, but I forced myself to take my time.

"Hey," I said, unable to resist eying him up and down as he stood in my doorway. His sleeveless black shirt showed off his muscular arms and the tattoos that adorned them. He had an Indian motorcycle on his left arm and a skull with roses in the eyes on the right.

"Hey yourself," Trace said, his dark eyes flashing with desire. He closed the door behind him and before I knew it, his lips were on mine and he was pressing me against the wall. Trace's kiss was deep, passionate, *forceful*. And I loved it.

Moaning deep in my throat, I threw my arms around his neck. We lost ourselves in each other, kissing as if our lives depended on it. Trace's rock-hard erection pressed pleasurably and painfully between my legs. Times like this I believed he *was* being faithful, because he was obviously horny as hell.

Though Trace was patient with my wanting to wait, his body often betrayed him like this. I felt terrible about holding back, but I simply wasn't ready. I broke off the kiss, still panting heavily.

A flicker of disappointment flashed across his face, but he quickly recovered. With a smile, he said, "Baby, you're gorgeous. You really know how to welcome a guy to your place."

Laughing, I gazed into his eyes. "It's about time you saw where I live. Of course, it's nothing compared to your house."

Scanning my small apartment, he said, "It's nice."

I took him by the hand and led him farther inside. "It's not a bad apartment. Suits my needs. That's the kitchen in there," I said gesturing to my left. "Bathroom down the hall. The bedroom's down that way."

Trace raised an eyebrow at the word bedroom but didn't comment. He was handling my reticence perfectly, making it clear that he desired me while not putting any pressure on me. I just hoped he knew how much I desired *him.*

For one brief second of madness, I thought about grabbing his hand and pulling him toward my bedroom. I was cautious, but I wasn't made of stone. I had needs too, and Trace was irresistibly sexy. Though it worried me to think of how many gorgeous women he'd been with, I also knew that meant he was a master in the bedroom.

But it was more than that. Something in his eyes told me it was okay to trust him.

I drew in a deep breath, and the moment of madness passed.

"Are you hungry?"

"Starved," Trace said with a grin. He clearly had no idea how close I'd just come to surrendering to my desires. My resolve was weakening by the moment, which was both exhilarating and frightening.

We ordered some pizza and devoured it when it arrived. Technically, Trace devoured more than half of it while I managed to keep to a slice and a half, despite wanting more.

Not long after our meal, we retreated to the couch to make out hot and heavy like a couple of teenagers. Trace's huge hands cupped my face as he kissed me long and hard, and I was amazed at how I'd gone from despising this man to wanting to feel him deep inside me. He was just so *different* from the type of guy I thought I'd fall for. I'd always seen myself with someone quiet and sweet like Matt. And now here I was, ready to give myself to a motorcycle man with tattoos. I was still afraid, but nowhere near as terrified as I used to be.

"Soon, Trace," I said breathlessly. "I promise. I'm just not ... I'm sorry, I—"

"Shhh," he said, gently touching my lips with his finger. "You make me crazy because I want you so badly, but it's okay. I'm not trying to pressure you into anything you're not ready for." With a sexy grin, he said, "I just get a little carried away when it comes to you. Sorry."

Trace drew in a sharp breath, and I watched as he tried to compose himself. Guilt tore through me knowing how frustrated he must be. Still, I knew from my therapy that guilt was a terrible reason to have sex.

"It's getting late," he said. "I should let you rest."

Trace still sounded frustrated, but there was a gentleness in his voice that told me he wasn't angry with me.

"I really will be ready soon. I know I always say that, but ... you're getting harder to resist."

"I do like hearing that, Sarah."

My body tingled all over when he said my name. It always did.

"I feel terrible getting you all riled up," I said.

"It's okay," Trace said, pulling me close. Then he murmured in my ear, "That's what my right hand is for."

I giggled, and he pulled back so he could look at me.

"I love making you blush," Trace said wickedly.

"I think about you that way, too," I said.

"You do?" Trace seemed so excited by the idea that I forcefully shoved myself out of my comfort zone. For his sake.

"Yes," I said, gathering my courage. "You've got your right hand, and I've got my shower massager. Sometimes I lean against the wall in the shower, close my eyes, and spray the water between my legs and imagine it's you pleasuring me."

My face felt like it was on fire at my deeply personal confession, and yet I still stared into Trace's deep brown eyes.

"Oh ... my... *God*," Trace said, collapsing back onto the couch, his erection straining the limits of his black pants. "I think that is the single sexiest thing I have ever heard in my life."

Sitting up, he looked at me, his eyes blazing with passion. "You make me *crazy*, Sarah. In a good way. I hope you know that."

He stood up and said, "I gotta go now before I burst into flames."

I laughed.

Trace pulled me in for a kiss and whispered in my ear, "Are you gonna have a shower after I leave?"

"Yes," I said softly.

He groaned and squeezed me tight.

"Make me *crazy*," he muttered. He headed for the door, then turned back around. "See you tomorrow night?"

I nodded.

Trace eyed me up and down like he was undressing me with his eyes before he rushed out the door.

You make me crazy too, Trace, my darling.

24

TRACE

Sarah was killing me. But in a good way. A *really* good way. I had never wanted any woman as much as I wanted her. Naturally, my sex drive was in *overdrive* because of her, but it was so much more than that. I wanted Sarah Asiago. All of her. She understood me in ways I never thought possible, and she really did not give a flying fuck that I was famous. She didn't seem to notice or care that I was a multi-millionaire. Sarah never asked for anything from me but my time and my company, and it had been a long time since anyone had valued me for just *me*.

No. Not just a long time. It was the first time anyone had *ever* valued me without wanting something in return. Just her, and maybe Flynn.

The motorcycle ride home gave me plenty of time to conjure up all kinds of fantasies of my beautiful Sarah. As much as I loved riding my bike, having a raging erection on a motorcycle wasn't the most comfortable thing in the world. I could hardly wait to get home and relieve the tension that had been building up all night.

I practically ran into the house when I finally got there.

At least with no one around to see, I didn't have to walk slow and cool like I usually did. The first thing I did was flop down in my bed and unzip my pants. It was slightly pathetic, I knew. The last time I'd felt this desperate, I was a teenager jerking off like ten times a day.

I took my phone out of my back pocket so it wouldn't fall out when I took off my pants, and I saw a message from Sarah.

Best shower EVER.

Groaning out loud with painful desire, I mentally thanked Sarah for that delightful image. Not that I had any shortage of sexy images to choose from when it came to her, but the visual of her showering was the best. Picturing her leaning against the wall with the shower massager between her legs, her eyes closed, moaning while she thought of *me*, was enough to make me come just thinking about it.

I grabbed my dick and started rubbing. Grateful I had no roommates, I could groan all I wanted while I released my sexual tension. I came with a sharp cry, making a mess everywhere, but it was hard to care. My breath heavy with relief, I knew it was only a temporary satisfaction, but it would do for now.

Staring up at the ceiling, I found myself fantasizing about how great it would be to cuddle with Sarah after sex. That was new. Usually after sex I just planned my escape. No doubt, Sarah would need extra reassurance given how unsure she'd been, but it was more than that.

The truth was, I couldn't even tell myself that it was just for her sake. I needed reassurance too, that this incredible thing between us was real. I was falling so hard for her, and I could only pray she felt the same way about me.

My phone was on silent, but out of the corner of my eye I saw it light up with a new message.

Thanks for being so patient with me. It means more than you know.

I smiled, imagining Sarah holding her phone in her delicate, feminine hands as she typed. I missed her already, wishing she was here in bed with me. My phone flashed again.

Maybe tomorrow night we can actually go out somewhere. Since it's the last night of the All-Star break, we should make the most of it.

My smile widened.

Anything you want, Sarah. Anything.

THE NEXT NIGHT, we went to a waterfront seafood restaurant in Annapolis. She drove to my place and we took my black Lamborghini. I still wanted to take her out on my motorcycle, but not yet. Baby steps were best for my baby when it came to getting her out of her comfort zone.

The hostess at Stoneyman's Crab House recognized me. It was pretty obvious by the way she blushed and giggled. It turned out to be a good thing, because she gave us a table outside right by the water.

"This is so lovely," Sarah said, gazing out at the water while I gazed over at her.

"My thoughts exactly."

I hadn't meant to say the words out loud, but I was glad I had when she turned to me with a smile that lit up her whole face. My God, she was beautiful.

We had a wonderful meal together, and it felt amazing to finally be out in public with her. Several people looked at us, and I could tell they recognized me. Luckily, nobody bothered us while we were eating. Sarah didn't seem concerned that people knew who I was. It was unlikely that anyone knew who she was or that she, too, worked for the Bay Birds organization. Unless one of the other players showed up here in Annapolis, our secret was fairly safe.

After we finished our crab cake dinners, Sarah reached across the table and took my hand in hers. Such a simple gesture, but I felt proud that she was getting more brazen about showing affection in public. I longed to tell the other guys that we were together, and it had nothing to do with proving a stupid point that I had won her over. I was just proud that a woman as incredible as Sarah was actually *into* me, and I wanted the world to know she was my baby.

Of course, I wouldn't breathe a word to anybody until Sarah gave the go-ahead. And that might not be for a long time.

When we left the restaurant, we walked hand in hand along the water. It was sweet and amazing and so *normal*. Real relationships based on emotion were a foreign concept to me. Up until now, my love life had been nothing but a series of one-night stands. And yet this, right here, was infinitely more satisfying. The only thing left to make this relationship utterly perfect was sex. Still, I knew Sarah would be worth the wait, no matter how long it might be.

"Oh my gosh, we should go to this," Sarah said, her eyes lighting up when she saw a club that had an '80s cover band performing tonight. "You love '80s music."

I was touched that she remembered. "Yeah, that would be fun."

We went into the noisy club and managed to find a table. I ordered a whiskey for me and a glass of wine for her. The band turned out to be really good. When they played an AC/DC song, Sarah turned to me and smiled.

In that precise moment, I realized I was in love with her.

The woman who had tolerated my arrogant attitude with grace and patience. The one who knew all my darkest secrets and cared for me anyway, and the one who remembered my favorite band because she always listened to everything I had to say.

My eyes watered slightly, and I casually sipped my whiskey to hide my tears.

I knew my Sarah. Telling her I was in love with her might frighten her off. Worst case scenario, she might even think I was saying I loved her just to get her into bed quicker. I grimaced at that thought.

Sarah was so strong, yet so fragile at the same time. I knew I had to handle her with care. Not my strong suit, but I would do my best.

25

SARAH

This was easily the best date of my entire life, and it wasn't even over yet. Being with Trace felt natural and wonderful, and we never ran out of things to talk about. We held hands as we walked back to his car, just as we'd held hands the entire night. I was glad we had gone out in public together. It felt like an important step in our relationship.

"What kind of car is this anyway?" I asked when we got back to the parking lot.

Trace chuckled.

"What?"

"I just think it's cute that you don't know. It's a Lamborghini."

My eyes flew open. "Wow. Pretty expensive, huh?"

Trace grinned and nodded. He seemed to like that I didn't care that he was rich. It just wasn't something I thought about when it came to him. There were so many other things to like about him, and I was discovering more every day.

I'd noticed a million little things. Like the way he paused

until I had my seatbelt securely fastened before starting up the car, as if he didn't want to rush me. And I could tell by the look on his face at the club that he was honored I'd remembered how much he liked AC/DC. Little things. Wonderful things.

"Annapolis is such a beautiful city," I said. "I haven't spent much time here before today. This was a great idea."

"I'm glad you liked it," Trace said.

I tried not to stare at him as he drove, but he was just so damned handsome.

"This really is a nice car," I said, admiring the sleek interior.

"Thanks. What I'd really love is to get you on the motorcycle, though."

"Sounds a little scary. But I guess I could try it."

"I have to admit, there is one other person who I want to ride with even more than you."

"Really?" I asked, feeling jealous already.

"Flynn," Trace said with a grin.

"Oh," I said, laughing.

"He's been going through a rough time lately." I could hear the worry in his voice. "He's starting to lose his hair, and he's pretty upset about it."

"That poor baby," I said, my heart aching for him.

"Yeah, it really sucks. Like he doesn't have enough going on as it is. Do you think I'd be allowed to take him for a quick spin on the bike? I know he'd love it."

"If there is any possible way, I'll make it happen," I said firmly.

"Cool. He said his doctors would probably be okay with it, but clearing it with his mama is another matter."

"Good point," I said. "Still, I'll make it happen."

Trace chuckled, and my heart soared with renewed

adoration for him. The way he cared for Flynn made him the sexiest man in the world to me.

When we got to his place, he shut off the car engine and turned to me.

"Did you want to come in for a bit? Or are you too tired?"

I gazed at him lovingly. He was always so thoughtful, and his low-pressure attitude meant the world to me.

"I can come in for a little while."

"Cool," he said, tenderly caressing my face.

The moment we stepped in the door, I pulled him close for a kiss.

"I had the most wonderful time tonight," I said, my voice sounding as dreamy as I felt.

"Me too," Trace said, dipping his head to kiss me again. His kisses drifted down to the sensitive skin on my neck, making me moan with desire.

"Oh, Trace," I said. "Feels so good when you do that."

I found myself wishing he could kiss even lower; open my blouse to suck on my breast. I wanted him to hike up my skirt, yank down my panties, and put himself inside of me.

And I was running out of reasons to not let him.

Trace had been nothing but wonderful ever since our first date. How many times did I expect him to have to prove himself? He wasn't the same cocky jerk he'd been when I first met him. And now I knew all the deeply personal reasons that made him act that way in the first place.

That, and I was tired of dating my shower massager.

"Let's go to the bedroom," I said breathlessly.

Trace shot up straight, making me feel cold without his warm breath on my neck.

"Baby, are you sure?"

My heart, along with my panties, melted when he asked

me that. As worked up as he was, he still wanted to make sure this was what I wanted.

"Yes," I croaked. "Take me to bed before I let you take me right up against this wall."

I must have looked as desperate as I felt because his eyes flashed with excitement. He knew I meant business.

"I would *love* to take you against the wall, but not for our first time."

Then he slid his muscular arms underneath my legs and swept me up off my feet. I stifled a moan of desire at the feel of his bulging arm muscles when he held me tight. I'd never had guessed in a million years that I would have sex with a tattooed biker, but there was nothing in the world I wanted more right now.

This was the first time I'd seen Trace's bedroom, not that I was paying much attention to the decor. My focus was on the dashingly handsome man who was carrying me in his arms. He lay me down on the bed with a black comforter and dark gray sheets. We tore at each other's clothes, desperate to get naked as soon as humanly possible.

Relieved of our clothes, Trace lay down next to me and slipped his hand between my legs.

"I need you so bad, Sarah," he said in a deep, husky voice. "But once I get inside you, I probably won't last too long."

"My fault," I said. "For making you wait so long."

"The wait is over." His dark eyes flashed with intensity. He slid two fingers inside me and moved them in and out, finding my g-spot right away.

I whimpered softly as he stroked, the burst of pleasure so strong it nearly brought me to tears. I threw my head back and closed my eyes, lost in the delicious sensations of sheer bliss. Then I opened my eyes and watched the tattoo on his arm flex with his thrusts. I'd never found tattoos sexy before, but I knew I'd never look at that skull with the roses the same way again. From now on, I would associate it with the orgasm that was quickly building up inside me.

"Oh Trace," I moaned. "Oh God, don't stop ... please ... I'm almost ..."

"Already?" he asked with that wicked grin I used to hate but now turned me on beyond all reason.

"Y—yes. I have a very ... sensitive ... g-spot," I managed to say. Most of my former lovers had taken a while to figure out exactly how to pleasure me, but Trace had zeroed in on the perfect spot right away. That, and he knew how to rub and massage me with the exact amount of pressure to render me completely helpless.

"Oh ... Trace." I writhed with his touch. I wanted to scream when my climax took hold of my body, but all that came out was a soft cry of relief. Squeezing my eyes shut, I allowed the swirls of ecstasy to crash over me until at last the waves of pleasure subsided.

Once I finally regained my senses, I suddenly felt utterly vulnerable. We were both naked, but I'd just had an orgasm while Trace had watched. I felt exposed. I glanced up at his face and saw deep pride but also concern.

"You're so beautiful, Sarah," he said softly. "So beautiful."

And just like that, my tension eased again. I felt safe with him.

Trace waited patiently for me to make the next move. I could see the strain on his face, and I knew his sexual need was intense.

"I need you inside me, Trace," I said, opening my legs.

He growled deep in his throat, the sound so erotic and primal that it sent a fresh tingling sensation vibrating through my lady parts. Without taking his eyes off mine, he leaned over and rifled through his nightstand and managed to grab a condom. It took him only a few seconds to roll it on, but it was enough time for me to indulge in the perfect specimen of masculinity before me. Trace's chest and arms rippled with muscles, and his cock was a work of art.

I could hardly believe this man was mine.

My man kissed me deeply, passionately, *wonderfully* before sliding into me at last.

I dug my nails into his back and cried out softly.

"Mmm, you *are* sensitive down there," Trace said, his hot breath on my cheek as he spoke.

"Yes," I said, losing myself all over again in the delightful sensations his cock gave me as it massaged my most sensitive spot.

"God, you feel good," he said as he thrust faster in and out of me.

I wrapped my legs around him, still digging my nails into his back. We breathed heavily as our lovemaking grew faster, stronger, and more desperate. All the pent-up sexual tension we'd both had since our first date was on the verge of explosion. Over and over again, Trace's cock hit that sweet spot inside me. Gripping his back tight, I mentally willed him to keep up that precise pressure.

Trace shifted his body, keeping me from reaching my climax. As frustrating as it was, I understood he'd done it to keep himself from coming too soon. Pumping hard in and out of me, he found another rhythm that was almost as pleasurable as the first. Trace grunted and groaned, and each animal sound he emitted only aroused me more.

Then he shifted back, massaging that sweetest spot inside me all over again.

"Oh Trace ... Oh God ..."

"Sarah, are you gonna—"

"Yes ... yes ... oh God, Trace, I'm coming again," I managed to say just before my body shuddered into another powerful orgasm.

Trace's eyes opened wide, and I had the honor of watching him lose control. With one last deeply masculine groan, he came. I could only hope it felt anywhere near as good as he'd made me feel.

He rolled off me and collapsed onto the bed. Then he laughed, but it didn't bother me in the slightest. I knew it was a laugh of sheer sexual relief.

"Oh my God, that was good," he said, turning onto his side to grin at me. "I knew you would be worth waiting for, but that was the best sex of my life."

"No way," I said. Considering all the women Trace had undoubtedly been with, there was no way I was the best. Then I realized my words might have sounded like I was saying there was no way *I* thought he was the best. I clarified quickly. "I mean, for me, yeah. No question it was the best for me. Hell, what you did with your fingers was better than most men could do with their whole bodies. But then I got the rest of you ..."

I ran my fingers down his chest, toward his cock.

"Your tattoos are so sexy, Trace."

"Baby, everything you got is sexy," he said, eying my naked body appreciatively. Usually, I felt self-conscious being naked after sex, but I didn't feel that way now.

Trace pulled me close and held me for a long time.

I HAD no idea what time it was or how long I'd been asleep. When I finally opened my eyes, I saw that Trace was awake. And grinning at me.

My blood went cold. My stomach clenched, and I felt the way I used to feel when he grinned at me like that.

Terrified and sick to my stomach.

"Took a lot longer than I'd thought, but I finally wore you down!" He jumped out of bed, still naked, and shot me another cocky smirk. "You were way more of a challenge than any other woman, but that just made it all the sweeter when I finally nailed you. And I nailed you *good.*"

"Wh—what?" I asked, sitting up in bed in horror. My head swam. I felt dizzy and faint.

Trace grabbed his pants and got dressed as he spoke. "Damn, I can't wait to get back to the clubhouse and tell all the guys that I *finally* hooked up with you. I certainly put the All-Star break to good use, didn't I?"

"Trace, what are you ... Wh—what—what are you talking about?"

"You are one sweet piece of ass, Sarah. I'll give you that." Trace still sported that sickening, wicked smile. "I can't wait to tell everybody all the juicy details, right down to the cute little noises you make when you come. And the best part?"

Trace leaned down to where I still sat naked on his bed.

"I can't wait to tell them all about the fun you have with the shower massager while you think about me."

I sat there, frozen in terror, while he laughed and laughed.

Then the room went black.

Breathing hard, I looked around. It was so dark, it took my eyes a moment to adjust.

Trace's bedroom. That's where I was. And that loud

noise was Trace snoring in bed. He was a heavy sleeper; my panting and jolting awake hadn't disturbed him.

It had been a nightmare, and yet it was all too real.

Trace had seduced me into his bed, just like he'd sworn he would. And at tonight's game, he would tell Matt and Brady and Rusty and Clay and everybody in the goddamn ballpark that he had slept with me. Everyone would know he had won. That I had willingly let him violate my body because I'd been stupid enough to actually believe he cared about me.

Shakily, I got to my feet. My heart pounded. I was sweating, yet chilly and clammy. I felt dizzy and nauseous. I had sharp pains in my chest.

I was having a heart attack.

Somehow, I got my clothes back on. My breathing was so heavy, I nearly hyperventilated.

It's not a heart attack. You know what this is.

Intellectually, I knew it was a panic attack. Certainly not the first time I'd had one. But it still felt like I was dying.

My body and my emotions spiraling wildly out of control, I managed to scribble a note for Trace before I stumbled out of his house.

I left as fast as I could, knowing I would never be back.

26

———

TRACE

Sarah was gone.

I stared at the four words she'd written on the back of an old grocery store receipt.

This was a mistake.

I felt like my heart had been physically wrenched from my body. As I stood there, holding this horrible note in my shaking hand, it occurred to me that this was karma. God knows how many times I'd left a note for a woman and slipped out without another word after I'd slept with her. It didn't feel too good to be on the receiving end of that kind of treatment.

Then again, none of those women had been in love with me. But I was hopelessly in love with Sarah. Clearly, the feeling wasn't mutual.

I sat down on the bed, naked and feeling utterly alone. I kept staring at the note as if there was some hidden clue on it that I'd missed.

What the hell happened?

I just couldn't make sense of it. I knew Sarah had been afraid to be intimate with me, and I'd been so careful not to push her. So many times it felt like she was ready, but then she'd pull back at the last minute. It had been frustrating as hell, but I'd done my best to be patient. I'd waited for her to make the first move, and last night she finally had. Hell, I'd even asked her again, to make sure it was what she wanted.

What does that woman want from me?

I crumpled up the note and stormed into the bathroom to take a shower. By the time I dried off and got dressed, my anger had cooled. The more I thought about the whole thing, the more I worried. Especially when a truly horrible thought occurred to me.

What if Sarah had been sexually abused the way my sister had been? I'd thought Sarah and I had told each other everything, but maybe she had been assaulted and it was too painful to talk about. Betsy's trauma had made her so despondent that she'd turned to drugs to kill the pain. Suffering that kind of abuse wasn't something you could just get over.

My chest ached at the thought that maybe having sex with me had triggered traumatic memories for her. More than anything, I needed to make sure she was okay.

I called her, but it went straight to voice mail. I left her a message, saying I hoped she was all right and pleading with her to call me back.

All my phone calls and texts went unanswered.

I had a game tonight, but that seemed so trivial compared to what was going on in my personal life.

Right now, Sarah was the only thing that mattered.

27

SARAH

I spent the entire day feeling like I was going to throw up. I didn't know what in hell I'd been thinking, sleeping with Trace. Ever since I'd woken up from that horrible nightmare, I'd been obsessing over what would happen when I had to face everyone on the Bay Birds team tonight. I didn't have a first pitch ceremony to oversee, but there was an important event scheduled. Andre Jones had paid for a bunch of inner-city kids to come to the game, and Andre's Kids would be on the field to sing the National Anthem.

No matter how humiliating it might be to walk out on that field when all my coworkers knew that Trace Ridgerton had finally gotten his wish and defiled me, I would not let Andre and the Baltimore community down.

In my mind, that horrible prom prank and sex with Trace had all melded together into one disgusting, twisted joke at my expense.

Challenge accepted.

Trace's response when I'd told him he would never have me echoed in my ears. If I'd actually gone to prom back in high school, I probably would have slept with my prank date, and he would have smeared my name all over school the following Monday.

Just like Trace was probably doing right now. I could just see him grinning and high fiving his teammates while bragging that he'd finally scored with me.

On the drive over to the ballpark, I broke down and sobbed. Somehow, I managed to pull myself together before shakily making my way through the back hallway inside Old Bay Stadium. Matt spotted me when he happened to be walking out of the weight room as I passed by. His eyes opened wide, and he rushed over to me.

And so it begins.

"Sarah, are you okay?"

"Y—yeah. I'm fine. Why?" I said, holding back tears of shame.

"You just look really upset." Matt's deep blue eyes filled with worry. "What happened?"

Maybe I hadn't managed to pull myself together as much as I'd thought, given the look of alarm on my friend's face. I realized it was entirely possible that Trace hadn't told Matt that we'd slept together. Many of the other guys on the team might slap Trace on the back and congratulate him on his conquest, but Matt wouldn't do that. That just wasn't his way. Plus, he never liked the way Trace pursued me. Matt didn't trust him, and he tended to be quite protective of me. Both he and Julia were aware of my difficult past, and they always looked out for me.

"I'm all right. Really. I had a panic attack earlier, and I guess I'm still recovering from it."

"Oh, I'm so sorry," Matt said gently. "Been a while since that happened, hasn't it?"

I nodded.

"Do you know what triggered it?"

"I ... uh, had a bad nightmare."

Matt opened his arms, and I graciously accepted his warm hug. I held him tightly and tried not to burst into tears. Eventually, I reluctantly let go.

"I'll be okay," I said with a forced smile. "I'm looking forward to tonight with Andre's Kids."

"Same here," Matt said. "It's fun to see the kids all excited to be on the field."

"Yeah. Thanks, Matt. I appreciate you checking up on me."

He nodded, still looking worried. I felt a bit stronger knowing Matt had my back. If Trace started too much trouble, Matt would kick his ass. And Brady would back him up on it, too. Trace wouldn't stand a chance if things got physical.

I continued down the hall. My stomach clenched when I walked by Clay Williams. He was pretty tight with Trace, and there was no doubt he was one of the first people Trace would tell.

"Hey, Sarah," Clay said with a friendly salute as I passed him.

That was a surprise. I'd expected him to shoot me a wicked grin like Trace often did, and then I figured he'd have a snarky comment. Maybe he didn't know what had happened.

But that seemed impossible.

Swallowing hard, I stepped outside. I usually loved that moment when I first stepped out onto the field. Being down here with all the players and being part of the excitement of professional baseball felt like a privilege. Now I just felt sick to my stomach, which made me want to cry. It was exactly the way I'd felt in high school when I'd forced myself to attend the next baseball game after half the baseball team had publicly humiliated me.

I was suddenly furious and sick to death of being afraid. Wanting to get the hardest part over with, I marched right over to the dugout to talk to the players.

"Hey hey," Brady said with a wink before popping his bubble gum. I tried not to read too much into that wink. Brady was always friendly, and possibly his wink hadn't meant anything. "Looks like the kids are all ready for tonight."

He gestured toward the warning track where Andre Jones was chatting happily with a bunch of adorable children. Just watching them helped calm me down. It was a sweet reminder of why I loved my job, and why I would not let anyone steal my joy from it.

A few of the other players glanced my way, offering a smile here, a quick wave there. Nothing seemed amiss.

Strange.

For a moment, I wondered if Trace was even here yet. But he must be. He was catching tonight; he would have been suited up in his baseball uniform hours ago for batting practice. My heart seized in my chest when I saw him near the third base line, throwing the ball with one of the pitchers.

Trace saw me too and froze, letting the ball strike him in the chest. He groaned and rubbed his chest. The pitcher cackled and yelled, "What the hell, Trace?"

Trace waved him off and started over toward me. I felt dizzy, like I might pass out. I drew in several deep breaths to keep steady, then forced myself to walk over to him.

We stood together on the warning track, far enough away from the others so we could talk privately.

"Did you tell anybody we slept together?" I blurted out.

Trace grimaced. "Of course not. Why would I do that? It's nobody else's business."

I stared at him, the realization finally sinking in.

"You really didn't tell anyone, did you?"

"No." He looked at me like I had lost my mind. "Did you really think I would?"

"Yes," I said without hesitation.

"How could you think that?" Trace asked with deep hurt in his eyes.

"Maybe because when we first met you treated me like a piece of meat, bragging to everybody about how you would stop at nothing to get me into bed."

Trace sighed, but a look of understanding crossed his face. "So you honestly think all of this—all this time we've been spending together—has just been some long con to get you to sleep with me?"

"Yes," I said, my voice barely a whisper. "I was afraid it was. I had a nightmare and then I had this horrible panic attack when I woke up in bed with you, and ... and ..."

"Oh, baby," Trace said, his voice gentle and loving. "So that's what happened."

Nodding, my eyes filled with tears. He gazed at me tenderly, and I knew if we hadn't been in public, he would have pulled me into his arms. Even now, he was doing his best to respect my boundaries.

"Sarah, it was terrible of me to treat you the way I did when we first met. I had no idea I had scared you so much. I'm so sorry. But a lot's changed since then."

"What's changed?"

"I fell in love with you, that's what changed," he said with the sweetest, most gentle smile on his face.

I gazed into his eyes, trying to make sense of everything. The warm, safe feeling I'd had when we were together last night washed over me again. I began to understand that my fear, my panic attack, and my past trauma had clouded my judgment. My terror had blinded me to the truth. Trace wasn't the monster I'd thought he was. He was a man from a broken home who was doing his best to survive. And he was in love with me.

"Turn around right now and look into the dugout," he said.

I did as he asked. A bunch of the guys were watching us from the distance, laughing and shaking their heads. When I turned back to Trace, he explained what was going on.

"They're laughing because they think I'm hitting on you again and that you're turning me down. Every time they see us talking, they think I'm striking out. They all say you're too good for me. Which is true, by the way," Trace said with a laugh. "When we're done talking here, I'm gonna go back to the dugout, and they're all gonna make fun of me. And I'm gonna let 'em. Because it doesn't matter what they fucking think. The only thing that matters is what you think."

"Trace, I'm so sorry. I'm sorry I messed everything up so badly. I—I— "

"Sarah," he said firmly. "It's okay. Don't stress about it. As long as you're okay ... as long as *we* are okay."

I nodded, and he let out a deep sigh of relief.

"Thank God," he said.

Trace turned and started walking toward the dugout. Then he turned back around and mouthed, "I love you."

As he headed toward the dugout, he threw his hands up in the air and shook his head. I could hear the laughter from the team from where I stood. I watched as Brady and some of the other guys chuckled when Trace returned to them. They slapped him on the back all right, but they were teasing him about not getting anywhere with me.

Now I was dizzy with relief, and not a little regret. My God, the things I'd put that poor man through. I had to find some way of making it up to him.

With a renewed sense of peace and purpose, I headed over to help Andre's Kids get ready to sing the National Anthem. I loved Baltimore. I loved my job.

And I loved Trace Ridgerton.

28

TRACE

During the seventh inning stretch, I went into the clubhouse to wipe the sweat and dirt off my face. It was hot as hell in mid-summer in Baltimore, even after dark. The Bay Birds were up 10-2, and I'd hit a home run so I was in a fantastic mood. I checked my phone and saw a text from Sarah.

Come see me in my office after the game if you're not too tired.

I smiled as I read and re-read her text. This whole day had been such a nightmare right up until I got to speak to Sarah and we were able to clear things up. I hadn't meant to tell her that I loved her yet, but I wasn't sorry I had. She'd been so upset that I figured she had probably needed to hear it. I tried not to read too much into the fact that she hadn't said it back. Could be because she actually didn't love me, but that didn't mean she never would. Or maybe she was still scared to trust this relationship. I needed to accept that she might not say those three words to me for a while. And it was possible she never would. I simply had to wait and see what would happen.

You're at work now? I texted back. Her work hours were

fairly flexible because she often had events at the ballpark and in the city on weekends and so forth. But I'd never known her to be in the office this late.

No. I'm still at the game. My throat is sore from screaming when you hit that home run.

Sarah added a smiley face and heart emoji.

I grinned, thrilled that she'd seen my moment of triumph.

I just figured my office would be a private place where we could talk after the game. But only if you're not too tired.

I'm never too tired for you, Sarah.

You have the patience of a saint, she wrote back.

That's the first time anyone's ever called me a saint, I assure you.

She responded with a laughing emoji.

Gotta run. I hesitated only a moment before adding, *Love you.*

I put my phone back in my locker and rushed to the dugout. So far today I'd told Sarah I loved her three times. She needed all the reassurance she could get, I supposed. And I understood. When you grow up with parents who didn't love you, it really fucks you up. You learn to not trust people, and you grow up with a deep-seated fear that you are inherently unlovable. Sarah and I had shared the same kind of pain, we simply responded to it differently. My response had been bravado, acting like I was better than everybody else so they wouldn't know how insecure I actually was. Sarah's response was fear, though she'd worked hard through therapy to overcome a lot of it.

I sat down in the dugout and looked out at the crowd. It made me happy to know Sarah was out there somewhere, watching the game and rooting for me. Not in my wildest fantasies did I ever think I would meet a woman who understood me the way she did. From the very beginning, she'd seen through all my bullshit. She'd figured out there was a reason I acted the way I had, and she'd given me a chance, even though she'd been terrified I would hurt her. How brave she was. And how lucky I was that she'd even given me a second glance.

I looked forward to seeing Sarah after the game. More than anything, I wanted to kiss her, hold her in my arms, and make sure she was okay. I needed to reassure her that I wasn't mad at her.

As soon as the game was over, I changed my clothes and rushed over to the building next to Old Bay Stadium where all the corporate offices were located. I didn't even shower— I hoped I didn't smell too bad. I just needed to see my baby.

I knocked on Sarah's office door and entered without waiting for a response. When I walked in, she was standing at the window, gazing down at the stadium below.

"Trace." She rushed over to me and threw her arms around me.

I held her close and said, "It's okay, Sarah. Everything's all right."

"I'm sorry," she said.

"I know, baby. I know. It's all right."

When she let go of me, she ran her fingers through my hair and gazed into my eyes. "I didn't mean it. I didn't mean to say that being with you was a mistake."

"I understand. Just promise me the next time you're upset, you'll come talk to me. Whatever it is, we'll figure it out. Together. Okay?"

"Yes," she said, her beautiful blue-green eyes filled with tears.

"God, when I first saw you today ... Sarah, I don't ever want to see you look at me like that again."

"Like what?"

"Like you're scared to death of me," I said softly, my heart aching just thinking about it. I knew I'd never forget that look on her face. She'd looked terrorized, like I was an intruder in her home there to do her harm. I *loved* her. I'd die before I'd hurt her.

Sarah nodded sorrowfully. "I'm sorry I'm such a mess."

"You can be a mess," I said, pulling her into my arms again. "As long as you're *my* mess."

She laughed softly, and I felt her tense body relax against mine. I looked forward to the day she was comfortable around me all the time. When she knew she was safe with me.

When she lifted her head, I took the opportunity to kiss her. She eagerly kissed back, and all traces of fear and anxiety were gone.

Thank God.

Pretty soon we were kissing, hot and heavy, like we'd done so often on the couch.

"I keep thinking about ... that fantasy ... you have," Sarah said breathlessly between kisses. "The one ... about ... having sex in my office."

I chuckled. "You remembered that, huh?"

I certainly did. It had always been my hands-down favorite fantasy during all that time when Sarah wasn't ready to go all the way.

"We should make the fantasy a reality," she said. "Right now."

I jerked back so quickly it startled her. "You can't be serious."

"Of course I am." The seductive gleam in her eye told me she wasn't kidding.

"That's crazy," I said, wanting nothing more than to

throw her down on the desk and bang her so hard she'd forget her own name.

But, as always, restraint was critical when it came to her. Baby steps. Wild sex in her office would be way too much, especially considering how upset she'd been this morning.

"I need to do something to make it up to you," she said. Now her eyes radiated sadness.

"Baby, I appreciate that. But it's not necessary. And the last thing I want is for you to do anything that makes you uncomfortable. It's been such a long day for you. Maybe tomorrow you can come over. Spend the night if you feel up to it. We can, you know, try again. Take our time. Take things slow. Take all the time you need to feel you can trust me."

"I do trust you, Trace. And I want to *show* you." The huskiness was back in her voice. She didn't sound uncomfortable with the sex in her office idea. "Unless you're too tired."

"I'm definitely *not* tired. I'm usually wired after a game anyway, and I'm especially pumped since we had such a great win tonight."

The final score had been 13-4, and I'd scored again in the ninth inning.

"You're *pumped*, are you?" She drew out her words, making me visualize pumping in and out of her. Which surely was her intention.

Sarah slid her hand between my legs and smiled wickedly when she felt my vicious hard-on.

"I'm always pumped for you, baby. But that doesn't mean we should get it on at your work."

"But I want to," she said with a flirty pout.

"It's not a good idea." My resolve was weakening by the second.

"Trace," she said, dropping the flirtatious act for a

moment. "I know you're worried about me, and that means a lot to me. But I'm okay. And the truth is"—she bit her lip shyly, blushing—"I really want to do this."

"Really?" I said, feeling more out of control than ever. I could only say no to an irresistible offer so many times.

"I know how your mind works, Trace Ridgerton. You really did think of me as a conquest at first." I was about to protest but she held up a hand. "That was at first. Everything's changed since then. I know that. But at first you liked the idea that I was like an uptight businesswoman who hated you. You wanted me to finally give in to my sexual desire for the bad boy catcher who took what he wanted."

Sarah had me pegged perfectly, as usual.

"You were never uptight, and you hated me for a good reason."

"I know," she said, and that devious gleam in her eye was back. "But I can pretend."

Sarah walked over to her desk and carefully moved her laptop to the safety of a nearby chair. Then she swept the rest of her things off her desk like something out of a movie.

"I give up," she said, her voice sounding desperate with need. "I can't resist you anymore."

Then Sarah Asiago lay down on her desk, knees bent, and *opened her legs.*

"Please, Trace," she begged. "I can't wait any more."

My teeth clenched, I said, "Christ, Sarah. I'm not made of *stone.*"

It was nearly impossible to turn her down now.

"From here it seems like a part of you is made of stone," she said. "And I need to feel it inside me."

That did it. I couldn't take anymore.

I rushed over to the desk. Then I bent over her and kissed her where she lay spread-eagled. I reached between her legs, slid her panties aside, and rammed two fingers inside her. She was *soaked*. Her eyes flew open wide, and she cried out with pleasure.

Sarah panted, opening her legs wider for me. I was riveted, watching her writhe at my touch. I couldn't wait to make her come. I hoped she would scream.

Then I remembered where we were.

"Shit," I muttered. "Hold on."

"Trace," she cried in frustration when I pulled my fingers out of her.

"Sorry. Sorry!" I jogged over to the door. Sure enough, it was unlocked. I doubted anybody was here in the office this late, but no sense in being utterly reckless.

After securing the door, I remembered I needed to secure my *cock*. I grabbed my wallet and pulled out a condom.

"I'm glad you're thinking more clearly than I am," Sarah said breathlessly. "Now come give me what I *need*."

The woman I loved lay on her back on her office desk, *begging* me to have sex with her. If this was a dream, I didn't ever want to wake up. I climbed up on the desk and yanked her panties down. She gasped, and I glanced up at her face to make sure she was okay.

Sarah's eyes were wild with desire, and I realized she was perfectly fine. She started to pull off her skirt.

"No," I said. "Leave it on."

I leaned down and murmured in her ear. "In my fantasy, you're dressed in work clothes except for your panties. And whatever you do, leave those high heels *on*."

When I lifted my head, I saw her suck in a breath. Her eyes flashed with excitement, and she nodded. I loved how *into* this she was. I realized this fantasy was only partly mine; it made her hot, too. I wondered if she'd given herself an orgasm with her shower massager while fantasizing about me fucking her on her desk.

God, I hoped so.

I managed to get my pants down and get the condom in place.

"I haven't showered," I said. "I hope I'm not too gross."

"Are you kidding me? You know how much I love sports. Athletes turn me *on,* Trace," she said. "And you're so sweaty from all that exertion from the game ..."

Sarah's words made me feel like the sexiest man alive. Like getting it on with the bad boy catcher from the Bay Birds was incredibly arousing to her.

"Are you ready?" I knew the answer but wanted to hear her say it.

"God, yes. Take me, Trace. *Now.*" The urgency in her voice drove me wild.

Grabbing her legs and throwing them over my shoulders, high heels and all, I rammed into her. She screamed and threw her head back. I hoped nobody was in the building, because they would not only know *what* we were doing, they'd know *who* was doing it since she kept repeating my name.

"Oh God, that's the spot," she gasped.

I know. I knew exactly where her most sensitive spot was, but I didn't want to ruin the fantasy by saying so out loud. This was supposed to be the first time the uptight executive surrendered to the bad boy.

I pumped in and out of her, making sure to hit her g-spot over and over again. The familiar, sharp pain of her nails digging into my back made me feel like such a badass lover. I hoped she would leave her mark all over my back. We were both so aroused, neither of us would last long.

Having sex on a desk was even more pleasurable than

I'd expected. With my girl flat on her back on a hard surface, I could penetrate her *deeply*.

"Trace, oh God I'm ... I'm ..."

I loved that she told me when she was coming. It was like her way of pleading with me not to stop, like any change of position might keep her from reaching orgasm.

And reach orgasm she did. Sarah didn't scream, but her nails dug into my back and she whimpered like she was fighting to stay quiet. I came explosively as I watched her come, my body shuddering hard as my intense climax roared through my body.

I was so perfectly satisfied that I was tempted to collapse on top of her, but I didn't want to crush my baby. Instead, I pulled out of her and quickly dispensed of the condom, wrapping it tight with a tissue and stuffing it deep down in the trash can. The last thing I wanted was Sarah's coworkers to know what she'd been up to in here.

Sarah still lay flat on her back. Moaning, she said, "That was amazing, Trace. I don't know why I didn't let you do that to me a long time ago."

I wasn't sure if she was still in uptight executive character or if that was the real Sarah talking. Either way, her words were a huge ego boost.

"Mmmm," I said, taking a moment to admire my gorgeous girl where she lay before picking up her panties from the floor. She giggled softly as I slid them up her legs. She pulled them the rest of the way on, sat up, and reached for me.

"I really don't know why I resisted you for so long," she said. The sadness in her voice hurt my heart.

Wrapping my arm around her, I said, "Because you were afraid. And that's okay. I mean, it's sad, but it's okay."

"I love you, Trace."

Sarah was the first woman to say that to me. I was shocked to realize she was the first *person* to say that to me. Tears formed in my eyes. Those words meant more coming from her beautiful lips than she could possibly know.

I kissed her sweet mouth and said, "I love you too, Sarah. I guess I'm the last person you ever thought you'd fall in love with, huh?"

"Honestly? Yes. But loving you is also even more wonderful than I could have ever imagined. Sometimes the most wonderful things in the world are unexpected."

I kissed her again and helped her down from the desk. Chuckling, I surveyed the damage to her office. Papers and office supplies littered the floor.

"We gotta fix this."

I started gathering stuff from the floor and Sarah put her laptop back on her desk.

"Wow. You'd never know what we did in here," I said when we were done.

"But I'll know." That wicked gleam in her eye had returned. "Every time I come in here."

"Cool. This was so amazing, Sarah. Thank you for doing this for me." I gazed at her with affection, admiring her strength and courage.

She let out a delicious, satisfied moan. "Not exactly a sacrifice, Trace. It was *wonderful.*"

I gazed at her smile, reveling in the way she made me feel like the sexiest man she'd ever seen and that I'd rocked her world. Just being near her gave me confidence. As if her love made up for some of the damage done by my family.

"I'm ready to tell everyone about us," she said softly.

"That would be great, Sarah. But don't do it because you feel you have to prove anything to me, okay? I'm so proud that you're my girl, but there's no hurry to tell people if you have any doubts."

"No doubts," she said. Her pretty eyes were full of peace and calm. Maybe she really was ready.

"Okay, baby. You tell anybody you want, but I won't say a word until you do. That way, if you change your mind ..."

"I won't."

I nodded, excited that people would know about us. I wanted the whole world to know how much I loved Sarah. But I had to admit, part of me was thrilled that the Bay Bird guys might have to eat a little crow. All this time they'd been teasing me about striking out with Sarah. Soon they'd know she was in love with me.

We left her office and headed toward the elevator.

"Do you really think sweaty athletes are sexy?"

"Oh yah," Sarah said. "Fer sure."

I grinned. Her midwestern accent came out strong when she was feeling especially safe and happy. I took it as a huge compliment.

"Then maybe I'll wear my baseball uniform sometime while we do it."

"Oooh, I think I'd like that."

The elevator arrived and we stepped inside.

"Mr. Devilbuss would have a heart attack if he had any idea what we did in your office," I said.

Sarah giggled as the elevator door closed.

29

TRACE

Flynn was dressed in street clothes when I arrived. In his jeans and T-shirt, he looked like a normal kid, except for the fact that he was nearly bald now. Seeing him in real clothes gave me hope that one day he would get the hell out of the hospital and be able to live a halfway normal life.

Today, he was dressed for our field trip on the motorcycle.

"Dammmn, you clean up good," I said, grinning. Flynn was excited, and he looked so *healthy*. I wished his mother had been here to see this. It would have done her good. I was just grateful we'd gotten her permission to take a spin on the bike.

"Thanks," Flynn said, eagerly sitting up straight on his neatly made hospital bed. Clearly, he was ready to go.

"I like this look. Not that I don't dig the hospital-gown Tiny-Tim vibe you usually got going."

Flynn cracked up. He had such a good sense of humor about his situation, and I believed that helped him cope with everything.

"Ready to roll?" I asked.

"Hell yeah!" Flynn said, getting down from the bed.

He was a bit shaky on his feet as he walked toward the wheelchair in his room, and I fought the urge to reach out and steady him. I worried about him, but I did my best to keep from showing it.

I headed over to the door, walking more slowly than usual to let him catch up, but otherwise I pretended not to notice his struggle with the chair. Though he was capable of walking, the wheelchair was hospital protocol.

A few nurses and doctors stood out in the hallway. My heart soared when I saw so many smiles as we emerged from the room. Flynn's medical team adored him, and they were happy he was able to go out on a little adventure.

"You boys have fun," said one of the nurses.

"We will," Flynn said excitedly.

His fingers fumbled a little as he rolled his wheelchair toward the elevator.

Affecting an English accent, I said, "God bless us, everyone!"

"Shut the fuck up," Flynn said with a smirk.

I chuckled as we got into the elevator. Downstairs, Flynn seemed steadier on his feet when he stood and left the chair behind. I guess you had to get used to walking when you were stuck in bed all day.

He took a deep breath of fresh air when we walked outside. "I almost forgot what summertime smells like."

I never realized how much I took for granted sometimes. I got to play baseball outside for a *living*, for God's sake. All while people were stuck in antiseptic-smelling hospitals for months at a time.

I glanced up at the crystal-clear blue sky. Thank God the

weather had cooperated. Flynn would have been crushed if it had rained and we'd had to postpone.

We walked out to the parking lot. Flynn's eyes bulged when he saw the motorcycle.

"Wow, this thing is incredible. I've seen pictures of your bike, but ... *wow*!"

Like Sarah, Flynn had a way of making me feel good about myself. It's quite an accomplishment to impress a fifteen-year-old boy.

"Indian Scout, 94 horsepower, liquid-cooled, V-twin," I said proudly.

Flynn nodded, eying my bike with admiration.

I opened the right-side leather saddlebag and pulled out the extra helmet.

"Come here," I said, and he stepped over to me. I secured the helmet on his head, tugging on it to make sure it was properly fastened. I went back to the saddlebag to retrieve some extra sunglasses and handed them to Flynn. "You'll definitely need these, 'cuz the helmet doesn't have a shield."

Flynn eagerly grabbed the sunglasses and put them on.

"Perfect. Now you look like a real biker," I said.

He grinned. "I can't believe I get to ride with you. This is so awesome, man."

"My pleasure, dude. Nothing I like better than showing off my bike. Let's roll."

I grabbed my helmet—the one with the skulls on the back—and fastened it securely. Then I climbed up on the motorcycle, flipped up the kickstand, and got the bike upright. "Hop on, my man."

I gave Flynn all the time he needed to get himself settled.

"You ready?" I asked.

"Yes."

"Hold on tight, dude. I mean, really tight, okay? And lean in a bit on the turns."

"Will do!"

Glancing in the side mirror, I made sure Flynn was gripping the handles tight. Had he been a woman, he would have wrapped his arms around my waist. Someday soon, I hoped to convince Sarah to take a ride with me like that.

I revved the engine hard, which I never did when I was in the hospital parking lot. But this was for Flynn's benefit.

"Yeah!" he yelled excitedly.

This was so *cool*. Sometimes I felt so damned helpless when I visited Flynn in the hospital, and I hated when he'd seemed depressed about losing his hair. It felt good to be able to *do* something to make him feel better.

No wonder Sarah loved doing charity work.

I fought the urge to tear out of the parking lot like a bat out of hell. Though Flynn would have loved that, I needed to drive respectfully until I was out of earshot of the other patients. I'd meticulously planned a half-hour motorcycle ride specially designed for my guy. Though I would have loved to keep him out with me for hours, I figured I'd better stick to the plan. Otherwise, they'd never let me take Flynn out again.

Once we were far enough away from the hospital, I turned on the radio to my favorite '80s station. I really cranked it up when we got out to the Baltimore Beltway. In what could only be described as a perfect moment, "Back in Black" by AC/DC came on just as I got the bike up to the fastest speed I was willing to go with my precious cargo on board.

"Yeah!" Flynn yelled, letting go briefly to pound my back with one fist.

I grinned. As a Bay Birds fan, Flynn knew "Back in Black" was my signature song at the ballpark.

After we got off the highway, I took him down some winding roads. I had to lean the bike to the side around some tight turns. I felt Flynn's body tense behind me, and I hoped he wasn't too afraid. Riding on a bike does take getting used to, and sometimes it can feel like the motorcycle's gonna fall over.

Flynn rode like a champ, though. He pounded my back again once we got off the twisty roads and said, "That was wicked!"

I chuckled, thrilled that he was having fun.

I turned the radio off as we approached the hospital, hating like hell that I had to return Flynn to this place. Seeing his excited face when he took off the helmet made me feel better, though. If nothing else, this was a little adventure he could tell his friends about.

"That was *epic*, Trace!"

"Glad you had fun, kiddo," I said, taking off my helmet.

Flynn looked at me with deep admiration, like I was a hero or something. Like Sarah, the kid had a way of making me feel important. Valued. Times like this, I wasn't sure which one of us benefited the most from our visits. The ride was over all too soon, but I'd try to take him out again when I had a break in my schedule.

"I did, man. That was wicked!"

"You're ahead of Sarah. She hasn't even been on the bike yet."

"How's that going, by the way?"

It was tough not to break into a big, goofy smile just thinking about my girl.

"Pretty damn good actually."

"Yeah?" Flynn said, opening his eyes wide. Then he

squinted at the sun in his face and shielded his eyes. I'd already put the helmet and sunglasses back in the bike.

"Better?" I asked as I stepped to the side to block the sun.

"Yeah," he said. "So, what's happening with you two?"

I wished like hell I could tell him about banging her senseless in her office; the kid would think of me as some kind of sex *god*. But even I knew discussing that with a fifteen-year-old would be highly inappropriate, not to mention disrespectful to Sarah.

"She told me she loved me."

"No shit?" Flynn asked, sounding impressed. "Wow. Do you love her?"

"Hell, yeah."

"Cool. Did you tell *her* that?"

"Yup. I said it first, actually."

"Way to go, dude," he said, fist bumping me. "I didn't think you had it in you."

"Me neither," I said with a laugh. "Oh hey, I almost forgot. I got something for you."

I opened my saddlebag and pulled out a Bay Birds cap, which I'd autographed in big writing across the front.

"Oh cool. Thanks, man," he said, smiling widely.

"Figured, you know ..."

"Since I look like Daddy Warbucks now?" he quipped.

"Well, yeah."

Flynn laughed.

"But you gotta wear it like this," I said, pulling out another cap and putting it on sideways.

"But of course." He arranged his hat to match mine.

"We gotta get a picture of us with the bike," I said.

I spotted an older lady getting out of her car and said, "Excuse me, ma'am?"

The lady jumped a bit when she saw me. She glanced nervously at my tattooed arms.

"Would you mind terribly taking a quick picture of us with my phone?"

She stared at me for a moment.

I mumbled under my breath to Flynn, "Get ready to turn on the Tiny Tim charm, kiddo ..."

Flynn opened his mouth, but the woman spoke first.

"Sure, honey," she said, ambling over to us. "I'm not great with this sort of thing, but lemme see if I can figure it out."

I took a moment to show her my phone and how it worked, hoping she would be able to get a good photo of us.

"Okay, get ready, boys," the nice lady said.

"Like this, Flynn." I posed in front of the bike and flashed the rock and roll sign with my fingers.

"Yeah, perfect," he said with a wide grin. We posed together and waited while the old woman took our picture.

"Thanks so much," I said, retrieving my phone from her.

"My pleasure, sonny," she said. As she walked away toward the hospital, she called out, "You Bay Birds are kicking ass this year. Keep it up!"

Flynn and I stared at each other, then quietly cracked up.

People could really surprise you. I was learning that every day.

30

SARAH

Thanks to a torrential downpour, the team got an unexpected night off. Brady invited us all to hang out in his basement, which made me happy. Trace and I arrived together in his Lamborghini, but nobody noticed when we walked in together. After getting a glass of wine from Brady the bartender, I headed over to my usual table with Lyric and Julia.

"Oh, this is nice," Julia said, leaning back in her chair. "Even with the All-Star break, I'm exhausted by this point in the season. Nothing like a bonus day off."

"Cheers to that," I said, clinking my wineglass to her beer mug. Glancing nervously from Lyric to Julia, I said, "This is kind of perfect timing. I've been wanting to talk to you guys about something."

"Everything okay?" Lyric asked with concern. Julia, too, looked slightly worried. My tension eased; I knew this was the right time to tell them about me and Trace. They were my friends, and they wouldn't judge me.

"Oh yah. Everything is great," I said. "It's good news, actually."

"Cool," Julia said with a warm smile. "Lay it on us then."

"It's about the guy I've been seeing."

"Finally! More details," Julia said, her eyes lighting up with interest. "You've been awfully vague about the man. I've been dying to press you for more info, but I figured you'd talk when you were ready."

"Thanks. I appreciate that. So, we've been getting pretty serious lately," I began.

"Can we meet him soon?" Lyric asked.

"Well, that's the thing. You kind of already know him."

"We do?" Julia asked, lifting her beer mug to her lips. "Who is it?"

Drawing in a deep breath, I said, "It's Trace Ridgerton."

Julia did a *spectacular* spit-take. I'd never seen anyone actually do that in real life.

I looked over at the bar. Trace had his mouth covered. His shoulders shook with laughter. We locked eyes, sharing a look of amusement before I turned back to my girls.

"Sorry, sorry," Julia said, wiping her mouth.

Lyric giggled as she watched Julia clean up her mess. Then she leaned forward. "Wow, Sarah. Believe me, I'm just as shocked as Julia. Trace Ridgerton ..."

"I know, I know. It sounds crazy. I guess it kind of is crazy."

"Sarah," Julia said, having finally gotten control of herself. "I want to be happy for you, but isn't this the same guy who was so obnoxious to you? The one who reminded you so much of those jerks who tortured you in high school?" Deep worry lines creased her forehead as she spoke.

"Yeah, that's the thing. He's not the guy I thought he was. I mean, he was at first, but ..."

This was harder to explain than I'd expected. I understood completely why they were so surprised at my announcement. As far as Lyric and Julia knew, Trace was still the jerk who wouldn't take no for an answer. The one who thought he was God's gift to women.

"Trace is just so ... different when you get to know him. Remember what I told you about our first date?"

"Yes," Lyric said softly. "You said he had a rough time growing up, and you two bonded over that."

"That makes sense," Julia said, nodding thoughtfully. "Explains why Trace acts the way he does."

"Exactly right." I felt relieved that my friends were beginning to come around. "I don't blame you for having a hard time trusting him with me. So did I for a while. Poor guy really had to prove himself. But he has. In, like, a million ways. You guys know how he used to brag about getting me into bed?"

"Uh-huh," Julia said, her voice taking on a hard edge. Clearly, she wasn't convinced yet.

Lowering my voice, I said, "Well, we have slept together. And he never breathed a word to any of the guys. Everybody on the team still teases him about not getting anywhere with me. And he just let them do it because he knew I wasn't ready to tell people about us yet."

I turned around to see Trace at the bar. He was watching me with my friends. I smiled and nodded, and then waved. He nodded back, understanding I was giving him the go-ahead to tell the men at the bar that we were a couple.

"That's good," Lyric said. "If it had been me, I would have been terrified that Trace would tell everybody the minute it happened."

"I was terrified," I said sadly. "In fact, I completely flipped out on the poor guy. I kept having flashbacks to high school and that awful prom prank. I was afraid that maybe this was some big joke to him after all."

"That must have been so hard," Julia said, reaching over and taking my hand to squeeze it.

"It was. I had a full-blown panic attack."

Julia gasped. "So that's what was wrong! Matt told me you mentioned a panic attack. Ugh, I feel awful. I meant to call to check on you, and I totally forgot. I'm so sorry."

"It's okay. I wasn't ready to talk about it anyway."

"Well, I'm glad you told us now," Lyric said.

"Me too," Julia agreed.

"Speaking of telling people," I said, turning to see how it was going with Trace.

Every man at the bar was staring at me.

Laughing nervously, I said, "Well, the cat's out of the bag now."

I saw Matt, eyes wide, exchange a look with his wife. Julia shrugged and held up her hands to show she'd had no idea about me and Trace either. I gestured for Trace to join us. He did, and now all eyes at the bar were on him.

"Hey, ladies." Trace said, grabbing a nearby chair and pulling it up to our table. With faux-innocent wide eyes, he asked, "So what's new?"

"Apparently a lot," Julia said, eying him curiously. She didn't seem judgmental exactly. Just cautious of Trace.

"Yeah," Trace said, gazing at me, his eyes filled with tenderness and love. It had to be hard for my friends to question his devotion when he looked at me like that. "I know it's gotta be quite a shock finding out the two of us are an item."

"You could say that," Lyric said with a smile.

"I mean, obviously Sarah is way too good for me." Trace grinned. "But somehow she fell for me anyway."

"That's wonderful, Trace," Lyric said, giving him the benefit of the doubt. She still seemed worried, but I could tell she was doing her best to keep an open mind.

"Wow," Julia said, glancing over at the bar. "Matt is *not happy* about this recent development."

Sure enough, Matt was white knuckling his beer mug, looking severely pissed off.

"What is the deal with you two anyway?" Trace asked me, sounding jealous. Quickly second-guessing himself, he said to Julia, "Sorry. That was dumb of me. I didn't mean to imply—"

"No, no," Julia said, reaching over and squeezing his hand the same way she had mine a moment ago. "It's a fair question, Trace. I can understand why you might ask."

Julia looked over at me, giving me the chance to explain.

"Matt and I did go out on a date once a long time ago."

"I know."

"You do?" I asked, surprised.

"Yeah. Matt told me."

"Oh. I hope you know I wasn't trying to hide that from you, Trace. It wasn't a big deal, and it was so long ago ..."

"I understand," he said, but I wasn't sure he did. He still sounded threatened by my closeness to Matt.

"It was probably the worst date I'd ever been on," I said, and Julia laughed. "Well, I mean not really. It wasn't *that* bad, since Matt turned out to be such a nice guy. But he basically bailed on the date halfway through. Said he couldn't go on with it since he was in love with another woman."

"I hope that woman was Julia," Trace said with a grin. I saw relief in his eyes now that he understood where I was going with this story.

"Of course," I said. "Matt said his head was totally

messed up, and he had to figure things out before he could even think of dating anybody else. He said he was in love with his best friend's sister and he wasn't sure she felt the same way about him. They'd been just friends their whole life, that sort of thing. I said he needed to just go for it. Tell her how he felt, and at least he could stop wondering about it. I'm sure Matt would have found the courage to tell Julia how he felt at some point no matter what, but I think he kind of credits me for getting him together with her."

"That's cool," Trace said with a nod.

"So after that date, he and Julia got together, and the rest is history. The three of us became really good friends. And Matt knows all about my childhood, too. My parents and the bullying at school and all that. He knew I was afraid of you, and he didn't take too kindly to the way you kept harassing me."

"Ohhhh, I see," Trace said. "That makes sense."

"It's gonna take some time for Matt to come around and accept the idea of us being together. But it has nothing to do with romantic feelings and everything to do with him being a wonderful, loyal friend. Okay?"

Trace nodded. "Yeah. I get that."

"He'll come around," Julia said, still sounding uncertain. "I guess we all will."

"I know it seems strange," I said. "But the truth is, we're very much in love."

Trace smiled and nodded.

"Wow," Lyric and Julia both said at the same time. We all laughed, and the tension that had hung in the air eased.

I looked up to see Brady and Matt approaching. Matt looked so angry that for a moment I was afraid he might punch Trace.

"It's okay, Matt. I promise," I said quickly.

"I hope so," he said grimly.

I loved him so much for caring about me the way he did. It made me understand what it might feel like to have an overprotective brother. He and Julia certainly were like family to me.

"I know it's hard to understand, but please believe me when I say I know what I'm doing," I assured him.

"Well, I do know you're a strong woman capable of taking care of herself," he said, still sounding worried.

"Trace, you always did say you were gonna sleep with her," Brady joked. He didn't mean to be offensive, but his comment embarrassed me. Brady, too, was a dear friend, but he didn't always think before he spoke. Lyric winced and was about to say something, no doubt to try to smooth things over, but Trace spoke up first.

"I did say that," Trace said, shooting me an apologetic look. "And it was stupid and disrespectful of me. Sarah deserves better than that. She's just so beautiful and so sexy that I couldn't help desiring her. And I got moody and defensive when she kept shooting me down. I acted like a stupid wounded kid. But lucky for me, she gave me another chance. One I didn't deserve. Then I couldn't help falling in love with her."

"That is kinda sweet," Brady said with a grin. "I didn't think you had it in you, Trace my boy."

"Neither did I," Matt said stiffly.

Trace and I stared into each other's eyes and a look of understanding passed between us. We were both glad to make our relationship public, but we knew it would take some time to convince our friends that our love was real.

But we knew. And that was all that mattered.

31

TRACE

I'd just checked into my hotel in Texas, and I was missing Sarah like crazy already. And yet, it was nice knowing I had somebody waiting for me back home. And for the first time, Baltimore was starting to feel like home because she was there.

I tossed my bags on the floor and flopped down on the bed. I pulled out my phone to text Sarah that I'd arrived safely. My heart dropped when I saw a missed call and a voice mail message from Mr. Devilbuss.

Shit.

Baltimore wouldn't be my home much longer if I didn't make things right with the big boss, and soon. Asking Sarah for help was still a last-ditch resort. She trusted me now, thank God, but it hadn't been easy for her. I didn't want to do anything to rock the boat. I wracked my brain to figure out something else I could do to get some good publicity without involving her. But doing some charity event without her would almost feel like cheating on her. She would be hurt if I didn't come to her for help, but I worried she might think I was using her to get back in Devilbuss's good graces.

Maybe I could just write a big check to some organization or something.

Nervously, I punched in the code to check my messages. No sense in putting off what the boss had to say.

"Trace!" the big man's voice boomed in the message. He didn't sound mad. "Nice going on that article in the Baltimore Bugle. I had no idea you'd been doing all that stuff. Good for you!"

What in the hell was he talking about? What article? And what stuff had I been doing?

"That's terrific publicity for you and for the team. Good job, good job. Talk to ya later."

Confused, I replayed the message. Had Mr. Devilbuss actually said *good job*?

Okay, so the big man was happy with me. That was all well and good, but I couldn't relax until I figured out what was going on. I jumped up from the bed and fished out my laptop from one of my bags.

I typed "Trace Ridgerton Baltimore Bugle" in the search toolbar. Sure enough, an article came up with today's date. The headline read "Bay Bird's Catcher Spreads Cheer at Local Hospital." My heart caught in my throat when I saw the photo of me with Flynn posing in front of my motorcycle.

With his hat on sideways and a huge smile on his face, I had never seen the kid look so happy and *healthy*. The idea that I had made him feel like that absolutely blew me away. It was the most incredible feeling. I skimmed the article. It talked about my frequent visits with Flynn and the bond we'd developed. I'd had my name in the papers lots of times for my sports accomplishments, but this was the first time I'd been proud enough to want to print out an article and frame it on my wall.

But how the hell did all this wind up in the papers?

I scrolled up to the top to see who had written the article.

Sarah Asiago.

My sweet Sarah had done this. My pride swelled further because clearly, she was proud of me too.

Forget texting. I grabbed my phone and dialed her number.

"Hey, you," she answered cheerfully. "You make it to Texas okay?"

"Yeah, yeah. I'm in the hotel. Sarah, I just saw the article."

"Do you like it?" she asked, sounding a little nervous.

I was too choked up to answer at first.

"Trace? You're not mad, are you?" She sounded afraid.

"No, I'm not mad. Of course not. It's amazing ..." I said, struggling to find the right words. "The picture ... I really love the picture, Sarah."

"Me too," she said, and I could hear the smile in her voice. "You two look great together. You can tell Flynn is so happy in that photo."

"Yeah," I said, still staring at the image on my computer. "Flynn's cool with this, right?"

"Oh yah. Definitely. He's the one who sent me the picture. I asked him about it first and then I talked to his parents. They thought it was a wonderful idea. They think the world of you, Trace. Especially Flynn's mom. Having a positive attitude is more important than most people realize when it comes to getting better. You give Flynn so much to look forward to in between treatments, and that means a lot to him. And it gives incredible peace of mind to his family."

"Mr. Devilbuss is happy about the publicity. He called and left me a message telling me that."

"Trace, why didn't you tell me you were in so much trouble with him?"

"What?"

"He told me he's been hounding you about doing more charity events. Said he warned you that you'd better clean up your act and do something to fix your bad publicity or you'd be off the team. All this time I thought the food drive had been enough, but I guess not. Why didn't you tell me what was going on? I would have helped you."

Sarah sounded hurt that I hadn't confided in her.

"I wanted to tell you. I just couldn't have you think for one second that I was using you to clean up my reputation. After all, you know that's why I started the charity work in the first place. I didn't want you to feel like that was the only reason I stuck around."

She sighed heavily. "I'm sorry you feel like you have to walk on eggshells around me. But I get it. Took me long enough to trust you, so I can understand why you were afraid to say anything to me."

"Though it occurred to me that Devilbuss would love the whole visiting kids with cancer thing, I didn't want Flynn to think I was using him either. I love that kid."

"I know you do," Sarah said with unmistakable pride in her voice. "I miss you already."

"I miss you too. Never had a girl waiting for me back home when I'm away on road trips before. Gives me something to look forward to."

"I'll give you something else to look forward to."

"Yeah?"

"I made an appointment with my doctor so I can go on the pill. No more condoms for you."

"Hmmm, I do like that idea."

"When you get home, I want to finally go on a motor-cycle ride with you. Then I want to ride *you*."

I groaned deep in my throat. "Now that *is* something to look forward to."

THE BAY BIRDS had games in Los Angeles after the Houston trip, so I was away for a whole week. After the day game on Sunday, we flew back home. I was utterly exhausted when I got back to my house late Sunday night. I texted Sarah to let her know I got home safely, and she texted back a heart emoji. Then she told me to get some rest. As much as I wanted to see her, I was grateful she understood how tired I was after the grueling trip. After a good night's sleep, we could celebrate our reunion properly.

I felt much better the next morning. Showered and dressed, I got coffee and some breakfast before going through the mail that had piled up since I'd left. I had a house sitter who came by to check on the place and get the mail for me while I was away.

Sitting on the couch with ESPN on the TV in front of me, I started sorting through everything. Some bills and mostly junk mail, but also a package had come for me while I was away. I didn't remember ordering anything, but it wouldn't be the first time I'd bought something online and forgotten all about it until it showed up on my doorstep.

My stomach tightened when I saw the return address. It was from Karol Ridgerton.

My mother.

What the hell could she possibly have sent me in the mail? For a second, I wondered if she'd actually sent me a gift.

"Better make sure the box isn't ticking," I muttered to myself as I opened the package. I found a note scribbled on a scrap of paper inside.

Found a bunch of your junk in the house and I'm tired of storing it.

That was it. It wasn't even signed. I pulled out a bunch of papers and found some old report cards and some drawings I'd done as a kid. Pretty sure I had saved them, because I highly doubted my mom or stepfather would have saved anything of mine for sentimental reasons.

I thought about Sarah, knowing she would understand how much this hurt when I told her about it later. Having your mother refer to your old crayon drawings as "junk" hurt like hell, no matter how old you were. Karol had a way of making me feel like I was five years old again every time I saw or spoke to her. And not in a good way. In a helpless, frightened way. I hadn't been safe at home ever. Especially when I was five years old.

My mom had included my high school yearbooks with the "junk." I supposed I should be grateful that she hadn't thrown them out. I grabbed the one from my junior year and started flipping through the pages. I paused, gazing at the photos from the freshman class that year.

Sighing deeply, I stared at the little girl who had the same haunted, dark brown eyes as me.

Betsy.

With the curse of hindsight, I now knew the little girl in that photo had already been sexually abused by my stepfather for years. I was still so goddamned angry at myself for letting that happen, but deep down I knew Sarah was right. We had talked about this a lot, and there really was no way I could have known what was going on. Still, I felt like I'd failed my baby sister.

I missed her so much.

The last I heard, Betsy was out of rehab. We weren't close, but perhaps it wasn't too late to change that. I would have to think on it some more, but maybe I would give her a call soon.

I grabbed my senior yearbook and flipped through the pages. Those days felt like a million years ago. I smiled when I saw the pictures from my old baseball team. Not all my boyhood and teenage memories were bad. School sports had offered a lifeline for me. I couldn't help being proud that I was the only one from my high school team to become a professional baseball player. It sucked that my parents weren't proud of that, though.

I looked over the senior class photographs, remembering my classmates. I gazed sadly at the picture of the boy from my senior class who had died in a car accident in college. Flipping the pages, it was crazy how many of the students I barely remembered. It hadn't been *that* long since I'd graduated, but my memory was shit.

My heart seized when my eyes landed on the photograph of a chubby girl with mousy brown hair. My brain simply could not make sense of it. No. It couldn't be. But I would know that face anywhere.

Sarah.

I had gone to high school with *Sarah*? That was impossible.

Wasn't it?

The girl in the picture had brown hair, not honey-blond like it was now. And she was much heavier.

Sarah had lost a lot of weight since high school. She'd said so herself.

The name next to the picture said Florence Sarah Robertson. And it was most definitely *my* Sarah. She had changed her hair, her weight, and her name. But it was her.

Florence.

My eyes flitting back and forth between that name and the picture, I wracked my brain to remember her from high school.

Then the truth suddenly slammed into me full force.

"No. No, no, no, no, no. It can't be ..."

I remembered her, all right.

Fat Flo. The girl my teammates and I tortured constantly.

I dropped the yearbook and cradled my head in my hands, rocking back and forth. I squeezed my head with my fists, willing myself not to remember everything that I'd done.

Oh dear God. Sarah was Fat Flo. And I'd humiliated her in front of the entire school when I'd mockingly asked her to the prom at a baseball game.

I didn't just remind Sarah of the bullies from high school.

I *was* the bully from high school.

And I hadn't given her, or any of the other kids I'd tortured, a second thought until right this moment.

I jumped up from the couch to pace on wobbly legs. I felt sick to my stomach, struggling to wrap my mind around this monstrous truth.

Had Sarah known who I was this whole time?

"Of course she did," I whispered.

After that horrible day, I'd gone on with my life like nothing had happened. Taken some skinny, hot girl whose name I couldn't even rember to the prom. I'd forgotten all about the incident that was no doubt burned into Sarah's consciousness for all eternity.

Everything suddenly made sense now. Why she'd

resisted me for so long. Why she'd seemed so afraid of me, and why she had completely flipped out after we had sex. No wonder she'd been afraid I'd just been messing with her this whole time.

Sarah knew exactly who I was, and she'd known what I was capable of.

Dear God in Heaven.

What could I possibly do now?

I did what I always did when I desperately needed to think. I ran out the door and jumped on my motorcycle to ride until life started to make sense again.

32

TRACE

I rode my bike through winding roads and sped down the highway as if that would miraculously provide me with answers. Somehow, I had to make this right. But what could I possibly do all these years later to make up for what I had done to my precious Sarah?

She'd obviously forgiven me. She was in love with me, for God's sake. Now more than ever I understood how hard that must be on her. As if she hadn't been through enough in her life, falling in love with her most hated enemy must really have messed with her mind.

Fresh nausea flooded my stomach every time I thought of the way I'd pursued Sarah when we'd first met. Well, when I'd *thought* we were meeting for the first time. I'd hounded and harassed her about hooking up with me. Horrified, I thought back to that day at Brady's bar when I'd said "Challenge accepted" when she'd shot me down yet again. Hell, even without the whole teenage bullying thing, it was a shitty thing for me to do. It was kind of sick, now that I really thought about it. Here I had a woman repeatedly saying no, and I had refused to back off.

What the hell was wrong with me?

Okay yeah, I'd had a fucked-up childhood. So had a lot of people. So had Sarah. And she didn't go around harassing and torturing people. What did that sweet, loving woman see in me?

Riding aimlessly, I soon found myself in the vicinity of the hospital. I hated to dump on Flynn, but I genuinely valued his advice. And the kid adored Sarah. He might be able to tell me what to do.

I parked my bike in the parking lot and hurried inside. I rushed up to the nurse's station so fast that I startled them.

"Sorry, sorry," I said, holding my hand up in apology.

"No problem," said one of the nurses. "We weren't expecting you today."

I normally called ahead to see if Flynn was up for a visit.

"Is he awake? Is it okay to go see him?"

"Oh sure. His door's open, so it should be fine to go right in."

"Thanks. Thanks a lot," I said.

I knocked on the open door. Flynn looked up from the television. His eyes lit up when he saw me.

"Hey, man," he said.

I closed the door behind me and walked to his bedside. His face fell.

"You look like shit," he told me.

"There's a reason for that."

"Okay, I'm listening." Flynn sat up straighter in bed.

"I fucked up with Sarah. I mean, *really* fucked up."

"Dammit, Trace," he said, throwing his hands up in the air. "You had such a good thing going with her. What did you do?"

"Something bad," I said, raking my hand through my hair.

Flynn stared for a moment, alarmed at my expression.

"What the hell did you do?" he asked. "Jesus Christ, you didn't rape her or something, did you?"

"Of course not," I said, louder than I'd meant to. It cut me to the core that Flynn could think for one second that I was capable of such a heinous act.

"Sorry, dude. I mean, I didn't honestly think you'd ever do something like that. You just look so freaked out."

"I know."

Flynn sighed. "Did you cheat on her?"

"No," I said. "I would never do that. I love her. I haven't been remotely tempted by another woman since I met her."

"That's good," Flynn said. He gestured with his hand for me to get on with it already. "But?"

I nodded and sighed, knowing Flynn might never look at me the same after my confession.

"Okay, so when I first started hitting on Sarah, she didn't want anything to do with me."

"I know," Flynn said with a smirk. "It was kinda funny."

I chuckled. "Yeah. So when I asked her what her deal was, she told me I reminded her of all the boys in high school who used to bully her. You know, cocky athletes on the baseball and football team who were popular and all that."

Flynn raised an eyebrow. "Yes. I am familiar with those type of guys."

"I always got the feeling Sarah was kind of afraid of me at first. It was weird and kind of sad. Anyway, it took her a while to warm up to me, but she finally did. And now we're together."

"You sleep with her yet?"

"Flynn ..."

"That's a yes," he said with a grin.

I debated for a moment about how candid I wanted to be with Flynn. Then I figured some details were important to the story. He needed to understand how badly I had wounded Sarah.

"Yeah. We slept together. And then after, she got really upset about it. She ... Well, she regretted it."

"Why?" Flynn asked, sounding surprised and sad.

"Because of those jerks in high school. One of them in particular. He was a hotshot baseball player on the team, and he pretended he was really into her and did one of those stupid prom-posals at the end of one of the baseball games. In front of the whole stadium. And it was all a cruel joke. Everybody laughed at her."

"Oh my God," he said softly. "That's so awful. Poor girl. She's so sweet. She didn't deserve that. I can see why that would really mess her up."

"Yeah. Sarah was a lot heavier in high school than she is now."

Flynn nodded grimly. "And I'm sure the kids were extra mean to her because of it."

"Definitely. She had brown hair back then. And she changed her name before she moved here from Minnesota."

"I guess she wanted a fresh start."

"Right. So ... she looks totally different now."

Flynn nodded, looking confused and wondering where I was going with this.

"That's why I didn't recognize her. I didn't remember ... until today. I was the one who did that prom thing to her."

My chest tightened as my words sank in and registered with Flynn.

"What?" he whispered.

"I know. I did that terrible thing to her all those years ago, and I'd forgotten all about it until now."

"But she hadn't."

Shaking my head slowly, I said, "No. Definitely not."

Flynn blew out a breath and lay back in his bed.

"I don't know what to do," I said.

"Have you talked to her since you suddenly got your memory back?" Flynn asked. He sounded angry.

"No."

He turned to look at me. "She said she loves you, right?"

"Yeah."

"Wow. You must be a great guy if she can forgive you enough to fall in love with you."

That was one way to put a positive spin on this. But I didn't deserve that.

"So what should I do?" I asked, not the slightest bit ashamed to be asking for advice from a teenager.

"You can start by telling her you're sorry."

"Do you really think that will help?"

Flynn sat up in bed again, wincing a bit as he did. Bald and fighting cancer, he was braver than I ever would be. He rarely complained about his lot in life, and now he was helping me with my problems.

His eyes met mine for a moment. Then he sighed heavily and looked away.

"When I was in eighth grade, one of the bigger boys grabbed me in the hallway, pulled my pants and underwear down, and shoved me into the girl's locker room. There were a bunch of girls in there and they saw everything."

Flynn's face turned a deep red, and he sounded like he was on the verge of tears. A sharp pain of anguish pierced my heart.

After a moment, he looked up at me and said, "If that guy showed up years from now and told me he was sorry?

Yeah. Yeah, it would help. It wouldn't change the past, but it would make me feel better."

"I'm sorry that happened to you, buddy. And I'm even sorrier that I was the type of guy who would have done something like that to you."

Flynn smiled sadly. "It's nice to hear you say that. Makes me feel like someday that guy might regret it, too. I know you feel bad, Trace. So tell her that. Tell her you're sorry for doing such an awful thing, and that you feel terrible you'd forgotten about it until now. And then tell her you love her."

His face brightened with a smile. "This is Sarah Asiago we're talking about. She's a sweetheart. She'll understand."

"Yeah. She probably will."

"Hell, she'll probably be relieved when you bring it up. The fact that you both went to the same high school was bound to come up at some point. She might be glad to get it over with."

"Good point. I'm really sorry for burdening you like this. It's the last thing you need."

"I don't mind, Trace. It makes me feel useful. Believe me, that's not something that happens often."

"Cool," I said, feeling relieved. "Talk to you later, okay?"

Flynn nodded, and I turned to head out. Turning back, I said, "Dude, if you tell me who did that to you, I can go kick his fucking ass."

He laughed. "Ooh, that is tempting. Can you imagine? The six-foot-two catcher from the Bay Birds coming at ya?"

I laughed heartily at that.

"Nah, it's cool. I'm not even back at school yet, and I'm already more popular than I've ever been. According to my friends, that article about you and me was a big hit."

"Oh, that's great. I swear, I didn't know anything about that until it hit the news."

"I know. Ms. Asiago told me she wanted to surprise you."
"She sure did. I love the photo."
"Me too," Flynn said. Then he yawned.
"Go to sleep, Tiny Tim. Catch you later."
He laughed as I shut the door behind me.

33

SARAH

I couldn't wait for Trace to show up at my place. It had only been a week, but it felt like forever since I had seen him. My heart jumped when I finally heard his motorcycle. I quickly straightened my hair and rushed to open the door before he got there.

Smiling, I watched him park his bike, take off his helmet, and shake his hair. He always looked so dreamy when he did that. Dressed in black as usual, he was as sexy as ever.

I could tell something was wrong the moment I saw his face.

He walked up to the door and gazed at me grimly.

"Trace, what's wrong?" I asked, fearing the worst.

"I know who you are. And I know what I did."

That was the last thing I'd expected him to say.

"Oh." My shoulders slumped. I'd known this conversation was inevitable, and at last the time had come.

Wearily, I gestured for him to come inside. I sat on the couch, feeling some measure of relief that we could finally get this conversation over with.

Trace slowly sank down next to me. "I don't even know what to say."

Neither did I, but I figured it wasn't my job to make him feel better about this. I wouldn't go out of my way to make it worse, but I'd be damned if I had to comfort him.

"Why didn't you tell me?" he asked.

My anger flared at that question. "I figured if it wasn't important enough for you to give it a second thought, why the hell should I be the one to bring it to your attention?"

"Yeah," Trace said, nervously wiping his hands on his pants. "You're totally right. I'm sorry. I didn't mean to imply you had any blame here because you don't."

Damn right.

"What suddenly jogged your memory?"

"The high school yearbook. I was flipping through and — God, you just look so *different* now."

"My weight, my hair, and even my name changed," I said charitably. "I suppose it makes sense you didn't recognize me. But tell me the truth, Trace."

I stared into his eyes, and he nodded rapidly, ready to do whatever I asked.

"Until now, did you give *any* thought to that girl you tortured in high school? Did she ever cross your mind?"

Trace thought for a moment. And then he said, "No."

My heart sank with his confession, but I wasn't surprised. "That's kind of what I figured. You did something to scar somebody for life and then you forgot all about it. That's really messed up."

"Yes. It sure is," he said somberly.

I hated this. I didn't want to be mad at him about the past. All I'd wanted was a happy reunion with Trace when he got home from his road trip. But I couldn't pretend I wasn't still hurting over what he'd done.

"I forgave you for it a long time ago, Trace. Probably more for my sake than for yours, but I did it."

"Everything makes so much sense now. I cannot imagine how hard it must have been for you to trust me," he said, his dark eyes filled with sorrow and regret.

"No. You can't."

Trace had long ago accepted that I'd struggled to trust him, but now he truly understood why I felt the way I did. That helped. It made me feel less crazy. I'd been so busy apologizing to him for not trusting him, I'd forgotten how legitimate my reasons were for that distrust in the first place. The bottom line was that it was *his* fault, not mine, that I'd questioned his motives.

"Sarah, I'm so sorry that I hurt you. And I'm sorry it took me so long to remember what I did."

"Thank you. It helps to hear you say that. It really does."

"Flynn said it would help."

"You talked to Flynn about this?"

Trace winced and nodded. "Yeah. Hope that's okay. I kind of went to him for advice."

I smiled. "I think that's sweet."

He let out a breath of relief. "He's crazy about you, and he likes that we're together. He wanted to help me fix this. Turns out he's been bullied too."

"Poor little thing."

Trace nodded. "This is gonna sound really stupid, but it's like for the first time in my life I'm starting to understand that everybody else has feelings too."

I frowned, trying to understand what he meant.

"It's hard to explain what I mean," he said, raking his hand through his hair. His vulnerability was endearing. "For most of my life, I've been focused on my own pain, you know?"

"You've been through a lot, Trace. That's understandable."

"Maybe so, but it's still no excuse for hurting people."

I agreed but saw no reason to rub it in by saying it out loud.

Trace took my hand and kissed it. "It took realizing I'd hurt the woman I loved to truly understand that everybody I meet on a daily basis is a real person. Flesh and blood, with real problems and hopes and dreams and fears and all of that. It's so easy to forget about people as soon as you meet them. Forget that after you talk to somebody and you go your separate ways, they go on living their own life. I guess it doesn't make any sense ..."

"No, Trace. It does. It really does. I read somewhere that some people act like they are the movie star in their own life, and they treat everybody else like they're just background players. I think ... maybe ... that's what you were doing?"

"Yes!" he said, sounding excited rather than mad. I laughed at his enthusiasm. "I love that you get me, Sarah."

"I do, Trace."

"Talking to Flynn, I get how his being bullied affected him, too. I'm so disgusted to think of all the other kids I did that to over the years."

"It's never too late to change."

"You really think?" he asked doubtfully.

I pulled out my phone. "Of course. You used to be Trace Ridgerton, bully. But this is who you are now."

I held up my phone and watched his eyes as they landed on the photo of him with Flynn and the motorcycle. His eyes filled with tears, and I didn't think I'd ever loved him more than I did in that moment.

When I put my phone down, he said, "It must have been hard for you. Seeing me go on to be so rich and successful."

"It was. For a while. But I learned long ago not to dwell on such things. We'd all like to believe that karma catches up with people eventually, but it often doesn't. I've learned it's okay to be angry, but if you dwell on that anger, you become bitter. And I was not going to allow myself to become a bitter person. My way of coping is to wish toxic people love and light but keep them at a distance for my own mental health."

"That was why you kept pushing me away."

"Absolutely. It's funny. I almost didn't apply for this job when Matt told me about it. Because I knew you were on the team."

"Wow," Trace said, shoulders slumping. "Makes you think, you know? About the ripple effect of doing shitty things."

"Yes, but the same holds true for good deeds. Just think about what Flynn might do in the future because you inspired him."

Trace looked doubtful, but I saw a faint glimmer of hope in his eyes.

"You've been through a lot in your life too, Sarah. But you don't go around treating people like crap. I don't know how you do it."

"I guess since I know what it feels like to be hurt, I don't want to ever make anybody else feel that way. Even if they might deserve it sometimes. I think on some level I always knew that you and other guys at school ... You did what you did out of pain and anguish. Happy people don't go around hurting other people."

"I guess that's true. I remember you telling me once that

you're nice to everybody because they might be fighting a battle you know nothing about."

"I did say that. Thank you for remembering."

I felt gratified that I might have influenced Trace to do better.

"I don't know what to do," Trace said, his eyes still so sad. "I feel like I need to do something big to make up for my whole life."

"Well, that's the great thing. You don't have to do anything drastic. It's not that complicated, Trace. Just be kind. Going forward. That's it."

Trace smiled at me, and a feeling of calm settled over me. I hated seeing him upset, even if it was necessary for his growth.

"I've learned a lot from you about being kind, Sarah. One of the happiest moments of my life was when I saw that article you wrote."

Placing my hand on my heart, I said, "Oh, I love hearing that."

"I wish there was some way I could make this up to you. I wish I had more words—better words—to tell you how sorry I am."

"Knowing that you're sorry helps tremendously. I think that's all I need. At least now we can put this behind us and move on. I consider this the end of this chapter, okay?"

I paused for a moment, thinking about how we could move forward from this.

"I want you to know that I will never throw this in your face. All couples argue sometimes, and this is not something we need to dredge up ever again. We can move on and heal from it."

Trace gazed into my eyes. "Is there anything else you want to say to me first? Before we do close the chapter?"

They were simple words, but so thoughtful. I loved that he wanted to give me the chance to say anything I might have kept bottled up all this time.

"Wow. There were so many things I always thought I would say to you if I ever saw you again after high school." Laughing, I said, "Most of them I would never say to you now."

Trace nodded but kept quiet.

"I will say that, well ... Since we've been seeing each other, there were times I just couldn't believe you could look into my eyes and not remember. That you could kiss me and make love to me and yet have no memory of your past with me. That prom proposal in front of the whole school ... You made me feel like I was a joke. And then everybody laughed, and I felt like the whole world thought of me as a joke."

I hadn't realized how upset I still was until I started to cry. Trace pulled me into his arms. He stroked my back and let me cry for as long as I needed. And I was grateful that he'd encouraged me to get it all out before we ended this painful discussion. He hadn't taken the easy way out by letting me wrap it all up quickly and let him off the hook. After all these years, I needed to express my heartache, and he knew it.

"I'm sorry, my sweet Sarah. So terribly sorry."

At last, my sobs subsided and I let go of him. I dabbed my eyes and the tension in my body eased. It felt like the storm had passed, and the calm that had returned was more peaceful than ever before.

"I'm a horrible person," Trace said, more to himself than to me.

"No, you're not. You've just been in pain for a very long

time. I forgive you, Trace. Now it's time for you to forgive yourself."

Trace shook his head in wonder. "After everything that's happened, the idea that you could open your heart enough to fall in love with *me*, of all people ... Sarah, you're the bravest, most incredible person I've ever known."

In this moment, it felt like a new beginning for us. Now that we'd hashed out the ugly past, I truly felt ready to move on.

"I missed you so much," I said, pulling him close. "I'm so happy you're home."

"Me too." He kissed me. "Been going crazy without you."

"Same here," I managed to say between kisses. Squeezing his hard arm muscles, my body quivered with renewed desire. Trace was holding back, probably cautious due to the emotional gravity of tonight's discussion. I needed to make it crystal clear to him that I was more than ready for makeup sex with him.

"My shower massager has *nothing* on you, baby," I said.

Trace groaned with need. He moved to straddle me where I sat. His weight was heavy on top of me, but it was a delicious sort of pain.

Kissing me, he said, "I love you so much, Sarah. And I want to show you how much I love you."

The sheer intensity in his voice made me shiver with anticipation. Grinning a deliciously sexy and wicked grin, he said, "Now I'm gonna get down on my knees and *beg* for your forgiveness."

I drew in a sharp breath and watched as Trace dropped to his knees in front of the couch.

He reached under my skirt, slid my panties off, and tossed them aside. Grasping my feet and opening my legs, he rested them on the coffee table. Kneeling before me, he stroked my most sensitive spot between my legs with his tongue.

I threw my head back and cried out loud in ecstasy. Sensations of intense bliss coursed through my body. Having Trace on his knees pleasuring me felt like an act of contrition...of *supplication.* I felt powerful over my former bully even while I was in a most vulnerable position as he controlled my pleasure. It was a thoroughly erotic experience.

My usual restraints during sex had vanished as I cried out, writhing under Trace's expert tongue.

Gripping the couch, I alternately cried out his name amidst other unintelligible sounds.

"Keep doing that." I relished feeling in charge. Getting caught up in the fantasy, I felt like royalty, ordering my subject to give me an orgasm. "Don't you dare stop."

Trace didn't stop. He sped up instead, swirling his tongue faster and making me scream louder. At last, I reached my peak of pleasure, screaming his name the whole time.

I still panted long after my body stopped shuddering. Trace got up from his knees to face me. The wild look in his eyes showed me he was as aroused by the act as I was.

Breathlessly, he asked, "You're on the pill, right?"

"Yes," I croaked.

"Thank God," he said, unbuckling his pants and pulling them down with his underwear. His cock was bigger and more swollen than I'd ever seen it.

"Take me, Trace," I ordered. "Now."

Straddling me on the couch, he plunged into me. I had to hold on for dear life as he thrust hard and fast in and out of me. Trace showed no tenderness in his desperation, but that was fine with me. There was a time and a place for slow, tender lovemaking. But this wasn't it.

He came quickly and came *hard*. I let him lay like that, collapsed on top of me, for as long as I could stand it. At last, I said, "Trace ... can't ... breathe."

Trace rolled off me. "Sorry, sorry."

Chuckling, he leaned back on the couch, his pants around his ankles.

"That ... was ... *awesome,*" he said.

"Yes, it certainly was." Still lying back against the couch, I turned my head to face him. "I love you so much, Trace."

"I love you too, baby."

He got up, pulled up his pants, and rebuckled them.

Glancing around the room, I said, "I have no idea where my panties got to."

"Me neither. You'll just have to go commando," he said with a grin.

I giggled. "Okay. Whatever." I stood up and pulled him close to me. Caressing his face, I murmured, "Trace, my darling?"

"Yes?"

"I'm starving."

"Same here," he said enthusiastically. "Thai food for delivery?"

"Yes, please."

"Cool." He grabbed his phone.

And just like that, we fell back into our usual rhythm.

I'd never been happier.

34

———

TRACE

The next morning, I lay in my bed for a while, alone and thinking about everything. I still felt terrible about what I'd done to Sarah all those years ago, but I was relieved that she'd forgiven me. I believed her when she'd said she was ready to move on, but I needed to do something more. Terrific sex hardly seemed sufficient compensation, especially since I'd benefited considerably from it.

Damn. Sarah was one red hot lover.

She'd really been on to something when she said I acted like I was the movie star and everyone else was just a bit player in my life. That was exactly what I did. And it needed to stop.

Eventually, I got out of bed and went about my day, puttering around the house, waiting to leave for batting practice. Unable to come up with anything I could do to show Sarah how sorry I was, I decided to ask her friends. I texted Julia, asking if I could meet her at her office at Old Bay Stadium, and would she mind asking Lyric to join us if she was available. I assured Julia that nothing was wrong, but that it was important.

Knowing Sarah, she would protect me by never telling anyone at work what I'd done to her in high school. She deserved so much better than somebody like me, but somehow, I was the one she'd fallen in love with. I would be grateful for that for the rest of my life.

It overwhelmed me to think about all the people I owed amends to, but one thing at a time. I'd never be able to reach everybody I'd wronged over the years, but every little bit would help. I kept thinking of Flynn saying he would feel better if his bully apologized to him.

My mind turned to Car Crash Girl, whose name I couldn't remember for the life of me. Like with Sarah in high school, I hadn't given that poor woman much thought at all. I tried replaying my conversation with Mr. Devilbuss in my head. He'd mentioned her by name several times, but I still came up blank.

I typed in my name and "car accident" into the internet search bar on my computer and winced when an article came up. "Florida Woman Sues Bay Bird Catcher Trace Ridgerton for Damages and Emotional Distress." Not a good look. No wonder Mr. Devilbuss had been mad.

Nancy Featherstone! Yeah, that was it. I tried not to think about how truly fucked up it was that I'd had sex with this woman and couldn't even remember her name.

Fortunately, I found her name listed on an attorney website where she apparently worked as a legal secretary. I felt bad about calling her at work, but it wasn't like I would find her cell phone number on the internet anywhere.

"Thank you for calling Norgan and Thorndyke Law. How can I help you?" said the woman who answered the phone.

"Hi, could I speak with Nancy Featherstone, please?" I said.

"This is she. How can I help you today?" Nancy chirped.

I faltered, realizing I hadn't thought much about what I was going to say. Maybe that was better, though. I should just speak from the heart and tell her how I felt.

"Nancy, this is Trace Ridgerton."

"Oh," she said. "Uh ... hi."

She sounded nervous; afraid, even. Between Nancy and Sarah, I wondered how many other people I had scared without knowing. I felt like such a monster.

"You should, you know, probably be talking to my lawyer instead of me," she said.

Then I realized she might be afraid because she thought I was mad at her about the lawsuit and had called to bitch her out.

"No, I really needed to talk to you personally," I said gently to put her at ease. "I just had to tell you how sorry I am about everything."

"I'm not dropping the lawsuit, Trace," she said, still sounding nervous but determined not to back down. Good for her.

"I swear, Nancy, this has nothing to do with trying to talk you out of the lawsuit. You have every right to sue me, and I will tell my lawyer I am totally fine with settling the case and giving you whatever you want."

Both my agent and my lawyer would be pissed about that, but screw 'em. It was my money, and I wanted to do the right thing.

"What?" she asked, understandably confused.

"I treated you like garbage, Nancy. And I just wanted to say that I'm really sorry. You're a nice person, and you deserve better than that. The car thing was just a simple accident, but leaving the way I did after we, you know ... That was a really shitty thing to do."

"Yes, it was," Nancy said, sounding like she was near tears. "I don't know. Maybe I overreacted by suing you."

"No. You didn't." The last thing I wanted was for Nancy to think my apology had anything to do with business. I'd hurt her, and I wanted to make her feel better. I had no ulterior motive. "You had every right to be upset."

"I don't know. Maybe ..." I could hear her sniffling, trying not to break down at work. "When all this happened, my grandmother was dying in the hospital. She—she passed away a few days after you left. We were really close. I mean, she pretty much raised me."

She'd been fighting a battle I knew nothing about.

"And I guess I took some of that out on you."

"Nancy," I said, going out of my way to use her name as much as possible. "I'm so sorry you lost your grandmother. That must be so hard. And I apologize from the bottom of my heart for everything I did to make your grief even worse."

"Thank you," she said, her voice stronger now. "It helps to hear you say that."

"I feel awful for leaving after we slept together. There was no excuse."

"It's just as well," Nancy said with a laugh. "I was so upset the next day, that this woman came up to me in a coffee shop and asked what was wrong. We've been together ever since."

"Together? You mean together, as in ..."

"Yeah. I'm bisexual," she said.

"Oh. I see."

This revelation was another reminder that Nancy Featherstone was a real flesh and blood woman with a whole life and personality and background I knew nothing about. Because I hadn't bothered to find out. Hell, I hadn't bothered to memorize her *name*.

"I'm happy to hear that. I hope it works out with you two."

"Thanks, Trace. And thank you for calling. I might ... Well, I'll think about dropping the charges against you."

"You really don't have to do that. But even if you do, I'm gonna pay you restitution. Whatever you want, Nancy. I really just wanted to tell you I'm sorry I was such a jerk."

"It's okay. I forgive you. And I saw that article with you and that kid with cancer." Laughing, she said, "Maybe you're not such a bad guy after all."

I wish I could believe that.

"Thanks. Take care of yourself, okay? Oh, and let me give you my cell phone number in case you need anything. That way you don't have to go through my agent or lawyer if you don't want to."

"Wow," she said, sounding surprised.

I gave her my phone number and we said our goodbyes. After we hung up, I felt so much better. And I hoped Nancy did, too, and that she would be as happy with her girlfriend as I was with mine. She deserved that.

JULIA'S OFFICE wasn't located in the same building as Sarah's, so at least I didn't have to worry about running into my girlfriend while I was meeting her friends. Julia's head groundskeeper's office was located inside the stadium near our locker rooms. I walked down the hallway that afternoon, dreading the conversation I was about to have. Julia and Lyric were still wary of trusting me with Sarah, and my confession about bullying her would not help my case. But making amends with Sarah was worth any discomfort I endured from her loyal friends.

Whatever Julia and Lyric dished out, I had it coming.

I knocked on the open office door and Julia looked up from her seat behind her desk. Lyric was sitting across from her, and both women looked concerned.

"Come in," Julia said.

I did, closing the door behind me. I took a seat next to Lyric.

"Is Sarah okay?" Julia asked.

"She's absolutely fine," I said with a smile. Lyric and Julia smiled back, looking relieved to hear that. "I just wanted to ask your advice about something for her."

"Ask away," Julia said happily.

I really hated to burst her good mood.

"Did Sarah ever tell you that she and I went to high school together?"

Both women looked shocked, which was what I'd expected.

"You were in school with her back in Minnesota?" Julia asked.

"Yeah," I said, gathering my courage. "The weird thing is, all this time, I didn't realize we went to the same school either. It wasn't until I was flipping through my old yearbook that I saw her picture."

"I guess you guys just ran in different social circles," Lyric said with a shrug.

"Well yeah, kinda. Back then she went by a different name. Sarah is her middle name, and she even changed her last name when she moved away from Minnesota. Plus, she was heavier back then."

"Right," Julia said. "She's mentioned that. I'm sure she

looks a lot different now. So it makes sense you might not remember her from your teen years." Her brow furrowed, no doubt wondering where I was going with this.

"The thing is ... Sarah remembered me. All this time she's known exactly who I was. Because the truth is, I was really mean to her in high school. I bullied her pretty bad back then."

"Oh wow," Lyric said softly.

Julia sighed sharply. She was more outspoken than Lyric, and I'd figured she would be the one to get especially angry with me.

"I didn't even remember what I'd done. The worst thing I did was at a baseball game once. You know how people do those prom-posal things?"

Lyric and Julia both gasped loudly. Lyric covered her heart with her hand and Julia covered her mouth in shock.

"That was *you*?" Lyric cried.

"Oh ... you—you know about that?"

"Yeah, we know about that," Julia snapped angrily. "She was traumatized by it."

"I know," I said sorrowfully. "She's carried all that pain inside and she never said anything to me about it. When I finally got my head out of my ass and remembered, we sat down and talked it over. And she forgave me for it because that's the kind of person she is."

I kept quiet for a moment, the same way I had done with Sarah when we'd first talked about it. I wanted to give Sarah's friends room to express whatever they needed to.

"I've seen teenagers come into the emergency room for suicide attempts over bullying like that," Lyric said, tears in her eyes. "We do what we can to save them, but they don't always make it."

Lyric wasn't even a doctor yet, but she'd clearly seen some horrible shit in her line of work.

I closed my eyes, letting her words wash over me. She was right. Given Sarah's horrific home life, I was lucky she hadn't tried to kill herself. There was only so much pain a person could bear.

I opened my eyes and said, "I don't know what to do to fix this."

Shaking her head, Julia said, "I can't believe it was you who did that prom-posal thing. I just ... I can't believe it."

She and Lyric exchanged looks of shock and worry.

"We all have been so worried about Sarah dating you and what might happen," Julia said, which made me wonder who "we all" referred to. She and Matt and Lyric at the very least, I figured. Probably more people now that I thought about it. Everybody loved Sarah around here, and they had every right to be worried considering the way I'd treated her at first. And now this new revelation confirmed their worst fears that Sarah's emotional well-being was in danger while she was with me.

"I don't blame you for being worried. Sarah has a huge heart, and that means she can get hurt sometimes. I still can't quite believe she picked me, but she did. We have an incredible relationship. We really do. I know it feels like it came out of nowhere, but that's because we kept it under wraps for so long. Mainly because Sarah, wisely, wanted to take her time and feel me out. Make sure my feelings were legitimate. She was so afraid at first and I didn't understand ... But of course now it all makes sense."

I jumped out of my chair and started pacing the floor in front of Julia's desk. "I'm just so goddamn mad at myself for having done something so awful. There's no excuse for me to not remember doing something so vile, no matter who the victim was." Turning to face Lyric and Julia, I added, "And you know that kid Flynn?"

"The child with leukemia," Lyric said softly.

"Yeah. He gets bullied in school too. That sweet little boy. And I picked on kids just like him. The ones who were so much smarter than me. The theater kids who didn't quite fit in. If I'd gone to school with Flynn, I'd have been first in line to torture him."

I realized my ranting was hardly helping my case, but I couldn't help spilling my guts. I felt like the worst human being on the planet, and I didn't care who knew it. All those baseball fans who adored me had no clue who I really was.

Sinking back down in my chair, I put my head in my hands. My heart ached so badly over hurting Sarah that I just didn't know what to do anymore. The room had gone completely silent, and I wasn't sure what to expect when I finally looked up at Lyric and Julia.

When I did, I knew immediately that the tone of the room had changed. I wasn't sure exactly what I'd said, but something had gotten through to Sarah's friends. I sensed more compassion than anger coming from them. Lyric, in particular, seemed moved by my words. Julia still seemed a tad skeptical.

"You've made mistakes in the past, Trace. But it's never too late to change," Lyric said.

"That's exactly what Sarah said."

Lyric smiled and nodded.

"Julia," I said. She looked both sad and worried. "I've seen the way you look at Matt. You know what it's like to love somebody so much you can hardly breathe."

She nodded slowly.

"We both do," Lyric said.

"I need your help to figure out what I can do to make

Sarah feel better. She said she's ready to move past it. That she forgave me a long time ago. She also said she feels better that I apologized, but I still feel like it's not enough. I can't change the past, but I want to do something to make it up to her. But I keep coming up blank."

Julia's expression softened as she listened to me. She was starting to believe my sincerity.

"You went to your prom, right?" Lyric asked.

I winced at the memory. "Yeah. Not with the girl I *wish* I'd gone with. But yeah."

"Do you remember one of the guys getting down on one knee and singing to his girlfriend at the prom?"

"Oh, I like where you're going with this," Julia said with a grin.

"Yeah, I remember. That was a buddy of mine from the team. He was high as a kite when he did that, believe me." I laughed and mimed holding a joint. "The girls went crazy over it."

"That's what Sarah said. It was all anybody could talk about at school," Lyric said. "She told us she couldn't imagine being the type of girl who guys serenaded."

"She's said stuff like that to me before," Trace said. "Like she wonders what it would feel like to be one of the pretty, popular girls for once."

"So Trace," Lyric began with a sly smile. "Can you sing?"

35

SARAH

Julia and Lyric invited me out to karaoke on Thursday night when the Bay Birds had an off day. I told them I was in, provided there would be no pressure to perform. I'd be happy enough to sit there and drink and watch other people make fools of themselves.

We went to a place just outside of Baltimore called Johnny Cee's Bar and Grill, and the food and entertainment did not disappoint. They had a crab cake to die for, and there was no shortage of drunken idiots getting up onstage to sing.

Not all of them were drunken idiots, though. Julia was brave enough to don a cowboy hat and sing an upbeat country song that really got the place going. I was so proud of her. She sounded pretty good.

Lyric and I eagerly high-fived her when she returned to her seat.

"That was so amazing," I told her excitedly. I was having such a blast with my two best friends. I felt at home with them, glad to be hundreds of miles away from Minnesota.

Maryland was truly my home now, due to all my loved ones I had here with me.

I could hardly believe my ears when the next song started up.

"Oh my goodness," I exclaimed, looking over at Lyric and Julia. "Now there's a song I *never* thought I would hear at karaoke!"

It was "Smoke Gets in Your Eyes" by The Platters.

"Sarah," Julia said with a laugh. "Look at the *singer*."

I turned to look at the stage and gasped. Lyric and Julia giggled.

Up onstage was none other than my boyfriend, Trace Ridgerton. He grinned at me as he crooned one of my favorite songs.

I was dimly aware that Brady and Matt had slipped in and taken seats next to their wives to watch the performance.

I stared at Trace, mesmerized. Clearly, a lot of thought and planning had gone into this incredible surprise, because Trace wasn't even looking at the words on the screen. He knew all the words by heart.

Trace had learned the song for *me*.

Tears filled my eyes as he slowly walked down from the stage, microphone in hand. He never broke eye contact with me, making it clear to every patron in the place that he was singing to me.

Having the man I loved serenade me in front of a whole room full of people was the most romantic thing that had ever happened to me. It was like a fantasy come to life. I could hardly believe it was real.

Trace was positively dreamy in his deliciously tight black jeans and jagged-cutoff shirt that showed off his tattoos. What made him look the most devastatingly handsome was the expression on his face as he sang. The way he gazed at me ... He was obviously in love.

I had never felt so beautiful, so desired, so *wanted* in my whole life.

He got down on one knee in front of me, microphone in one hand, gesturing dramatically with the other as he sang the powerful finale of the song.

All these years I'd wondered how it would feel to be the type of girl whose boyfriend sang to her at the prom in front of the whole class. And now I knew exactly how it felt.

Better than I could have possibly imagined.

As I wiped the tears from my eyes, the whole place erupted in applause. He stood up, put the microphone on the table, and then he kissed me. For which he received even more applause.

"I wish I had taken you to the prom and sung to you then," Trace said.

And that's when I realized why he had done this. I hadn't told Trace how much I'd longed to be that girl at the prom with the song that was just for her. But I *had* told Lyric and Julia.

I could not have asked for more loving, loyal friends.

"This is better," I told Trace, meaning every word. This wasn't some high school dance where most of the couples probably weren't together anymore. Trace wasn't just a teenage date. He was the man I loved. And he loved me.

Trace and I gazed into each other's eyes. Eventually, somebody retrieved the microphone so the next person could perform.

Crossing his arms, Matt chuckled. "Okay, *that* was pretty cool."

Matt was smiling, seeming on board with our love affair for the first time. It wasn't every day a man made a fool of himself in front of a crowd, and I was sure Matt never expected Trace of all people to do such a thing.

"Holy shit, that's Brady Keaton!" some guy yelled. "And Matt Jovey!"

"And Trace Ridgerton was the karaoke guy!" somebody else called out.

No wonder Brady and Matt had entered the place quietly after Trace had begun to sing. It was the only way they wouldn't be noticed.

"I think we've been spotted," Lyric said with a rueful laugh. This happened to her *all* the time.

"Damn," I muttered, hating to see the magic of the evening end so abruptly.

"Hey," Brady said, sitting up in his chair. "Why don't you two kids take off? We'll handle this crowd."

Matt nodded, and I turned to Trace.

"Is that okay?" I asked.

"Of course," he said, grabbing my hand and pulling me toward him.

"Thank you, guys. So much!" I called to my friends as Trace ushered me out.

"You're welcome, girl," Julia called back.

I'd thank my friends properly later, but right now we had to make a quick getaway.

When we got to the parking lot, Trace said, "Oh ... I've got the motorcycle. Is that okay?"

"Yeah," I said, tenderly caressing his face. "That's more than okay. Trace, this was so amazing. In so many ways."

"I know it doesn't make up for everything," he said. "But it's a start I guess."

"More than a start. Oh, Trace, this was so *romantic*," I said dreamily, pulling him in for a kiss.

I could have kissed him there in the parking lot all night, but some people came out of the bar.

"Let's get out of here. I don't want to share you with anybody right now," I said.

"Fair enough." He pulled another helmet out of the bike's leather bag and secured it on my head, tugging on it to make sure it was properly fastened. He also slid on a pair of clear glasses as a wind shield for my eyes. "You ready for this?"

"I guess," I said with a nervous laugh. I really was ready, though. Riding a motorcycle meant a lot to Trace, and it was about time I shared that experience with him.

He put on his helmet and got on the bike. I climbed on behind him.

"Hold on tight, baby," he said.

"Don't worry. I will," I said, before we zoomed off into the night together.

Riding with Trace was incredibly exciting. He took it easy with me at first, repeatedly glancing in his side mirror to check on me.

"You okay?" he called out when he started picking up speed.

"I'm great! This is fun," I called back.

I held on tight to Trace as we went down some winding roads, which was exhilarating and scary at the same time. Kind of like my relationship with Trace, although I was no longer afraid. I trusted him now. I trusted *us*.

Trace took me back to my place and we made love. I remembered thinking there was a time and place for slow, luxurious lovemaking.

And this was definitely that time.

I was more in love with Trace than ever before. Just thinking about the way he'd looked when he sang to me aroused me beyond all reason. All I wanted was to give myself to him, over and over again.

So that was exactly what I did.

We made love several times, gratifying each other, falling asleep, and then waking up to do it all over again. The perfect end to a perfect night.

36

TRACE

I stood at a crosswalk downtown, waiting for the light to change. I was meeting Sarah for lunch. We'd wanted to make sure we got a chance to see each other before the team left for Chicago.

The light finally changed, and I headed toward the restaurant, smiling to myself the whole way. The karaoke thing had gone even better than I'd hoped. I'd been nervous as hell, despite the fact that I performed in front of crowds all the time. But that was different. I was actually *good* at sports, but I wasn't the world's greatest singer. But Sarah hadn't cared. She had cried when I sang to her, and the look in her eyes had made any discomfort more than worth it.

Lyric and Julia had really come through for me and for Sarah. I had forgotten all about that guy at the prom. Once Lyric mentioned it, I remembered the girls going crazy over it. It was the talk of the school on the Monday after prom, and all the girls were excited and jealous. Strange how it hadn't seemed like a big deal to any of us guys. The band had been playing some love song, and my buddy just got down on his knee and started singing along to his girlfriend.

Now that I thought about it, I realized it was kind of like when a woman receives flowers at work. All her coworkers go crazy over it, and the girl always gets really excited. It might not seem like a big deal to the guy who sent them, but that simple gesture clearly can have a big impact.

It's not that complicated, Trace. Just be kind.

Maybe so, but Sarah had deserved far more than a bouquet of flowers after what I had done. Hopefully I'd given her a special memory she would carry with her for the rest of her life. I knew I would never forget it.

Especially with the guys on the team ragging me about it. Naturally, Brady had told everybody. Not that I really minded. Good-natured teasing from my teammates was a small price to pay for making Sarah happy.

When I got to the pizza place, I saw Sarah sitting alone at a table. She looked sad.

I rushed over and sat down across from her. She smiled when she saw me, and it made me happy to know that seeing me made her feel better.

"You okay?" I asked.

"It's been a rough morning," she said wearily. "So glad at least I get to see you. That makes it better."

Our server arrived to take our order. After she left, I asked, "So what's going on?"

"Out of nowhere this morning, I got a call from my mother," she said.

"Oh wow. That's crazy."

Sarah had cut her toxic family out of her life altogether. It hadn't been an easy decision, but it had seemed the best option. Her mother in particular was awful. The woman did nothing but cause her daughter pain. As far as I knew, neither of her parents knew where she was, and Sarah liked it that way.

"How the hell did she even find you?" I asked.

"The Baltimore Bugle printed a picture of me with that article I wrote about you and Flynn. Somebody she knew saw it and told her about it. My mom didn't even know I'd changed my name until now."

"That must have been really upsetting. To get a call from her from out of nowhere."

"It was," Sarah said softly. "But that wasn't the worst part."

She swallowed hard, and I could tell she was trying not to cry. Just then, a young woman wearing a Trace Ridgerton jersey started heading toward our table.

Shit.

I held up my hand to stop the woman and shook my head, mouthing, "Sorry." Fortunately, Sarah was looking down and didn't see the exchange. I took Sarah's hand, giving her my undivided attention. She was always patient with my fans, but she didn't need that kind of hassle right now.

"What did she say?"

"She started out saying she was glad she found me. That she missed me," Sarah said, squeezing my hand. Her voice shook as she spoke. "Told me she knew we had our problems in the past and that maybe we could patch things up. Make a fresh start."

I nodded as I listened, my stomach tightening. I was afraid to find out what came next.

"And like an idiot, I believed her. Just like that. It was like I'd forgotten everything she'd done to me. Everything that had happened in my life. She has a way of doing that, you know? Making you forget."

"She's manipulative," I said.

"Yes. Exactly. She can make me forget everything she's done or make me feel like it's all in my head."

I nodded again, knowing the type very well from my own upbringing.

"So my mom's talking to me about letting go of the past and all that. She sounded so sincere ... And then she mentioned you."

"Me?" I asked.

"Yeah. She started talking about my job and how great it must be to work with all these famous baseball players. And I guess some gossip rag somewhere must have mentioned that you were dating the Director of Community Partnerships and Events for the Bay Birds, and ... Long story short, my mom loves the idea that I'm dating a millionaire baseball player and she was trying to see what she might get out of it."

Sarah's tears started to fall, crushing my heart in the process.

"Oh, baby. I'm so sorry," I said helplessly. She had let go of my hand to wipe her eyes, so I wasn't even touching her anymore. As much as I wanted to leap up from my seat and hold her close, I didn't want to make her uncomfortable in public. She was doing her best to compose herself, drying her tears with a tissue and checking her makeup with her pocket mirror.

"I feel so stupid, you know? For falling for it. I mean, for a minute I actually believed—" Her tears threatened to spill again.

"Of course you did. We all want to believe our parents are gonna come through for us. That after everything that's happened and despite all evidence to the contrary, we still hope our mom and dad will someday tell us they love us and they're sorry for everything they did to us. I don't think you ever stop hoping for that. It's just human nature."

Sarah nodded sadly, but she was calmer now. If nothing else, she knew these weren't just idle words. I knew what I was talking about.

"My mom popped up fairly recently too," I said.

"Really?"

"Well, she didn't call me or anything. I got a package in the mail from her. And like you, for a few seconds I thought maybe she'd done something unselfish for once. Like she saw something in a store somewhere and thought of me and mailed me a present." Laughing bitterly, I said, "Nope. She was getting rid of all my 'junk,' as she called it, including drawings I'd done for her over the years. Said she was tired of storing it. Times like these, I can't even imagine what it's like to have normal parents. Ones who are actually proud of their kids. The kind who hang up their kids' drawings on the refrigerator instead of just throwing them in the trash."

"I know what you mean. I'm so sorry she did that to you, Trace."

"You're not stupid for hoping your mom could change, Sarah. You're just an optimist with a huge heart. And it's a testament to your strength as a person that you never gave into bitterness despite everything. And if nothing else, this proves you did the right thing by cutting your family out of your life."

"I love you, Trace," she said softly.

"I love you too. Feel a little better?"

"You always make me feel better," she said. "I'm glad you're here."

The server arrived with our pizza.

"And this makes me feel better, too," Sarah said with another smile as I took her plate and served her a big slice.

Sarah ate more now, and I loved that. She was still careful about the foods she ate and how much, but she seemed more at ease now with her diet. She'd even put on a few pounds, and I liked to think maybe I had something to do with that. Like she was so comfortable around me that she let her guard down a bit. I wanted to see her enjoy life, and I didn't give a damn how much she weighed.

The young lady wearing my jersey was still watching us, so I motioned for her to come over. Her eyes lit up, and she grabbed a black magic marker from her purse before walking over.

"Uh, Mr. Ridgerton ... Would you mind signing my jersey for me?" she asked nervously.

"Sure, be glad to. Thanks for waiting. My girl's having kind of a rough day, so I had to make sure she was okay first," I said, smiling at Sarah. Ever since our first disastrous date when I'd disrespected her by putting my fans first, I made sure Sarah knew she always came first now.

The girl stretched out the front of her jersey, flattening it so I could sign it.

She squealed with glee. "Thank you. Thank you so much!"

"You're welcome."

The girl turned to Sarah and said, "I hope you feel better."

"Thank you," Sarah said with genuine gratitude in her eyes. "I appreciate that."

The happy fan wandered off, and nobody else bothered us for the rest of the meal.

After lunch, we lingered outside on the sidewalk.

"I'm gonna miss you," Sarah said as I held her in my arms.

"Me too. But it's only for a few days. Then think of all the time we'll have together in the off-season."

Sarah sighed happily. "That will be lovely. I guess I better get back to work."

I kissed her and touched her cheek gently. "Sarah, whatever happens, I'm your family now. Okay? Me and Lyric and Julia. We're always gonna be here for you."

"Thank you, Trace," she said, tearing up again. This time, though, they were happy tears.

We headed back to Old Bay Stadium together, hand in hand.

I had enough time to kill before the game tonight to go back home for a little while. Sitting on the couch, I thought about my sister. I figured I should at least give her a call, try to reach out.

Just as I was gathering up the nerve to call her, my cell phone rang. It was Jake Belcourt, my agent.

"Hey, what's up?"

"Good news," Jake said.

"I could use some good news. Lay it on me."

"Nancy Featherstone's dropping the charges."

"Oh wow," I said. I was relieved to have my legal troubles disappear just like that, and it warmed my heart that she was letting me off the hook. She was a nice person, and I guessed she had forgiven me. We'd had a great conversation when I called her, and I hoped this meant she wasn't upset anymore.

"Yeah, you sure caught a break."

"That's great. I'm gonna pay her anyway."

"Say what now?" Jake asked.

"I'm gonna pay her anyway. Every penny she asked for. She deserves it. I was a jerk to her, and I want to make it right."

"Oh. Well, um, okay ..." my agent said, sounding understandably confused. I stifled a laugh. His reaction reminded me of the end of *A Christmas Carol* when everybody wondered what the hell had gotten into Ebenezer Scrooge.

"Thanks for letting me know, man. Mr. Devilbuss will be happy. You can probably start hashing out my new contract with him."

"Already on it," he said enthusiastically.

"Cool. Thanks again."

After the call with Jake, I felt like anything was possible. I knew what I had to do.

I dialed the number quickly before I lost my nerve.

"Hey, Betsy? It's Trace ..."

"Hi," she said, sounding shocked to hear from me. "You okay?"

"Yeah, I'm fine. I just ... Look. I know things have been really screwed up between us for a long time. But that was our parents' fault. Not ours. Maybe we can, you know, start over. I've really missed you."

My sister fell silent for so long that I was afraid we might have been disconnected.

Then she said, "I've missed you too, Trace."

37

TRACE

Around noon on a Wednesday in mid-September, I got an unexpected knock on my door. I heaved myself up from the couch and opened it to find Sarah standing there, tears running down her face.

My body shifted into panic mode. "Are you okay?"

She nodded as she rushed inside, but she didn't look okay. Sarah sat on the couch, and I sat beside her.

Tears still streaming, Sarah turned to me and asked, "Did you really mean it when you said you were my family?"

"Of course I did," I said, wondering what had suddenly made her question my sincerity.

"Good. Because I'm pregnant," she blurted out, fear in her eyes.

"Wh—what?" I struggled to process her words.

"I'm pregnant, Trace. I'm so sorry. This is all my fault," she said, dabbing her wet eyes.

Still trying to wrap my head around this news, my top priority was calming my hysterical girlfriend.

"Now, baby, I don't think it's physically possible for this

to be all your fault." I laughed gently. "That's not how it works."

Sarah's tense shoulders relaxed a little. Had she expected me to be angry? My emotions were all over the place, but the last thing I felt was mad. But she'd come from a family who'd blamed her for everything that went wrong, ever. Old habits—and fears—died hard.

"I am on the pill, but I guess I'm still not used to taking it. And I must have forgotten once or twice, because ..." Her body hitched and she looked ready to break down again.

"Hey hey, come here," I said, pulling her into my arms. "It's all right. Don't cry, baby. Everything's all right."

After trying to soothe her for a few minutes, I let her go so I could face her.

"Of course we're family. Our family's just gonna get bigger, that's all."

Sarah's lovely eyes lit up with hope.

"I mean, that is, if you're sure you want to—"

"I do," Sarah said, putting a protective hand over her belly.

"Me too."

"Really?"

"Yeah," I said with sudden conviction. "Hell yeah."

"But Trace, we don't know what the hell we're doing. Our families were so screwed up ..."

"Sarah. I love you. You love me. And we're gonna love the *shit* out of this baby."

Her face grew calm, gentle. "I already do," she whispered.

"Remember what you told me when I said I was probably the last man on earth you ever thought you would fall for?"

Sarah shook her head.

"You said sometimes the most wonderful things in the world are unexpected."

She smiled. More tears filled her eyes, but the good kind.

"It's funny. I noticed you'd gained a little weight," I babbled on excitedly. "And you look great with more curves, by the way. I thought it was maybe because you were happy and comfortable with me and you were able to eat more without worrying. But now I know the real reason."

Sarah stared at me.

"What?"

"It's kinda too early for me to have put on baby weight," she said.

"Ohhh," I said, realizing how badly I'd just put my foot in my mouth.

I was about to apologize, but she laughed.

"No, no. It's okay. I'm glad you said that." She grew quiet for a moment. "I do worry about that sometimes. What would happen if I gained weight and started looking like Fat Fl—"

She stopped herself before she used the cruel nickname I'd once given her. She had promised she would never throw my past in my face again, and she hadn't. But that didn't mean she could just forget all about it.

"I mean, if I got heavy again."

"You don't ever have to worry about that. At least not as far as I'm concerned. I mean, I think you're happier and healthier now that you're eating a little more and taking good care of yourself. But other than that, I don't care how much you weigh. You're always gonna be my sexy girl."

Sarah smiled, and her look of calm returned.

"You're gonna be the sexiest pregnant lady in the world," I said excitedly.

She laughed. "We'll see I guess."

"Should we get married?" I blurted.

Sarah drew in a sharp breath. She looked stressed out and a little afraid.

"It's okay, Sarah. It's too much too soon."

"Yes." She looked relieved. "I'm sorry, Trace. I just—"

"You don't have to explain, baby. I understand. I told you, we're already family. I don't need to put a ring on your finger and get some piece of paper to prove that."

Sarah nodded. "I'm not saying never. I just ..."

"I know. We love each other. And that is more than enough," I said, stroking her pretty hair.

Her eyes shone with joy. "You know, the baby was probably conceived that night you sang to me."

"Oh, I love that," I said. "We did have a wonderful night together."

"Yes, we sure did."

"We made that baby with a lot of love, and that's how we're gonna raise him or her."

"Yes," she whispered. She snuggled up against me on the couch. I tenderly stroked her belly as we held each other close.

38

SARAH

It was the last game of the baseball season. Sadly, but not surprisingly, the Bay Birds had not made the playoffs. They'd come close to making it to the Wild Card race but had come up short. Still, the team had played much better than they had in years, and the boys had a lot to be proud of.

The time had come for the last ceremonial first pitch of the season. Trace was catching, making the game even more fun for me. Nobody knew I was carrying his child yet, and he'd said it was up to me when to make the announcement. We were nervous about being parents, but also really excited. Fortunately, we would have the off-season to prepare as much as possible.

I wasn't sure if it was pregnancy hormones, but I seemed to be always tearing up. And today's first pitch ceremony was particularly meaningful; I was even more emotional than usual.

Hand over my heart, I watched Flynn Bishop throw out the first pitch to Trace. The ball made it all the way to the plate, showing how strong he was getting lately. He'd been recently released from the hospital, and his prognosis was good. Watching Trace jog up to the mound and hug the boy was too much for me. I broke down in tears.

Laughing and with his arm still around Trace, Flynn called over to me, "It's okay, Ms. Asiago. Don't cry."

Naturally, that made me cry harder. I walked over to them and we had a group hug. It was perfect and lovely and wonderful. Trace and I would be lucky if we had a kid who was half as amazing as Flynn.

After the game, which the Bay Birds won 7-3, a bunch of us headed over to a seafood restaurant overlooking the Chesapeake Bay. Brady, Matt, Trace, and a few others had pitched in and rented a room and had food catered for the wives and families of the team. A last hurrah before we all went our separate ways until next season.

Trace got there ahead of me because I still had to finish out my workday after the game was over. I'd also wanted a chance to change out of my work clothes since this was a casual event. I was one of the last ones to arrive. The party was in full swing when I got there.

"Oh ... my ... God," Trace said when he saw me, clutching his chest and staggering backward dramatically.

I laughed. It was a bit of an overreaction, but I loved it. As a surprise for him, I'd bought a motorcycle outfit. The top had leather fringes on it and the pants were leather, too. I was greeted with a bunch of wolf whistles from the guys on the team.

Trace positively beamed with pride. He'd taken a lot of crap from the team when it came to our relationship, and I'd wanted to make a statement to show my support. I figured this would be a nice visual image to show his influence on me.

"Sarah, you look *gawdge-gous*," Brady said enthusiastically, kissing my cheek.

"Girl, I am loving this look on you," Julia exclaimed.

I waited until the commotion died down a bit. "Yeah, well don't get too attached to this outfit. It's not gonna fit me for very long." Placing a hand on my stomach, I looked over at Trace and said, "We're expecting in the spring."

More whistles, hoots, hollers, and definitely some gasps.

Trace grinned proudly, mouthing, "I love you." He eagerly accepted handshakes from his teammates.

"I still can't believe you managed to win this girl over," Rusty said, slapping Trace on the back. He turned to me and smiled. "The way you looked at him during the food drive, I thought you'd never want anything to do with him."

"Honestly, neither did I." Gazing at Trace lovingly, I added, "Crazy how things can change."

"That's for sure," Rusty said. "But seriously, congratulations. I'm really happy for you both."

He engulfed me in a warm hug, which I eagerly returned.

"What about you? Are you still dating Emily Martindale?" I asked.

"Yep," he said, and I was suitably impressed. Emily Martindale was a pretty famous actress, well known for her work on a popular cable television show. I hoped I would get the chance to meet her at some point.

And yet, something in Rusty's eyes said he was underwhelmed by his girlfriend. My instincts told me not to get too attached to the idea of them as a couple.

"I can't believe it," Julia exclaimed before pulling me into a hug. "Congratulations!"

"I'm so happy for you, Sarah," Lyric said with a warm smile.

They both eyed me curiously.

"What?"

"Sorry, I just have to ask …" Julia said, eyes wide. "Was this, you know, an accident?"

"Well, ye—" I stopped short. "No. Not an accident. And certainly not a mistake. It was a *surprise*."

Both my friends nodded.

"I'm excited, but I'm also kind of terrified."

Lyric put her hands on my shoulders and said, "Sarah, you know we are here for you. Anything you need."

Julia nodded in agreement.

"Yes. I do know that."

They truly were my family. Every bit as much as Trace was.

"How would you like to be called Aunt Julia and Aunt Lyric?"

Both women squealed so loud it made everyone turn around to look at us. We dissolved into laughter.

Now that Trace's sister was back in his life, our baby had three aunts to love him or her.

Trace made his way over to me.

"Come on, let's get you something to eat. You must be starving."

"I am," I said.

Lyric and Julia watched as Trace put his hand on my back and led me over to the buffet table. I saw my friends smile, and I knew they trusted him now. I was in good hands with him, and he was going to make a wonderful father.

"I'm so glad we got to share the news with everybody," Trace said giddily.

"Me too." I kissed him, then grabbed a plate.

His grin suddenly widened and his eyes lit up.

"What?" I asked.

"Now I can tell Flynn. I can't wait."

"Oh yeah, you're right. He's gonna be so happy."

Looking me up and down, he said, "Damn, you look fine in leather, baby."

"Thanks," I said as I filled my plate. Trace led me over to a table where he'd saved me a seat.

"Oh, I almost forgot. I got something for you." I got up and grabbed the plastic bag I had set down near the door.

"What'd you get? What'd you get?" he asked like a little kid.

I pulled out a tiny black onesie with a motorcycle on it.

Trace stared at it for a long time. For a moment, I was afraid he was upset for some reason.

"Trace?"

"I love it, Sarah. I just ... I love it. And I love you."

"I love you too," I said, watching Trace fight back tears.

In that moment, I knew everything was going to be okay. Like all parents, we would make mistakes. But we would love our baby and we would love each other.

And that was more than enough.

THANK you so much for reading the third book in The Boys of Baltimore Series. I hope you will continue on with the next book in the series, Batting Fourth!

Heartfelt thanks to you for reading!